Alexandra Jordan is the author of ***Snowflakes and Apple Blossom (the 1st Benjamin Bradstock Tale, shortlisted for the Writers' Village International Novel Award)*** and ***High Heels in the Sand,*** a whodunit set in the beautiful Peak District. She lives in the Peak District with her husband and their twin boys.

Contact her on Twitter @Alexjord18 and Facebook

SEASALT AND MIDNIGHT BRANDY

A Benjamin Bradstock Tale

ALEXANDRA JORDAN

ISBN-13: 978-1539950400

I wish to dedicate this book to one of my most ardent readers, always first on the phone to congratulate me on my latest work.

Known to us all as Uncle Glen, he is the kindest, bravest and most honest person I know.

God bless.

Acknowledgements

A great big *Thank you* to all the people who have encouraged and supported me:

To Angie and Liz, my amazing proofreaders

To the lovely people who trusted me enough to buy my very first novel

To Grace at *House of Play,* Doncaster, for my wonderful cover design

To my wonderful family, and all my friends.

FOREWORD

In order to illustrate this, my second tale, I would like to offer a beautiful quotation from Mahatma Gandhi:

'I cannot think of permanent enmity between man and man. Believing as I do in the theory of rebirth, I shall live in the hope that if not in this birth, in some other birth I shall be able to hug all humanity in friendly embrace.'

Let's hope this will one day be possible.

Benjamin Bradstock, Edinburgh

1

Enid Phelps

WE lived in Dorset at the time, in a small tumbledown village at the edge of the sea. We were only there six months while Dad, a plasterer by trade, worked on new houses for the council. Nice they were, with iron gates and shiny front doors.

The year was 1959. A year of firsts. The first Barbie doll (I got one for Christmas), the first Mini travelling the roads, the first hovercraft launched. Woodstock and the Moon Landing were still a long way off, ten years into the future.

Me, I was seven years old. Each day, after school had finished, I'd find Mum waiting for me in the playground. We'd walk home hand in hand, chatting away, the salt of the sea and the squawking of seagulls filling the air around us. On the way, we'd pass this beautiful old house. It was derelict, ramshackle, but I loved it. Standing at the corner of a lane leading down to the beach, it had its own plot of land and a driveway of small white pebbles. I'd comment on how sad it looked, how it could do with pretty flowers in the garden and lace curtains at the windows. I'd chat about it, dreaming that one day we'd live there, or that I'd grow up, get married, and move in.

Then one day, one gloriously sunny day, with the sky as blue as Mum's eyes and the sparkling waves roaring in my ears, I realised Mum thought I was making the whole thing up. She couldn't see the house. Not one bit of it. She was merely pretending to, filling in the details in her lovely cockney accent. But the details were all wrong. She wasn't describing the house I could see, with broad windows either side of a black front door, two enormous steps leading up, and flakes of old paint hanging from the eaves. No. The one she described had pretty window boxes, flowery curtains, and a navy-blue door with a shiny brass letterbox.

I remember looking up at her, to see if she was joking, to catch the amused smile on her face.

But no. She thought *I* was the one making it up.

I realised suddenly, my heart thumping, that the house wasn't really there. I checked. I got Sam, my brother, to come with me, pulling at his arm so he couldn't escape.

The house had a big garden, but there were no flowers, just long strands of grass dried brown by the sun. A huge apple tree guarded the entrance, its strong branches and tiny fruits hanging above the path enticingly. It seemed such a lovely old place, the kind that should have a family living there, with children running round and a sun-kissed gardener looking after it.

'What do you think to this old house, Sam? Isn't it lovely?'

He looked around. 'What house?'

'Sam, stop messing! This house here.' I waved towards it. 'This great big house here. You can't exactly miss it.'

'Enid, what you talking about?' He stared at me, his expression the same as the time he had a gobstopper stuck inside his cheek. 'There's nothing there, stupid! Just a bit of old land!'

I let go of his arm to study his face properly, screwing up my eyes against the light.

'You can't see a house? A great big house with big, massive windows? Can't you see anything, anything at all?'

'Come on Enid, stop messing. Let's get back.'

Sam is five years older than me. He was my protector and my best friend, so I knew he was telling the truth.

I finally knew with absolute certainty that I could see the house, but no-one else could.

My heart began to race like a pigeon's. I touched both steps first to make sure they were real, to make sure I wouldn't fall into nothingness like *Alice*. But they were definitely there, solid slabs of cold grey stone. So I climbed them, turned the brass handle, pushed open the door and stepped inside, leaving the door ajar.

Immediately, I heard a sound like a small thud. It seemed to fill the hallway. Rooted to the spot, I held my breath. Then a soft sigh, a whisper, a trailing fragment of sound, reached my ears, echoing around me.

'Ohhhhhhh ...'

Terrified, I waited, expecting to hear something else. But nothing happened. The house was completely quiet.

I remember I was shaking with fear. But I was determined to continue, to explore, to see what was inside this house, this house that only I could see.

I continued along the wide entrance hall and stepped through the first door on the left. It was a gloomy drawing-room of some kind. I looked around, expecting to see someone, a face, a smile. Surely the sound had come from here. But no. I turned back, running in and out of the other rooms. A sunlit dining room, a spacious kitchen, a neat and tidy drawer-filled study. Still there was no-one there.

I began to shiver, despite the warm day outside, and automatically pressed my left thumb into the centre of my right palm, something I'd seen Dad do, something I knew was supposed to calm me.

Despite this, my breath was coming fast, my skin crawling with fear, so I ran back to the front door. But I can't just leave, I decided, not without knowing if anyone lives here. I knew I'd never have forgiven myself, would have branded myself a coward the rest of my life. So I stood inside the entrance, closed my eyes and turned around, three hundred and sixty degrees. I think I expected someone to suddenly appear when I opened them. But there was no-one, nothing. Of course. Clenching my damp fists, I stepped back, ready to turn and run.

But a sudden intuition filled my lungs, and I called loudly.

'Who is it? Who's there?'

'It's me ...'

The house echoed with the pain of her sigh. It chilled me to my very bones.

Then I saw her.

A child. In the corner. Near the kitchen. Her dress was dark, plain, and she clutched a large doll as if it would fall and break.

'It's me,' she said again. This time loudly, confidently.

'Who are you? I don't know you.' I stepped towards her. 'Do I?'

I was supposed to be out playing with the other kids. We lived in a wood that bordered the beach, the lapping of the waves a constant and calming repetition in the background, interrupted only by the screech of birds as they dived for fish. I loved that place.

And our caravans were always the smartest, the prettiest, the best. Mum made sure we were always clean and smart too, especially for school. She knew the teachers looked down on us because we were Romani, and that each school had its own curriculum, so if we weren't careful we'd miss out, moving around as we did. So she made sure to liaise with the teachers, filling in any gaps in our education with books borrowed from school libraries or collected from second-hand shops. That's how we came to do so well. Sam became a schoolteacher and I qualified as a nurse, an SRN in the Queen Alexandra's Royal Army Nursing Corps. Sounds posh, doesn't it? It was. It was lovely.

But I'd left home that afternoon with no interest in the future that lay ahead of me. I was intent on checking out that house.

She must have been about four years old, the girl. She'd been crying, her eyes puffy and sore. I stared at her. Her face looked familiar. She looked a bit like me. Big, dark eyes. Long, wavy hair. Except her skin was brown, and she had a birthmark on her left arm, just above the crook of her elbow. I remember admiring it because it was a perfect star-shape. I liked her doll too. It had a silk ribbon wrapped around its head in the most beautiful crimson colour.

'Who are you?' I asked again.

'Will you help me?' she asked, tears filling her huge eyes.

'Why? What's wrong?'

'I'm lost.'

Stepping towards her, I smiled. 'Well, where are you trying to get to?'

'I want my mummy …'

A sinuous curl of mist flowed from her lips.

And she disappeared.

The house was icy cold and damp. As I'd stepped inside I could hear the drip, dripping of water in the background that reminded me of a cave Dad had taken me to on the East Coast. The hall had a smooth bannister curving up to the first floor like a snake. There was a smell too, with a trace of something acrid, bitter and grey.

I can taste it even now.

I remember looking up. Cobwebs hung from the ceiling like huge strips of lace. But I could see no spiders. I touched the painted walls with my fingertips. They didn't really exist, I knew, yet I could feel them. Cold, like marble. Damp, like melting ice.

For some reason, none of this had frightened me enough to make me leave.

But the girl did. I ran for my life. Back down the steps, along the road, and home.

Sam was playing on his bike with the others, racing up and down the field. He called out as I ran towards our caravans.

'Hey – Enid! Where've you been?'

'Joan McCready said she'd meet me at the corner shop, but she didn't turn up,' I lied.

'What – you went without Mum?'

'Don't tell,' I pleaded, removing my shoes and diving into the warmth of my parents' caravan. Mum was cooking tea and Dad was smoking a fag.

Mum wiped her hands on her apron. 'Enid, be a doll and put out the dishes, will you?'

'Okay.' Happy to be back on safe ground, I agreed willingly for a change.

'But wash your hands first. Look at you - you're filthy.'

I held up my hands. My fingertips were black bright. Which surprised me. I wouldn't have thought it possible to collect dirt from an invisible house.

'Sorry, Mum.'

I washed them in the bowl of soapy water Mum always kept at the bottom of the caravan steps. We had to be careful not to trip over it as we walked in and out, but Mum was so proud of her lovely caravans she wanted to keep the dirt outside. So we had to take off our shoes and wash our hands and keep everything clean and tidy. They were nice, though, our caravans, with plum red paint and bright yellow wheels. Inside, there was beautiful paintwork everywhere, and comfy seats, and little gaslights with pure white mantles.

We had two caravans. One for me and Sam to sleep in, and one for my parents. Theirs was bigger, with a tiny black kitchen range and a battered old alarm clock on the mantelpiece. This is where Mum did all her cooking. My favourite was sausage and mash. Not very exciting, I know, but Mum always made it taste delicious, with thick onion gravy. And apple crumble, the apples picked from any trees we could find. Those few months in Dorset we camped in a farmer's field. I remember it vividly. Waking to the murmur of tractors. Eating our evening meals with the scent of honeysuckle tickling our noses. And listening to the roar of waves lashing the beach in the silence of the night. Mr Jackson, the farmer, always had a big smile on his face. Most people don't like the Romani, but he did. He even fed our horses with hay, free of charge. Even now I remember the scent of Topper, my horse. The sweet smell of harness oil, the touch of his soft warm nose, and those velvety lips that would grab every potato I offered. How well I remember.

Nowadays there are no horses, no caravans, except the ones that pass through on their way to the Caravan and Camping Club in Folksbury. No. Just me in my little cottage in Pepingham, my herbs and flowers, my spells and incantations. And Genevieve, of course. Genevieve is fifteen years old, quite good going for a cat. The Romani consider cats to be unlucky; you'll never see them anywhere near one. But when Peggy brought her to me, a tiny bundle of black fur and green eyes, mewing gently, she just won my heart.

Peggy Fleming is an old and very dear friend. She lives in Folksbury, the next village along on the main road to Grantham. We go back a long way, me and Peggy, to when I first lived here. I was out shopping, getting to know the area, and we began chatting in the fruit and veg shop where I bought my potatoes. She still works there, you know. You can see her outside in all weathers, rearranging the produce on the old cart, her fingers wrapped in thick woollen gloves. But it lets her keep an eye out as to what's going on. And boy, does she see some things. But then, it means she can help people.

And that's where I come in. If she needs me to help too, she just asks.

Which she did. Last night. It was nearly nine o'clock and I was in the kitchen feeding Genevieve (she likes her bowl in just the right place, under the table so she can eat in private) when the doorbell rang. Now I get a bit nervous on my own at night and it doesn't get any easier as I get older. But I'm luckier than most - I do have Genevieve. So off she skips towards the front door, tail held high and proud. I followed quickly, my heart in my mouth. We're a small village, but there have been times when people travelling through have taken it into their heads to just come and help themselves.

Genevieve turned, giving me the nod. It was Peggy, I knew it was Peggy. So I opened the door, the cold December night hitting me with a blast like cold steel.

'Enid. How's things?' So in she stepped, the peppered scent of patchouli oil wandering just ahead of her, and wiped her boots on the mat.

'I'm okay, thanks, Peggy. And you?'

'Fine, fine. Mm, smells good. You still baking, then?'

Pulling my cardigan around me, I locked the door. 'Just a few more to do. You still got room in your freezer?'

Hanging her coat on the hook, she followed me into the kitchen. 'Of course. Well, there's only me, and I don't eat much. Not these days.'

I scraped the tin clean for Genevieve, placed her bowl onto the floor, and watched her disappear beneath the crimson tablecloth.

'Tea?' I asked.

She sat back, crossed her long slender legs, and smiled. 'That would be just dandy.'

I lit the tea-lights I always keep on the table, and filled the kettle in a bit of a daze, wondering why she was calling round on such an awful night and at such a late hour.

'How are you *really*, then?' I asked.

'Just got one of them sheepskin coats for the winter. Off of ebay, it was. Ian helped me find it – I don't do online, as you know. Wasn't too bad a price, either, and it fits just right.' She rubbed her hands together gleefully, the huge gold ring she always wears shining in the candlelight.

I pulled down two cups and placed a bag into the teapot. 'Nice. You should have worn it tonight. What colour is it, then?'

'A kind of biscuit colour. Gorgeous, it is. I really bought it for the shop. It'll get dirty quickly, I know, but it'll keep me lovely and warm.'

'Just what you need, then.' I poured milk into a jug. 'So come on, Peggy, out with it. What brings you all the way here on such a miserable night?'

The smile fell from her face. 'We've got trouble, Enid.'

2

Tori Seaborne

Thursday December 10th

WHAT is it with ripped jeans? My knees are fucking freezing!

I do love them, though. I mean, they're not designer or anything. Well, Mum can't afford H&M, and Nan just flat-out refuses to buy them. Which I kind of understand, to be fair.

'I'm not wasting good money on brand new jeans,' she says every time I ask, which is all the time, really. 'Not when they've already got holes in them. Ridiculous, I call it. Waste of money. They can see you coming, young lady ...'

So I've made my own. Well, okay, I've cut rips in my old jeans, the ones from Primark, the only ones that still fit me. Wish I hadn't, though. Because here I am, stood here, freezing cold, my knees literally purple, waiting for Raff to appear. Rafferty. Shit name, yeah? You've got to ask yourself what his mum was thinking. And he's *still* in the pub, him and two of his mates. Getting pissed, no doubt. Jack and Jacob. What is it with boys these days – their names all begin with J? Except Raff, of course. Obvs. Anyway, he's still in the Royal Oak and I'm still stood out here in the cold crappy fresh air. The only thing warming me up is my fag, and it's nearly my last one. The landlord threw me out an hour ago. Only reason I bought the fags, too. I don't really smoke, I'm not hooked or anything, just thought it would lend a certain gravitas, make me look more grownup - you know. I borrowed the money from Mum's bag, so I hope she doesn't notice. Well, if she does I'll defo pay her back.

When I get a job.

Pity about the last one, although it did last three months. I was only late a couple of times as well, but any excuse to get rid. Miserable cow. Calls itself a coffee shop. More like a greasy spoon. She's no more an idea of how to make a latté than I have. And luxury hot chocolate? She's having a laugh. Cheapest stuff she can get, and *then* she waters it down.

I can see him. Yeah, he's at the door. About time too. Freezing out here. 'Hi!' he shouts, and I'm in his arms before you can say 'give us a hug'. We run all the way back to his place. His parents are away for a few days, Norfolk, I think, so we have the place to ourselves. Nice house, too. Massive. His dad sells posh cars. I've only been here once before, when his dad was at work and his mum was off shopping in London. I am impressed, of course I am, but it's not home. It's a cold kind of a house, not cosy like our apartment.

We say hi to Fudge, their chocolate lab, climb the stairs, and are snuggled up in bed before midnight. Raff places a bottle of real champagne in a silver ice bucket and a pack of Benson and Hedges onto the bedside table. For before and afterwards, he says. So we drink the champagne, which is totally awesome. Then we have sex, which is just amazing, because Raff drops ice cubes from the bucket down my back and we end up in fits of giggles. Raff is so beautiful. I do love him. Then we smoke a ciggie between us - well, I pretend to. I never inhale, it's just rank.

Raff always uses a condom after the scare we had the first time. I mean, I did tell him I was on the pill, but he was still scared shitless. It was unplanned, you see, we were rat-arsed, did it without thinking. On his neighbour's white sofa, as well. Raff was babysitting and I'd only popped round for a chat. As you do.

Anyway, we use one this time, so he's not so worried. And yeah, it's good, awesome.

I wake up at two, check my phone, yelp, and fling on my clothes. My texts and missed calls are going crazy. Mum! I kiss Raff goodbye and run home through the dark, my feet barely touching the ground.

She's sat there in the kitchen waiting for me, an open paperback and a cuppa on the table, half the pack of biscuits gone. Nan's in bed, sock out.

'Where've you bloody well been?' Mum murmurs through gritted teeth.

I never could lie.

'Raff's', I pant, out of breath.

'You could've let me know, Tori. I've been worried sick.' Her soft green eyes are wrinkled with fatigue, her face is pale, and her left hand's clutching her phone like it's trying to escape *I'm a Celebrity*. 'I never know whether or not to ring the bloody police.'

'Sorry.' I throw my hoodie onto the sofa, hug her quickly and slump onto the chair beside her. She obviously wants to 'talk'. The table's littered with old magazines and dirty cups, so I pull a Woman's Own towards me and devour the fashion pages while Mum lectures. On and on and on. And on. She goes from crying one minute to practically screaming the next.

'If your father was here, not that he was much bloody use when he *was* ...'

'I love you. And the thought of you out at all hours with all kinds of boys ...'

'Just promise me one thing. That you'll work bloody hard at school, that you'll do better for yourself than I ever did …'

Still reading, I nod. 'I promise, Mum.'

When she's finished, she yawns, then kisses the top of my head tearfully. 'Come on, bedtime. School in the morning. Night-night, my darling, God bless.'

She heads towards the bathroom, but I stay where I am, tired but happy. And not a bit concerned. You see, Raff has just said he loves me. I am ecstatic. I am loved. I am over the fucking moon.

I pull open the fridge door. I'm starving and fancy something really sweet. The only thing I can see is the jar of strawberry jam Nan bought at one of those farmers' markets. I drop two slices of bread into the toaster and push down the handle.

Then I feel it. That sensation. It's really weird, I've felt it before. As if someone's watching me. Always when I'm on my own. A coldness, a shadow at the door, like someone has taken the flat and emptied it out, leaving just me and the kitchen. It's difficult to describe, but it really, really freaks me out. I'm so scared I'm holding my breath.

Leaving the bread in the toaster, I force myself through the doorway, down the hall and into my room. Pulling on my PJs, I crawl into bed, a slow unearthly shiver still running down my spine.

My alarm goes off at seven. As I reach for the clock my duvet slips to the floor and I grab it, pulling it back over my head and trying to return to the awesome dream I've been having. I have some really weird dreams too, but I never, ever want to return to them. They're like, so *real*. Mum says it's from eating too much cheese at bedtime, but I don't, not really.

I'm quite looking forward to chatting to Mum before school, but she's already mad at me for leaving bread in the toaster. Wasting food again.

'You'll eat it, madam, cold or not,' she says, slapping it onto a plate.

I eat it, covered in thick yellow butter and Nan's jam. Cold toast isn't that bad, to be fair. But what I don't understand is this. Mum's always telling me off for wasting food, but when I do eat it she goes on at me for *eating her out of house and home*. I can't win.

I catch the bus to school, as per. Danielle's in her usual seat at the front, looking out for me. Billie, Dorothy, Nicky and Beth sit further back while Jake, Jacob, Jack, Joe and Jamie are on the back seat, messing around. No surprises there, then. Do boys' names begin with a J because it's a soft sound, I wonder, mothers trying to make their sons gentler, more empathic? Well, it doesn't work, I can tell you. No way does it work.

I shout 'Hi' to Billie and the other girls, then crash onto the seat beside Danielle, holding my Hollister

me a favour. I'd have been pushing a buggy round the streets and putting out rank nappies for the bin-men by now.

Danielle and I chat about her and Chris for the twenty minutes it takes to reach Grantham, then I just have to tell her.

'I've got news of my own,' I venture, hardly able to contain my excitement.

'What?'

The Y3s are *really* noseying now.

'He says he loves me.'

'What?' she repeats, the bus doors opening noisily.

Scurrying off my seat, I shout at the top of my voice.

'He loves me! He says he loves me! Woohoo!'

Miss Kilfoil's our French teacher. She's a real sweetie, better than the last one who ended up separating me and Danielle for talking all the time. Miss Kilfoil just lets me and Danielle get on with it, practically encourages us to talk. We're supposed to be coming up with loads of adverbs this morning. Most adverbs are just the adjective with 'ment' added, so they're dead easy, and Miss Kilfoil's letting me and Danielle help everyone else as she has work to do. Mock exam stuff for January or something. But it's great, I love it, walking round the classroom, people holding up their hands. Doesn't make me want to be a teacher, though. No way. I think it would drive me mad, all those hormones whizzing round, teenage girls messing with their hair, spotty boys leering if you so much as wear a tight tee-shirt. Yuk!

Oh, my God! A message from Raff. Inviting me to his place on Saturday for dinner. It's his mum who's inviting me, too. I've only met her the once, and she's already putting my feet under the table. Shit, what the hell do I wear? Practically everything I own is too small, or worn out, or torn. I've got that red dress, the one that's a bit see-through, that Nan bought me for a school party a couple of years ago. But honestly, I can hardly move in it, it's so tight. That'd look alright, wouldn't it, leaning over for the gravy and the back of my dress ripping apart? I suppose I've got those weird black trousers Mum bought me, but I hate them, and they're not exactly the kind of thing you wear to dinner, are they? I need something sexy, something that makes me feel good. Something really special.

We've come straight back to Danielle's after school. We did have to pick up her kid brother from the childminder's first as her mum's still at work, but that's cool. Christian's only just started school, so he does mornings there and goes to the childminder's for the afternoon. He's alright, actually, is Chris. A bit sniffly and cries at the slightest thing, but then he is only five. Danielle says he takes after his dad for that, because he's always moaning about things too. But he's not her real dad, her mum's remarried, so she can say that and get away with it.

I busy myself making cocoa-flavoured biscuits, so we can eat. Mrs Harrison refuses to buy biscuits and cakes, so Danielle and Chris have to snack on grapes and Babybels and stuff. Not very filling after a hard day at school. But the biscuits are so delish I burn my tongue on the first one. We scoff the lot, at the same time entertaining Chris with his new finger puppets. I'm the wicked witch out to steal the biscuits, while Danielle plays the princess, and Chris the prince. The prince wins, of course, bashing the witch on the nose and knocking her out. As I roll back onto the carpet, Chris is laughing so much he's actually crying. He's really quite cute. He's got Danielle's huge eyes and long, dark eyelashes.

When Mrs Harrison gets home, she takes care of Chris so we can go up to Danielle's room. It's all sugary pinks and ivories, but it's actually really nice, always neat and tidy. We fall onto the bed, a massive king-size, put on some music (Olly Murs, of course), and check out Facebook and stuff. Billie's posted a picture of her new dog, a West Highland Terrier, on Instagram, and we admire its cutie-pie face. Beth's posted pictures of the new bike she's getting for Christmas. It's black with bits of silver all over. I don't know why she's getting it now, though. I mean,

I like surprises for Christmas. But hey, she's really sporty so I'm sure she'll have fun.

Then it's time to get down to the important stuff. Basically, what do I wear to Raff's on Saturday?

I try on some of Danielle's clothes. She's really cool, slim, always looks just so. But her clothes don't look good on me. In fact, they look awful. It must be the colours, we decide. I mean, I usually wear black, grey or dark blue, sometimes a splash of red or purple. Danielle wears pastel colours, soft greens, apricots, pinks and blues. She looks fab in them, like a model. I look horrendous, and end up throwing everything to the floor in a temper. Within twenty minutes her bedroom looks like mine, a heap of dresses, skirts, jeans, tops and metal coat hangers that cling to everything like the tendrils of a giant sea anemone. Suddenly, though, Danielle has this brainwave.

'Here. Try this.' She pulls a black dress from her under-bed drawer. It's slim-fitting, with long sleeves made of lace and a length that sits just below my thighs. I *totally* love it.

'It's way too short for me,' she continues. 'That's why it's in there. Bien sûr.'

Pulling it on, I twirl before the mirror, cringing at my bony white legs. Black leggings. Defo. Even if they are slightly too small for me, they'll still look awesome.

'It's fab, Danielle. I really love it. Can I borrow? Please?'

'You can keep it. I hate it.'

'What?' I shriek. 'No …!'

'It's yours. Forever.'

I can't believe it, I'm nearly in tears. I step over the piles of clothing to hug her. 'Thank you, thank you, thank you! You are the bestest friend in the whole wide world.'

Laughing, she pushes me away. 'Hey, you're doing me a favour. Mum bought it, so she might make me wear it, but if it's no longer there she can't. To be fair, I *was* thinking about taking it to a charity shop or something.'

I pull back. 'You're saying I look like a charity case?'

'No,' she laughs. 'Actually, you look totally amazing. That dress cost a fortune, but it looks awful on me. But on you …' she gazes at me thoughtfully. 'You look like a film star. Glamorous. Tall and sexy, and flaming gorgeous.'

Stunned, I sit back onto the bed.

I mean, I've never thought of myself as glamorous. I am *not* glamorous. But as I stare into the mirror behind her I can see what she means. A kind of Nina Dobrev look. Sounds big-headed, I know, but I can see it. Me. Like a film star. Oh, my God!

Tears fill my eyes. 'Thanks, Danielle.'

'You silly. Don't.'

3

Melissa Slater

Friday December 11th

SO that's it. I've invited her. Much to Ed's delight. But if he thinks I'm going to be all fussy-fussy over her, he's got another think coming. I'm going to show her up for what she is, a two-bit scheming little cow. What right does she think she has to seduce my son? Okay, he wasn't exactly a virgin when he met her. I know that, I'm not stupid.

But now he's fallen for her good and proper. Hook, line and bloody sinker. And after all that expensive private school education, he's going to end up married to some little slapper who lives in a rented apartment on Fulbeck Street with her mother and grandmother, and not two pennies to rub together.

And that, right there, is the attraction to my Raff. Obviously. She marries him, he takes over the business when Ed pops his clogs, and hunky dory – she's made for life. Unless he gets bored, of course. Which is highly likely, seeing as she's thick as two short planks. Hardly said a word when she came round that time. I'm not expecting great things tomorrow.

Well, I've finally sacked the cleaner. About time too. She never was any good. Don't know why we took her on in the first place. Teenagers. No idea how to clean a house. Leaves fingerprints on the windows, dust on the surfaces, and as for the en-suite sink - don't ask. Okay, I know she has a baby to look after, and she was a bit upset when I told her, but what can you do? No, I've appointed that firm that advertises in the village magazine. Hot Dollies, they're called. The owner seemed okay when I spoke to her, and they use that eco-friendly stuff too.

I'm off to meet Maxine and her friend Stacey for lunch. We're eating at Visocchi's, that new place on the high street. It's supposed to be *really* good. But then they always are when they've just opened. Give it six months or so, then we'll see what it's like. We're going shopping afterwards because Stacey's got a wedding coming up. A Christmas wedding too, how exciting is that? She wants something in keeping, long sleeves and fur jacket or something. She's okay is Stacey, a bit snobby, but quite down to earth really.

So.

Time to decide on the menu.

I'm thinking roast beef and Yorkshire pudding. Then that chocolate tiramisu cake I made last Christmas. Delicious. Knowing Raff, though, it'll end up being vanilla ice cream and orange jelly with sprinkles.

4

Enid

Saturday December 12th

I'VE known Peggy most of my life. Since I moved to Pepingham, anyway. She's known as old Mrs Fleming around here. As if she's always been old.

I was only twenty-one, a sweet nothing, when me and my Peter decided to settle down here. We used to run a bed and breakfast, you know. Ran it for nearly thirty-seven years. Until he went off with Mrs Lucy Conanby, one of our guests. The tart. What he saw in her I'll never know, and how he could do it right under my nose.

But that's by the by, so I'll stop now.

We made a good living out of it, brought up our kids on the income. And we had all sorts of people visiting. Lovely young couples for romantic weekends, retired bachelors on walking holidays, families itching to explore the area with their kids, or just folks staying for weddings at the local church.

The Parish church in Pepingham is quite special, dating right back to 1561. History books document it as quite a plain building originally, but it's had a few additions along the way, so now it's really beautiful. Even the grounds have something, they're so lovely and peaceful, and they look magnificent on the photos. So you can understand folks wanting to get married there.

But our B&B guests, bless them, would sometimes have marital problems of their own. I could sense it, as soon as they walked through the door. Genevieve, too, would wander round the house knowingly, her ears pricked and her tail high. Not this house, not the one I live in now. No. We owned a beautiful place back then, extended it when we first started out so we could take people in. No, the one I live in now is a small stone cottage, two-up, two down, with a kitchen extension, an extension for a bathroom upstairs, and a small conservatory to one side. That's where I grow my herbs. It's just off the main road, not far from the greengrocer's. The greengrocer's wife, Abigail Croxley, knows Peggy quite well, both of them in the same trade. So I always stop to chat when I get my groceries of a morning.

I do like my cottage. It's called Chimney Cottage and is the end one in a row of four. It was built in 1790, so the floors are a bit creaky, but it's just right for me, not too big to look after now I'm on my own, and it's along a little cul-de-sac with an unmade road leading to beautiful woodland. I like it best in the autumn when the leaves have turned gold, the light's a soft grey, and the air has the musky scent of wood-smoke. Gorgeous, it is.

I very nearly bought an apartment, you know. On the main road. When I think about it now, the thought of living there drives me crazy. I'd have gone mad, with nothing to do but watch the telly all day, or listen to the traffic flowing along outside. No. I changed my mind at the very last minute when I saw the *For Sale* sign go up on this place. Snatched their hands off, I did. So now I can get out, potter in my garden, wander along to the shops, take a walk through the woods, and chat to people. Old Bill Mitchell always stops and talks, brings me flowers from his garden, maybe a bit of rhubarb in the winter and some raspberries in the summer. He does love his garden. He's a bit of a drunkard, truth be told, but his heart's in the right place. But no, I think if I'd had to climb up to that apartment with my bits of shopping every day, I just wouldn't have got out and about so much. It would have been too big a deal. My Carol wanted me to move down to Nunhead in London to be near her, you know. But I resisted. She doesn't want to be worrying over me day and night. That's not what you bring your children up for. No. I'm much better being independent, and I have my friends, and Genevieve.

As for the guests with their marital problems, it really unsettled me at first. I'm kind of sensitive that way. Any little eddies, any disturbances in the air, cause my toes to twitch, my skin to crawl, like termites in the sand. I've always been the same.

So Peggy and I decided to do something about it, to try and help them. She usually takes care of Folksbury while I look after Pepingham, but she wanted to help.

We're witches, you see. White witches. Wiccans. There's at least one in every village and many more in every town. Where there isn't one, we take it in turns to help out, whenever the need arises.

It was the Seventies, the era of David Bowie and T-Rex, cheesecloth shirts and flared trousers. We'd wait until the guests had gone out for the day, for the wedding and the reception afterwards, tottering along in their platform shoes, their long permed hair (women and men) blowing in the wind. While they were out, we'd place muslin bags inside their pillowcases. One for him and one for her. It was a bit of trial and error at first, I must confess. But eventually we found the ultimate remedy. Each bag was filled with three garlic cloves and two red rose petals, then we'd soak them in violet leaf essential oil. It was always a bit of a rush - you couldn't make them too far in advance or the oil would dry out. But we did it, and it worked every single time. You could tell. They'd come down to breakfast the following morning, laughing and joking, unable to keep their hands off each other. It always pleased me to see it, although Peter never liked me doing it, said I was interfering. He never got much involved in the business anyway, apart from the practical stuff, DIY and suchlike. No, he preferred to sit there all morning after the guests had gone out, with the wireless blaring and the paper spread across the kitchen table, leaving me and the girl we had in to clean the rooms. And he never liked Peggy. But she's a real friend and I don't know what I'd do without her these days, now I'm on my own.

Last Tuesday evening, however, I knew there was something very, very, wrong.

'What do you mean, Peggy? What kind of trouble?'

'Young girl. Been here before. Suicides.'

Tut-tutting, I poured steaming water into the teapot.

'Oh, dear.'

'I've been contacted. She has a great-uncle who's been keeping an eye out. Apparently she's committed suicide before, she's in danger of doing it again, and he wants it to stop.'

I stirred the tea with a spoon and replaced the lid, covering the pot with the blue hand-knitted tea cosy I got from that vintage place up the road. 'How old is she, then?'

'Only sixteen.'

'The poor kid.'

'But it means we have work to do.'

'Biscuit?' I offered her my tin of cinnamon shortbread. Cinnamon's full of manganese, very good for us old folks.

'Thank you.'

'Do we know what happened before?'

She nodded her approval of my baking. 'Mm. Good.'

'Thank you.'

'She was a good witch, a wiccan. A kind of you and me. Some people didn't like it, set out to destroy her. It was the beginning of the war, and she was due to help out.'

'Which war?'

'The Great War, the First.'

'That's a long time ago.' I poured tea, handing her a cup.

'Thanks,' she murmured, pouring in some milk and stirring, her old hands wrinkled with rich blue veins. 'But that was only the first suicide.'

A shiver ran across my shoulders, an unseen hand brushing softly by. I returned to my seat and Genevieve jumped onto my knee. I stroked her dark, soothing fur.

'So what happened, exactly?'

'Obviously, I only got the name and date from Great Uncle John. I've had to do a bit of digging myself.'

Uttering a deep sigh, she took a few sips of tea, pulled some wayward hair from her face and tidied it back into the grey bun she always wears.

'I've written it down.' Pulling a sheet of folded paper from her bag, she read. 'She was named Clotilde Dourdos, born at home in July 1893 in an area of Paris called Arcis. She had an English mother and a French father. Bilingual. Useful. She was twenty-one when the war began, still at home and still doing the paperwork for her father's taxi business. But he was asked to use his taxi cabs to help transport French troops to the front. It was the First Battle of the Marne. I remember the story from my schooldays.'

I grinned. 'Wow. That's some going, Peggy.'

'Now then, Enid,' she warned, looking up and smiling.

'Sorry ...'

'It was General Gallieni who requisitioned them, hoping to defeat the Germans. Six hundred cabs they used, to carry three thousand men. Unfortunately, Clotilde's father fell down some stairs, broke his ankle, couldn't go …'

'So she did it,' I volunteered.

'She dressed as a man, flat cap, trousers, leather brogues, and set out to drive a group of men to the front line. Then she drove home again. Quite a feat for a young girl in those days.'

'Well done, her, I say.'

Peggy shook her head grimly. 'No. Not really. She ran into a group of Germans. They'd become lost, detached from their squadron or whatever they call them in Germany. They were tired, hungry, disillusioned. They raped her, one after the other.'

I went cold. 'My God …'

'She came home, and never told a soul. The only way anyone knew what had happened was when a farmer's wife came forward after Clotilde died. She'd called at the farmhouse to clean herself up before going home. She was the only child, you see, and very precious. The knowledge would have completely destroyed her parents.'

'I can understand that …'

'So of course when she discovered she was pregnant, she couldn't face telling them that, either. She took an overdose of the morphine her father was taking for his ankle.'

Sudden tears ran down my face. 'Oh. Peggy. That poor girl. Her poor mother.'

She placed her hand upon mine. 'She was twenty-one. Innocent. I can't imagine what it must have done to her.'

Distraught, I went to fetch my handbag from the sitting room, pulling out the small bottle of frankincense I keep there. Standing at the table, I dabbed some onto a hankie and breathed in. Genevieve, I noticed, had retired to sit beneath the radiator on the other side of the kitchen.

'You want some?' I asked.

Peggy nodded, and I poured three drops onto a clean tissue. I mix my own oils, this one with just a little sweet orange. It always lifts me, helps me feel better. Right then though, I could have done with the entire bottle.

'You want more tea?' I asked.

'I could more do with a tot of brandy, I don't know about you.'

'Aren't you in the car?'

'I know.' She shrugged her shoulders. 'Never mind, I'll have one when I get home. It helps me sleep.'

'I've got some wine in the fridge,' I offered. 'Half a glassful won't hurt, will it?'

She nodded. 'That'd be lovely, Enid. Thanks.'

I poured two glasses of ice-cold Pinot Grigio, and we clinked our glasses together.

'Cheers, Enid.'

'Cheers, Peggy.'

But its delicate flavour was lost on me. The spicy, peppery scent of the frankincense was all-pervading. Wonderful stuff. So before long, what with the frankincense and the wine, I found myself relaxing, a soft sigh escaping my lips.

'So, go on. What happened after that?'

'Well, she was born again three years later - not long, you notice - into a very wealthy family. Father a businessman, the mother a flibbertigibbet type ...'

'A social butterfly?'

'You could say that. According to Great Uncle John. Anyway, she grew up and married into another wealthy family. She was living in Yorkshire by this time.'

'Where you were born, Peggy.'

She smiled. 'But her husband went off to war, came home shell-shocked, psychologically damaged, a drunkard. He beat her about, bless her. Black and blue, she would have been. Rather than suffer the hell of her marriage or the stigma of divorce, she committed suicide. Threw herself off the bridge and drowned. Left two beautiful children behind.'

The atmosphere in my cosy kitchen suddenly changed. The tea-lights had blown out and Genevieve was sitting up, staring at me as if she'd seen a ghost.

I shivered involuntarily. 'Some people.'

'She has lived other lives, of course. Happier, more fulfilled lives.'

'According to Great Uncle John.'

'Yes. Obviously I'm only going on what he's told me.'

Peggy has this very special gift. She communicates with the other side. Actually no, they communicate with her. She's the legally ordained Wiccan High Priestess, you see. And, of course, she communicates with me. I do sometimes sense things around me, but not like she does. It's more with the people I've known. Like after my dad died, I could sometimes smell his cigarettes in the room, as if he was visiting, wanting a chat. And I'd talk to him, telling him all my troubles, all my joys. But I could never actually 'communicate' with him, much as it distressed me at the time.

'So what's happening now, then? Is she being beaten up again?'

Draining her glass, Peggy shook her head. 'No. She's a bit of a manic depressive, by all accounts. Boys. Sleeps around. Drinks. Low self-esteem and all that. Got a bit of a reputation, by all accounts.'

'Where does she live, then? What's her name?'

'She lives in that house on the corner of Fulbeck Street. You know the one. It's been made into two flats now. She lives with her mum and grandma in the upstairs flat.'

I remembered it. A lovely old building, built in the 1800s. It had lain empty for years, until someone from London with plenty of money bought it, did it up, and rented it out.

'I know the one. So what's her name, this girl?'

'Victoria Seaborne. Her grandmother's lived in Pepingham all her life, is well known around here.'

'Oh. Who is she, then?'

'Christine Jacobs. You know her?'

I nodded. 'I've heard of her, yes, I have.'

I'd heard her name mentioned at the greengrocer's – I think she's friendly with Abigail Croxley. But I'd never seen her to chat to.

'Her daughter Elizabeth moved down south when she got married. Then moved back after a rather nasty divorce.' Peggy grinned. 'You know me, Enid, been doing some research. She and her mum have been renting that flat for a while now, I think, because the only one that ever comes up in the paper is the lower floor. Nice apartments, they are though. Spacious, roomy, and there's a nice back garden for them to use.'

I pictured the scene. A grandmother, her daughter and her daughter's daughter. All living in the one place. Was there love there, or shame? Was Victoria able to take her pals round, have fun, play loud music? Was her mother house-proud, her grandmother the kind who makes cakes and biscuits?

Or did they sit in front of the telly all day, out of work, unloved, unwanted, feeling sorry for themselves?

'So how do we know she's suicidal?'

'Her boyfriend's about to finish with her. Again. Great Uncle John says she sleeps around, one lad after another after another.' She sighed deeply. 'Why do they do it, these young things? Why are they in such a rush to grow up, do everything before they're twenty?'

'I don't know, Peggy, I really don't.'

I sighed heavily, thinking of me and Peter when we were courting. All very innocent, it was. Well, apart from the odd fondle beneath my bra at the pictures on a Saturday night. And we thought that was naughty. But we were nineteen, not sixteen. And I was really, truly, madly in love, married him two years later.

'I suppose we got married earlier, kept ourselves out of trouble. Do you think?' I asked.

'I suppose.'

'Or maybe we just kept it all quiet, tried not to get pregnant and found out. We did get pregnant though, sometimes, didn't we? I remember a girl in the QAs had to leave because she was expecting a baby. The father was already married, so couldn't make her respectable. I don't even know what happened to her after that. Poor girl. She was a really good nurse, too.'

'These things happen for a reason, Enid, they really do,' she murmured.

'You mean she wasn't meant to be a nurse?'

'She probably fell in love with some gorgeous hunk willing to take on the baby, and is nicely settled down now, with a houseful of kids.'

'I do hope so.' I stood up. 'More tea?'

'Please.'

I busied myself with the teapot. 'So - what's your suggestion for this Victoria? Any ideas?'

'We have more than Victoria to contend with, I'm afraid. There are people out to encourage her, the very same people who prevented her from helping out during the war. She was destined for great things, according to Great Uncle John. What with her language skills and her bravery. She might have shortened that war by quite a few months, saving thousands of lives, all told.'

My blood turned cold. 'Which people, Peggy? They've reincarnated? Exactly what do we have to contend with here?'

Her eyes filled with sudden tears. 'Dark magic, Enid. Very dark magic.'

5

Tori

Sunday December 13th

IT'S happened again. That shadowy thing in the doorway. It was after I got home from Raff's last night, just before midnight. Mum was waiting up for me, as per, while Nan snored her head off. We chatted for a while over a cuppa, then she went off to bed. I made the big mistake of staying up for a while, messaging and stuff. And that's when I felt it. Someone watching me. Again. It really, really gives me the creeps.

I'm sure this place is haunted. It's scaring the shit out of me, but what can I do? I can't exactly ask if we can move out, can I? It'd cost a fortune. Besides, we've lived here for years and I doubt whether Nan would want to move now.

The church bells are going off on one again. Really good at waking me up after a night out, they are. Every Sunday morning. Without fail. I pull the duvet over my head, but it's no good, I can't get back to sleep. I check my phone instead, but Raff's not replying, must still be asleep. Danielle too. And Billie. Lucky things. In fact, the whole world must be asleep, apart from me. Why do we have to live right next to a church? I mean, what idiot would put a house *here*?

Last night was just awesome, though. My dress looked totally fab. The way Raff looked at me. I can tell he loves me, just from his eyes. And what totally amazing eyes. Deep blue, navy, the kind that melt your insides, dry your mouth, quicken your pulse, and make you want him right there. Right there on the kitchen floor. But his mum had to be there, didn't she? And his dad. Oh well, another time.

Actually, his dad was alright. A laugh really, just like Raff. But his mum. Oh, my God. Overboard. Trying too hard, the smile totally false. Just like the nails and boobs, I reckon. And when it came to her asking me about my parents, I found it really difficult.

She was so *obviously* checking to see if I was good enough for her precious son.

To be fair, I don't even remember my dad. Mum goes on about him as if he was a total loser, but he can't have been so bad. I mean, she married him, didn't she? And Nan never says a bad word about him, other than the fact that he never provides for us. Mum took him to court years ago, but he lied about his earnings. You can do that when you're self-employed, she says. He's a sports trainer of some kind, apparently. Mum says that covers a multitude of sins, but I don't ask, because she really doesn't like talking about him.

So when Raff's mum asked about my dad, I just had to say something, didn't I? So I made the whole thing up. Mrs Baker, my English teacher, she'd have been so proud of me. I sat there and told them all, right in the middle of dinner, how my dad was a manager at Jaguar Land Rover in Coventry. We've been studying the motor industry in Economics, so I know all about it, where the head office is, even how much GDP they produce. And Raff's parents took it all in. They squirmed a bit, though, when I said he'd taken out a huge mortgage, so couldn't afford to send Mum much money, which is how she comes to be working at the post office part-time. Then I embellished the whole lot by telling them how she got four A-levels at school and could have gone on to *be* somebody, but decided to stay home and look after me instead. And now she had Nan to look after, too. Mr Slater was lovely, said I was to call him Ed, said how much he admired women who gave up their careers to look after the kids, how his mum had done the same. And look where *he* is now. But she, Mrs Slater, smiled and sneered all at the same time, saying how unfortunate it was that Mum could only work at the post office, what with all that intelligence inside of her.

We had roast beef and Yorkshire pudding for dinner. Not like my Nan's Yorkshires. A bit too crisp for me. Pudding was nice, ice cream and orange jelly with sprinkles. Raff asked for it specially. Then we had coffee made in a machine that you put capsules into. Posh. If me and Mum want to be posh, we just make coffee in the percolator we bought at Oxfam. To be fair, it doesn't taste much different.

So then me and Raff went up to his room. To binge-watch *Skins*, we said. But within two minutes we were snogging each other's heads off.

'God, you look beautiful,' Raff kept saying. 'Wish my parents were out.'

His hands were all over me. Like he'd never wanted me so much in all his life. Like he just couldn't wait.

An hour later, we heard his mum climbing the stairs. By which time we were actually watching *Skins*. Brilliant stuff. She brought us some drinks, beer for Raff and orange juice for me. As if I was a kid.

'Come on, we'll share,' laughed Raff after she'd gone.

'Your mum!' I said, picking up his beer and drinking some.

'Well, you are only sixteen.'

'You're only seventeen!' I retorted, pretending to pour it over his head.

So when I got home at midnight, I felt really, really good. We'd had an amazing evening. Totally awesome. I think his mum and dad really liked me – well, his dad defo. But when I felt that *thing* in the doorway again, I felt so sick. I had to literally force myself through it to get to bed. Just the thought of it makes my stomach tighten and my skin crawl. As if there's a caterpillar making its way down my back. Ugh!

There's definitely something going on here.

After the bells have finished clanging and banging, I crawl out of bed, pull on my dressing gown, put on some socks, have a wee, and go through to the kitchen. Nan's already up, heated curlers in and cup of tea in one hand, listening to Steve Wright on Radio Two. Sunday Love Songs. A load of soppy stuff, if you ask me.

She smiles as I sit at the table. 'Cup of tea, love?'

Pulling my sleeves over my hands to keep warm, I nod. 'Please, Nan.'

She pours it from the pot. Old people don't make it in the cup like normal people. Economising, I think, you can use one bag instead of two. Probably the result of living through the war, when they didn't have much. Although Nan's not that old. Anyway, it's still nice and hot and I'm looking forward to drinking it. I watch the steam rise as she pours.

'Thanks, Nan.' I hold it between both hands and sip, warming my fingers, revelling in the heat. She's already opened the curtains, so I can see out to the street below. It's frosty, the cars and shop windows sparkle in the weak sunshine. I'm suddenly reminded of that ghostly feeling I had last night.

'Nan?' I say.

'Yes, love?'

'How long have you lived here?'

'Since your mum came up from Islington. I had a cottage along the road there,' she nods in the direction of the church, 'but it was only small, so when she and your dad split up, I sold it and we moved in here. It's got an extra bedroom and lots more space for you to run around in.'

'So that's about – what – fourteen years, then?'

'About that, yes.' She looks across curiously. 'Why?'

Putting my cup down, I lean forward, arms folded. 'Have you ever seen a ghost here?'

She laughs out loud. 'What? What makes you ask that, you funny'un?'

Embarrassed now, I shake my head. 'Just ... it's nothing.'

But she becomes suddenly serious. 'Sorry, love. Go on. Just what?'

So I blurt it out. 'I think there's a ghost, Nan. Here, right here in this kitchen.'

She looks round, at the window, the fridge freezer, the cooker, the washer. Finally, her eyes rest on the entrance to the hall. 'You think so?' she whispers.

A cold hand runs down my body. So I was right.

'You know, don't you? You know something?'

Her blue eyes, as calm and clear as the sky on a sunny day, assess me carefully. 'What have you seen, Tori?'

'Nothing. I've actually *seen* nothing. But I've felt it. A - a presence. A thing. I dunno, Nan ...'

She sits beside me, taking my hand. 'Tori, whatever it is, it won't hurt you. It will never hurt you. And yes, I have sensed it. Quite a few times. It's been here for years, ever since we moved in, really. It did used to scare me, but now I just accept the fact it's there, that it'll probably always be there, and I don't let it worry me.'

Stupidly, I burst into tears. 'But Nan – it scares *me*. I'm terrified to go to bed some nights.'

She pats my hand with her old wrinkled one. 'Don't cry, chick. I wouldn't let any harm come to you. I'd even move us out if it came to it, even though I love living here.'

I blink the tears away. 'Do you?'

'What, living beside that beautiful old church? You've got to be kidding. Who wouldn't love it? Churches have an aura about them, don't you think? Kind of peaceful. I thought it would do us good, take care of us, living beside it. And besides, I have my gorgeous genius granddaughter - good alliteration, yes? - living here with me. So what's not to like?'

Nan and her alliteration. She does make me smile.

'So what do you think it is, Nan? Is it really a ghost, or something more sinister?'

'Like what, young lady? Just what is going on in that head of yours?'

'I don't know. A – a poltergeist or something.'

'Aren't they the ones that throw things around?'

I have watched all the films. 'Yes, Nan.'

'And have you *seen* anything being thrown around?'

'No, Nan. Not yet,' I mumble.

'Well then …'

'You know what it is, don't you?'

'What I do know is that it won't hurt you.'

I jump up. 'What is it then, Nan? Who is it?'

She shakes her head mournfully. 'This is a very old house, my darling. We don't know what's happened here before, what can have caused dead spirits to hang around.'

I'm just about ready to scream. 'What have you seen, then? The same as me?'

'I've *felt* something, yes. In the middle of the night, if I can't sleep and come out to make myself a cuppa. And there are footprints on the floor sometimes, kind of frosty and white. But they've always gone by the morning.'

I've never, ever seen footprints on the floor. Now that really freaks me out.

'But Nan, that's *so* creepy. Isn't there something we can do to make it go away?'

'You shouldn't be scared, love. It will just be a sad old spirit hanging round, unable to find peace. For some reason. We mustn't be scared, we must just feel sorry for it.'

I sit back down. 'But we need to find stuff out, don't we? Can't we get rid of it, help it move on, or whatever they call it?'

Picking up the teapot, she empties it into the sink and refills the kettle, the old tap making its usual gurgling noise.

'You'd have to appoint some kind of exorcist, a ghost hunter or something. And Tori, love, we don't have that kind of money. Best leaving well alone, I think.'

'But Nan – it scares me.'

She turns, looks me in the eye. 'Then the only solution is to go straight to your room before midnight, avoid the kitchen altogether. Stay away from it.'

Her ageing face is bathed in sunlight from the window. Her calming presence soothes me.

'Okay, Nan. I get it. Nothing we can do.'

'That's right, my love. Another cuppa?'

It's alright avoiding the kitchen, I realise afterwards, but what about doors closing when I've purposely left them open? Or opening after I've shut them? And the times I smell something weird, like alcohol, like from a whisky bottle, when there's no-one there? No, it, the thing, might not be hurting me, but it's terrifying the hell out of me. I mean, Nan's obviously used to it, but the sooner I move out of this place the better, I think.

I concentrate on my maths today, algebra and simultaneous equations. I think I'm getting the hang of them now, after going through it with Danielle a million times. Her stepdad's a whizz at that kind of thing, so he shows her what to do, and she shows me. Algebra's just like a puzzle, really, you've got to break the code to find the answer. That's how I see it, anyway.

At one o'clock Mum pokes her head around the bedroom door. I'm stretched out on the floor, headphones in.

'You coming out, Tori?'

I groan inwardly. She obviously wants to 'talk'.

'I'm studying, Mum. Like you're always telling me to.'

'I mean, are you coming outside? It's beautiful out there. Thought we could go for a wander.'

Sitting up, I push my books away. I'm still in my PJs, I realise, and the cups and plates from the tea and fried egg butties Nan made me are still on the side.

'Okay. But I need to get dressed. Five minutes.'

So twenty minutes later we're outside in the fresh air. It is a beautiful day, she's right. Bright and sunny, not a cloud in the sky.

We walk along the main road towards Folksbury, enjoying the sun on our faces, the breeze in our hair.

'Just thought you should get some sunshine,' Mum says, 'before winter really sets in.'

'What about when you're always telling me to put sun-cream on?' I retort.

'That's when it's hot, in the summer, silly. You don't want wrinkles, do you?'

'No, Mum.'

She turns to me. 'I am very proud of you, you know – the amount of work you're putting in for your mocks. I just want you to know that.'

I'm embarrassed, but she smiles, that toothy grin she has where her oh-so-sad face just lights up.

'Thanks, Mum.'

'I just want you to have a nice life.'

That always gets me to thinking. What went wrong with *her* life? How come she's not done much with it?

'Mum?' I ask as we approach the zebra crossing.

'What?'

'What was my dad like?'

'A bastard, that's what he was like. Going off with other women, that's what he was like.'

'No. I mean before that. What was he like when you fell in love with him?'

Crossing the road slightly ahead of me, so I have to lengthen my stride, she sighs deeply.

'What was he like when I fell in love with him? Let me see now.' Another sigh. 'I met him in a bar. In St John's Wood, in London. I'd gone there with a couple of friends from work, just on a night out, as you do.'

'Where were you working?'

'I was temping. All over London, I went, lots of different offices. That time I was working for a firm of solicitors. Big place, it was. Important.'

'So how did you get to talking?'

'Oh, I fancied him straightaway, knew he was the one for me. It was Sonia who introduced us, though. She was the one who got talking to him, and I suppose it just went from there.'

'Was he good-looking, attractive - you know?'

Tucking her hands inside her pockets, she nods quietly. 'He was. You get your eyes from him.'

I grin at that. 'So where did he work?'

'Work? You're lucky if he's ever done a bloody day's work in his life. No, not that one. He had the brains, just couldn't be bothered to get them out.'

'So why did you marry him, Mum?'

'Got myself pregnant, didn't I? With you.'

'Sorry.'

Pausing, she turns to me, ruffling my hair. 'Not that I'd have it any other way. You know that. I love you, Munchkin.'

Embarrassed, I pull back and we carry on walking. 'So what kind of person is he, then? What kind of things does he like doing?'

'He likes listening to music, that's what he likes doing. Flat on his back if he can.'

'Mu-um ...'

'Sorry. Okay, he played the keyboard. He played in this band for a bit.'

Now that sounds interesting. 'Did he?'

She pushes her dark hair behind her ears, preening. 'He liked cars, and he liked to go out to the seaside on a Sunday afternoon for fish and chips.'

'What kind of car did he have?'

'Oh, he didn't own one. No, he just admired other people's.'

'So how did he get to the seaside?'

'We'd go to Brighton on the train. Loved it, I did. Very romantic.'

I shiver with delight. The fact that my parents were so much in love when they had me makes me feel special.

'How long did you know each other before you got pregnant?'

'Just a year. Not long, really. By then, he said he'd got work as a car mechanic, had to work long hours. So I wasn't seeing so much of him. At least, that was his excuse. I know better now. Still managed to get bloody pregnant, though.'

'But how? Weren't you on the pill?'

'What do you think I am? Bloody stupid?'

'Sorry.'

'No, I'd had the flu, been sick everywhere, for days. Pill must have come up with it. It wasn't like it is now, where they stick it in your arm.'

We've reached the turnoff to Folksbury, so we stop and turn around.

'Come on, let's get back home,' she says. 'Sky's clouded over.'

So has her mood, I notice. I take her hand.

'But Mum ...'

'What?' she asks.

'You did get me out of it.'

She smiles, and suddenly we don't need the sunshine.

'You're so right, Munchkin. I did get you.'

6

Melissa

Monday December 14th

WELL, the little bitch did alright, didn't she? I asked her all the right questions, but she still talked her way round. Father in management at Jaguar Land Rover indeed. Fat chance. Little toe-rag. No, he's probably skulking away in some prison somewhere. I know her sort.

I do wonder where she got the dress, though. It's definitely designer, but not your Ted Baker catering for the masses kind. No, something much more upmarket. Possibly Finders Keepers or even a Sonia

Rykiel. Obviously expensive. Probably stolen. Or borrowed. Mind you, who would lend to *her*? Oh, I don't know, maybe I'm wrong. Maybe it's just something she picked up in Next. Looked good on her, though. She's not bad looking, I'll give her that.

Rafferty's totally obsessed, you know. When I went up to his room afterwards, ostensibly to take up some drinks, her mouth was red raw. They must have been snogging the whole time. Watching *Skins*, my arse. Ed says he has to sow his wild oats somewhere. But I *mean*.

Stacey bought the most beautiful dress. It's only Dior. Dior! Pale blue with long sleeves and a v-neck. Just short of seven hundred pounds, it was. She bought shoes and bag to match, and plans on wearing her grey fox fur over the top. Faux, of course.

I only managed to get a couple of things for our trip to Bruges. A silver blouse and the softest cashmere jumper, in pale blue. We're going over there for a few days with Ade and Imogen. Ade's an old friend of Ed's, they practically grew up together. He married Imogen in his early thirties. She's a bit younger than him, but it all seems to have worked out. He owns his own business too, a builder by trade, and a good one at that. No shilly-shallying as far as Ade is concerned. Does everything by the book.

Maxine brought another friend with her for lunch. Eva, she's called. She came over, all hugs and kisses

So yes, as I sat there in my kitchen last Tuesday, a second cinnamon shortbread in my hand, my mind wandered back to my childhood, to happier times, times before I knew what the words *dark magic* meant.

'Penny for 'em?' murmured Peggy in her watered-down Yorkshire accent.

I smiled. 'Just thinking about my mum.'

'Funny how you still miss them, even after all these years.'

Peggy's mum was a nightclub dancer, back in the day. Even though she gave it up when Peggy was on the way, she still managed to instil in her a sense of the dramatic. Peggy loves her carmine-red lipstick. Bright red nails, too, when you can see them. The shop-work she does, dishing up mud-encrusted potatoes and carrots, means she has to wear woollen gloves most of the time. But even they have brightly coloured stripes.

'Life can be so short, can't it?' I said.

'Now don't get maudlin, Enid. We're here to help another life, to make sure she has one to live. And a good one at that.'

I chewed on my biscuit. 'So what's the plan?'

'We get to know her. We bear down on the family, throw a circle of light around it.'

I grinned. 'Like in the olden days?'

She nodded. 'Like in the olden days.'

'Duk Rak?'

'Duk Rak.'

Duk Rak is the Romani way of protecting the home, like a guardian spirit. My parents never used it, but I know of it from old Grandma Delaney. She'd always use it around the camp, wherever she went. Whenever we camped with her, I'd follow her round, watching as she placed flat stones on the camp boundaries, one in each corner, and one at every door and gate. She'd use egg-white to paint the ancient occult symbol of the pentacle on the stone, forming a protective seal. It was invisible once it had dried; they looked just like old stones sitting there. But you can use your hand instead of egg-white, if you prefer. There are minor chakras in the palms. Psychic energy can be either drawn or expelled from them. Like when healers lay on their hands to cure people. You can direct this energy into protecting a place or a property too, but you have to be quite experienced in the art. These centres of energy can be powerful tools of perception and healing. Unfortunately, they can also be used for evil purposes, including the Dim Mak, the death touch, although a really powerful aura is needed for this.

'It won't be easy, will it? It's not a very big garden,' I replied.

'It doesn't have to be. We can use the pillars on the garden gate and there's plenty of space at each corner, just inside the walls. The thing is to get in there without attracting attention.'

'So just who is it we're guarding against?'

She stared at me as if she'd seen a ghost. 'Someone I thought I'd seen the back of years ago.'

'Really?'

'Flora Middlewood.'

I was puzzled. 'Do I know her?'

'According to Great Uncle John, she and her cronies were around in Paris during the Great War. They sorted out Victoria in that incarnation, good and proper. And now they're back, to do more damage.'

'Does she live round here?'

'That's just the trouble, Enid. We don't know how she's incarnated herself into this life, who she is. She could be anybody.'

'Right. How do we handle that, then, an unknown enemy? It's alright using Duk Rak, but the poor girl can't stay in her apartment forever.'

'I realise that. She's still at school, she's young, she'll have to be out and about.'

'Right,' I repeated, wondering where on earth all this was going.

'No. We get to know her. Make friends. Infiltrate.'

'Peggy, with the best will in the world, I'm just a little old lady, you're an even older lady, so how …?'

'Now that's where Josie comes in.'

'Josie?'

'Victoria's mother and Josie work in the post office part-time. They work on different days, but they must surely have met each other.'

Josie and I have been friends for years. She lives in a two-up, two-down, not far from me, just a five minute walk. It's newer and smaller than mine; it's never been extended. But it's beautiful inside. A decorator friend of mine did it up for her a few years ago. Lovely, it is.

The following morning we were shouting through the letterbox to gain Josie's attention. It transpired she was out the back pegging out washing. The sky was grey with cloud and they'd forecast rain, but Josie's always good with the weather, knows exactly when it's about to pour. Without fail, I'd say.

It was nearly lunchtime, so I'd taken round one of the apple and sultana pies I'd made, thinking we could eat it with some custard. They were for a charity event the week before Christmas, so I'd been making them in advance and freezing them.

'Well, it's good to see you both,' Josie enthused, her Geordie accent cheerful, inviting.

We followed her into her kitchen, small but cosy, with warm terracotta tiles on the floors and walls. There was the faint scent of oregano oil, a useful herb to have in the wintertime. It acts like a disinfectant, good against the flu.

'Cup of tea?' she asked.

'I'd love one,' I said. 'Here, I've brought you an apple pie. I thought we could eat it now, if you fancy it.'

She winked at me in that wicked way she has, her brown eyes sparkling.

'I am feeling a bit peckish, now you come to mention it. I only just realised the time when I heard you knocking. Here, I'll make us a bit of custard to go with it.'

Peggy stretched herself out on a kitchen chair. She does remind me of Genevieve sometimes.

'So how are you, Josie? I've not seen you around for a while,' she said.

Josie pulled a Pyrex jug from the cupboard.

'Oh, you know. Been here and there, the usual, looking after the grandkids and stuff. I'm doing a bit of part-time work at the post office now, you know.'

'That's exactly what we've come about,' I murmured, removing the defrosted pie from my bag and placing it on the side.

'Really?' asked Josie, pouring milk into the jug.

'Really,' I nodded, filling the kettle for her.

Peggy smiled. 'You know Elizabeth Seaborne, don't you?'

'Lizzie? Well, we do a shift together now and then, if that's what you mean.'

'That's exactly it,' said Peggy. 'So you've already got a foot in the door.'

Josie pushed the pie onto a plate, placed it inside the microwave and pressed some buttons. Turning to me, she asked, 'Okay. So what's going on?'

Peggy relayed the whole story as we sat there, safe and warm, the cold December wind locked outside and the threat of danger to that poor young girl receding with our every word.

The pie was delicious, even if I do say so myself. Josie's rich custard stuck to the crust like glue, but the pastry remained crisp and crunchy. Just how I like it. I'd added a few drops of lemon balm tincture to the mix. It calms the nervous system, lowers blood pressure and soothes digestion. And a good helping of Tulsi to blow away any grumpiness over the festive season. Because, let's face it, Christmas can be damned hard work. The folks of Pepingham are definitely going to have peace on earth and goodwill to all by the time I've finished with them.

Josie licked her spoon clean. 'Nice bit of pie, that, Enid. You say you're selling them?'

'At the village fayre. It's in aid of the NSPCC. Nicole Brunewski's organising it all. I've made some gluten-free as well. Working with that rice flour, though, it did my head in.'

'Right, ladies,' interrupted Peggy. 'A plan of action. What we need to do is think of ways we can take Victoria and her mum into our confidence. Without scaring them shitless.'

We have to excuse Peggy's turn of phrase. Age has made her belligerent. But could I hell as like think of how to communicate with Victoria, let alone get her on side.

'How about inviting Lizzie and Victoria round for tea or something?' asked Josie.

'I can't see how that would help, to be honest,' replied Peggy. 'It needs more, something long-term, something that can happen over a period of time.'

'It might start up a nice little friendship – you never know,' I replied.

'What, with a teenage girl?' said Peggy.

Then Josie had her brainwave. 'How about offering Victoria a part-time job? Her mum was going on about her losing the one at the coffee shop a couple of months ago. There's your shop, Peggy, or I could ask at the post office. Or she could come and help with your pies, Enid?'

'Or do a little gardening. Or something,' I faltered.

'That's it!' exclaimed Peggy. 'Josie, could you ask Steve at the post office? I'll ask at the shop. They've never said anything about wanting someone extra, but I can ask for nothing.'

'Steve's never said anything either,' admitted Josie.

'I *could* do with some help in the garden sometimes,' I said thoughtfully, 'and she could even help with my pies, although I like to do my own baking. I like a nice bit of music playing in the background. But if it's going to keep her alive, then she's very welcome to come and help.'

'No guarantees there, but everything's worth a try. Definitely worth a try,' murmured Peggy, reaching for more pie. 'Now. We need to organise this Duk Rak.'

Josie waved goodbye through the sitting room window as we left. I remember it well.

But I remember it only because the glass made her lovely smile look all wrong. It sent a shiver through me, unexpected and cold. I waved back all the same, as though nothing was untoward. Little did I know.

It was only after I'd seen Peggy off in her car and had reached the gate to my house that I began to think about my ridiculous offer. How on earth do you keep a teenage girl occupied with work when there's only one of you? It's not like I've got an enormous house or a family to look after, or a busy B&B. That's it, I realised. I could take in a couple of guests at weekends. It wouldn't take much doing. I have a spare room with a shower. Admittedly, it's small, but there's a nice view, and I've done it all before. Victoria could come along, make beds, clean rooms, even make breakfast. She has worked in a café, after all. And the money I make could pay her wages. Genius. Smiling, I mentally patted myself on the back.

Genevieve brushed against my legs as I pushed open the door.

I bent down to stroke her. 'Hi there. You missed me?'

I could have sworn the blinking of her eyes was a nod.

8

Tori

Wednesday December 16th

RAFF was out with his mates last night. At the Royal Oak. Again. But I've got this awful cold, been coughing and sneezing all over the place, so didn't feel like going out. Plus my nose was red and sore from blowing, which is *not* a good look. Plus it was raining. Again. I did feel bad, though, not seeing him. I don't get to see him during the day, you see. He doesn't go to our school, it's not good enough for his nose-in-the-air mother. No, he goes to Abbey Hill, the private one that costs literally thousands of pounds.

All the money in the world wouldn't make me wear that uniform, though. No-one would want to wear that uniform. It's totally, and I mean *totally*, gross. I've seen them, yeah, wandering round town. Purple, with a lilac ribbon trailing round the edge of the blazer. I mean, *purple* blazers. How could they?

To be fair, there are definite advantages in going to private school. They have much longer holidays, for a start. They broke up for Christmas last Friday when we had a whole week left to do. You'd think if they're paying for their education they'd have shorter holidays, not longer, so they get their money's worth. So typical.

So there I was last night, in the kitchen, feeling sorry for myself, chatting to Danielle on the phone, when something caught my eye. There was someone moving outside. Someone in our garden. Near the wall. I peered out. It was a woman, an old woman. There was an old woman sneaking round in our garden.

I called out. 'Nan! Nan! Quick! Look!'

Half asleep (I think she'd been having a nap, bless her), she rushed over to where I stood.

'What's wrong, love? I can't see anything out there, if that's what you're looking at.'

'There's a woman out there. I've just seen her. Oh my God, there's another one. Look!'

There were *two* women in our garden, one much taller and younger than the other.

Nan followed my eyes. 'I can only see the one, love. Looks like she's checking something, I don't know.'

'Well, we need to go out. We need to see what they're up to.'

'Oh no, love. You're full of cold and I'm half asleep. Anyway, it's chucking it down out there. You'll catch your death.'

Shaking her head, she began to fill the kettle. Now I'm not gonna lie, she lives on tea, my Nan.

'But Nan, it could be anybody,' I insisted. 'What are they *doing* in our garden, anyway, out in all that?'

On impulse, I grabbed my coat from the hook in the hall and ran down the stairs to the back door.

'Oi!' I screamed, shielding my eyes from the rain. 'Oi – what are you doing here? It's a private garden, this is!'

The tall woman straightened up to stare at me. She was older than I'd thought.

'Victoria?'

Stunned, I paused in my tracks. 'Yes?'

'It's okay, I'm a friend of Josie's. She works at the post office with your mum. She said it was okay for us to take some of your nettles. We use them for our nettlespud soup, you see. Very nutritious, they are.'

I was immediately suspicious. 'But why our garden? There's loads of nettles around.'

'Well, they can be hard to track down after everyone's finished with their gardening. Besides, we know these haven't been sprayed with insecticide. Organic, that's how we like them.'

I still wasn't convinced. She had nothing in her hands, and no gloves on to protect her skin. It all looked very suspicious to me. And the smaller woman – I was sure I'd seen her around the village.

'Organic nettles?' I replied. 'You've got to be joking me.' But the exertion had got to my lungs and I began to cough loudly.

The small woman walked up to me and I knew where I'd seen her. She lives in one of the cottages on the road leading to the woods. Me and Raff see her chatting to the neighbours sometimes, when we take Fudge for a walk.

'I'm really sorry if we've disturbed you,' she was saying. Her voice was gentle and soft, kind of calming. 'You sound like you shouldn't be out here, anyway. You need to go back inside where it's warm.'

Even through the rain, even in the dark of the night, I could feel her presence, her coal-black eyes burning into mine, insistent, demanding. It *is* what you need, they were saying. It *is* what you need …

Confused, I blinked and shook my head. 'It's only a bit of a cold. I'll be fine.'

She took my arm. 'Come on, you don't want to catch your death out here. I promise we'll leave, just as soon as you're all nice and warm.'

I let her lead me to the back door, a solid glass contraption with leaded lights. She took me up the stairs and knocked on our apartment door. And it's only now that I wonder – how the hell did she know where I lived? We could have lived in the downstairs apartment for all she knew.

Nan opened it immediately. She'd obviously been watching from the window.

'Come in, come in. It's Enid Phelps, isn't it?'

The woman nodded, and I pulled my arm away abruptly as she entered our hallway.

'Cup of tea?' asked Nan.

'Enid' was sat at our kitchen table before you could say *bugger off and go away*, so I headed to my room.

Half an hour later, my cough had settled, I'd dried my hair off, and was on Instagram. Raff was still at the pub and Danielle was doing her homework, along with half my maths class.

Nan knocked at the door. 'Tori?'

I pulled it open. 'You okay, Nan?'

She nodded towards the kitchen. 'Come and meet Enid Phelps, love. She has a perfectly pleasant proposition for you.'

Her alliteration made me smile, but I hesitated, wishing I was down the pub with Raff. Not that they'd have let me in.

'Come on, love. It won't take long,' she encouraged.

So I sat down, grabbed a chocolate digestive, and let her make me a cuppa.

Enid Phelps smiled at me. She has a nice friendly smile, even though her teeth are old and a bit wonky. I admired her huge brass earrings and the row of heavy gold bangles on her wrist.

'I like your rings,' she said. 'Very pretty. Vintage, are they?'

She sure knows how to get round someone. I looked at my fingers. I have a ring on each one, apart from my third finger, left hand. Obvs.

'They're Nan's,' I replied. 'She gave me them for my birthday in November.'

'Seven solid sacred charms, that's what they are. To bring you luck,' said Nan.

Enid smiled. 'They're lovely. And you wear them all at the same time?'

'Yeah,' I shrugged. 'Don't see why not. I never take them off.'

My rings are my pride and joy, I love them. And they are vintage. From Nan's teenage years and then her marriage to Grandad. Two of them are real diamond, one has a pearl, and the rest are gemstones, two blue, one purple, and one with a deep red garnet. I think they look really cool, all next to each other. Better than cheap nail varnish any day.

She smiled again. 'I've been chatting to your nan, as you may have gathered.'

'Where's your friend?' I asked, suddenly realising how long she'd been here.

'She'll have gone home. I shouldn't worry about her.'

'So what *were* you doing, sneaking around our garden?'

'Collecting nettles, like we said. They're chock full of vitamins. Peggy uses them for her gout.'

I still didn't believe her. 'Right. So she can pick nettles without gloves on, can she?'

'Of course not. She had plastic gloves in her pocket, all ready.'

'And she's your friend, is she?' I gratefully sipped the tea Nan brought, and picked up another digestive.

'She is, and a very good friend too.'

'So what is it you want to talk to me about? What's this proposition?'

'I'm looking for someone to help around the house, and your Nan said you might be available. I need someone who can maybe do a bit of cooking, make the beds, do some gardening.'

'What, like a home help?' I retorted.

'No, Victoria. The thing is, I used to run a bed and breakfast, and I've thought I might start one up again. Maybe just weekends at first. You know, taking in couples who want to go walking or visiting local villages and so on.'

I shook my head. 'Well, if you're asking me to do it, then I don't know. I'd have to think about it.'

'I pay good money,' she coaxed.

I didn't trust her. There was something about her that wasn't quite right, as if she was lying out the back of her wonky old teeth. I avoided her gaze, which was definitely trying to win me round.

'I – I need to ask Mum first.'

Mum was still at the post office, stocktaking or something.

She stood up. 'Well, let me know, once you've decided. I'm on Canwick Lane and it's Chimney Cottage, last one on the right. When you're ready.'

When Mum got home, I told her to sit down while I made her a cuppa and warmed her dinner in the microwave. Nan and I had already eaten.

'What's all this about?' she asked, bemused.

'Nothing, really …'

She patted the chair beside her. 'Come on, Miss. Sit down.'

So I sat. Nan was on the sofa behind us, watching telly. A documentary on Norfolk, some ageing actor who couldn't get acting work.

Mum smiled. 'Come on then, Munchkin. Out with it.'

'Well, we've had this woman round. Really weird, she was, totally unbelievable. There were actually two of them, out in the garden digging up nettles. So they said. Out in the pouring rain.'

'Really?' I could tell she wasn't taking this seriously.

'The other woman says she knows someone called Josie who works with you. Is that true?'

Pushing food into her mouth hungrily, she nodded. 'Actually, Josie did mention someone called Enid, just before I left. Something about a job.'

'Okay.' I digested this. So they *were* telling the truth about something.

Nan joined in, one eye still on the telly. 'She's offered Tori a job – that's what all this is about.'

'No, it isn't,' I protested. 'I just thought they were weird, digging up nettles in the rain and not even asking first.'

Mum put down her fork. 'Doing what?'

'Bed and breakfast,' Nan replied.

'You're still at bloody school. And why would they ask *you*, anyway?'

'Right. Thanks, Mum, done a lot for my bloody ego, that has. To be fair, it is only weekends.'

The idea of earning money for new clothes seemed suddenly attractive. I could buy lots of little black dresses. Just so Raff can rip them off.

'Weekends? Well, I suppose you could just about manage that. So long as it doesn't interfere with your schoolwork. How many hours?'

'I dunno, Mum, I didn't ask. I just said I'd think about it.'

'Well then, you'd better find out, hadn't you? I don't suppose they'll pay much, but it's better than nothing.'

'I'll call round after school some time, shall I?'

'That reminds me – have you done your schoolwork yet, Tori?'

'No, I didn't feel like it.' I coughed to emphasize how bad my cold was.

'No excuses, young lady. What have I told you? Your French teacher, Miss Tinfoil – she …'

'Kilfoil.'

'Miss Kilfoil - she's told me she wants you to do it for A level next year, and another language, maybe Spanish. Says you've got a knack for it. She's thinking you might do a Middle Eastern one in the evenings, too. They're doing after-school stuff now, you know. She thinks you've got a real flair for languages, it could take you a long way if you work hard. So give me that bloody phone, and get yourself to your room.'

School today has been totally boring, and I don't feel at all well. In fact, I'm tempted to bunk off and go round to Raff's, despite my sore nose. But Mum will kill me if she ever finds out, and school are bound to ring her. So I sit here, disgusting green tissues piling up in my bag, and get through two hours each of Maths and Physics. Gross. And I've got French and English this afternoon.

Actually, languages are alright most of the time. I quite enjoy them, really. In French, me and Ross Bachchan, whose mum and dad come from New Delhi, end up in stitches at the back of the room. We've been teasing Danielle because she has a love bite on her neck. And she's not happy.

Miss Kilfoil has given us a comprehension to do, so we're all busy writing, but we're allowed to talk and ask each other questions.

'What's love bite in French?' Ross asks Danielle.

She blushes, pushes me away because I'm sat next to her, and continues writing, all the while avoiding my eyes.

Ross looks across to me, and we both feel really bad.

'Sorry, Danielle,' I whisper. 'We're only joking.'

She grins cheekily, and we're all friends again.

Once English is over, I catch the bus and dash round to Raff's. He's arranged for some friends to come over – the usual crowd – and is up for a party. But when I arrive, his parents are still there and there's only Raff and Fudge to greet me at the door.

'Where is everyone?' I ask.

'Not coming. Mum and Dad are upstairs. They were supposed to be going to Bruges for a long weekend, but it's been cancelled. One of the friends they were going with is in hospital.'

Instead, we get the bus into town and wander round the shopping centre. I look at clothes, as per, then sit in Costa for ages with a mocha latte and toasted teacake. Raff buys because currently I'm penniless. The shops are dead, everyone's gone home, and it's freezing outside, a biting wind, and I haven't brought my coat. Mum would kill me if she knew (I hide it in my room when I'm at school), but it's a total pain having to carry it everywhere. The coat-hooks are all in the science block, so unless I have physics, biology or chemistry as my last lesson, I have to dash to the other end of school to get my coat before I catch the bus. And I always miss it.

Anyway, Raff's messaged Josh and Dylan to come and join us in Costa. Dylan, who drives and actually *owns* his own car, brings along his girlfriend, Megan Harvey. She's in the year above us, doing A levels. She's the sophisticated type, all shiny hair, French manicures and Ugg boots. She's alright really, I suppose, but can be a bit stuck-up sometimes, which makes me feel totally intimidated. Especially when we get to talking about school hols and what everyone's going to be doing. I mean, my God, her parents are taking her to Switzerland for Christmas. They have family over there, so they're spending the whole holiday with them. Oh my God. I've never been as far as fucking Scotland.

So by the time we get back on the bus, I'm feeling dead miserable, am coughing and sneezing, and need a great big hug. Raff's parents have by this time gone to visit their friend in hospital, so we have the house to ourselves. He makes omelette and chips in the microwave, and we end up in bed together. But I'm feeling really lousy by this time, so we just fall asleep. At ten o'clock I wake up and make my way back home.

I've had the weirdest dream, though. Seriously. I told you I have weird dreams sometimes? I see Megan, Dylan's girlfriend. She's crying, that's all I can see. She's crying, really, really upset. Strange. It's what's wakes me up, to be honest.

So I get home just after ten, my nose running with snot. I'm freezing cold and wanting to soak in a really hot bubble bath. Mum's still up, watching the news, something to do with the Paris bombings. Terrible stuff. Looks like they've found some evidence or something. Anyway, I walk in, telly blaring out, Mum on the sofa, and Nan in bed.

'Where's your coat, young lady?'

'In my room.'

'I know it is. I just found it, screwed up in a ball under your bed. That bloody birthday present I spent a bloody fortune on in Hollister. And you can't be bothered to wear it?'

Shamefaced, I put the kettle on. 'Sorry, Mum. I do really like it, honest. It's just - I have to carry it round school with me and it's really bulky.'

'Don't they give you pegs to hang things on? It's no wonder you're full of cold. You look dreadful. Come on, run yourself a bath and I'll make you a drink. Here, take some vitamin C.'

And she pushes two tablets and a glass of water into my hand. A bit late now, I think.

Swallowing them down, I run a bath with the Body Shop bubble bath left over from Mum's birthday. She doesn't mind, and she'll probably get more for Christmas anyway. I soak for ten minutes or so, until my white fingers turn pink and my body thaws out. Mum knocks on the door.

'Cup of tea and toast on the table, love. I'm off to bed.'

'Okay. Thanks, Mum. Won't be long.'

I sit for a bit longer. But as I do so, the bathroom door begins to open, all by itself, as if I'm being told to hurry up and stop messing.

'Oh my God,' I murmur, pulling out the plug and heaving myself from the bath. I grab a towel, wrap myself inside it, and run to my room. Clean PJs are on the bed (Mum's obviously been tidying up), so I put them on and snuggle up inside my dressing gown. My breath is shallow with fear and I'm shivering again.

'You alright, Tori?' calls Mum from her bedroom.

'Fine, Mum …'

I can't tell Mum. She wouldn't understand like Nan does, it would terrify the life out of her. Minutes later, I'm safe and warm, a cup of tea in my hand and two slices of toast and butter in my tum.

I make sure I'm in bed just before midnight.

9

Melissa

Thursday December 17th

I was really looking forward to Bruges as well. Damn Ade and his damned heart attack. I've suggested to Ed we go away on our own, but he says that would be unseemly, with Ade so poorly in hospital and everything. So instead of riding around Bruges in a horse-drawn carriage, calling on the Walstraat for hot chocolate with brandy and waffles, and choosing a very expensive Christmas present, we've had to visit the bloody cardio ward and sit with Imogen, poor thing, while they operate.

He was just getting ready for work and there it was. A massive heart attack. Thank goodness he survived, that's all I can say. But I'm sure he'll be fine. They work miracles these days.

And now that Victoria's bloody well turned up again. My Raff could really do a lot better for himself. No, really. He definitely needs to finish with her. And soon. Before she goes and gets herself pregnant. Good grief, can you imagine it – her mother turning up at the wedding in M&S or something?

There's that daughter of Maxine's, I suppose. Now *she's* sophisticated, with silky long blonde hair and plenty of money. They could get out and about more, splash the cash. That's the kind of lifestyle he needs, my Raff. Not sitting at home, waiting for the *girl next door* to show up when she feels like it. And always in the same bloody clothes. Ripped jeans that have seen better days. And that bloody awful grey hoodie. It has to be a hand-me-down, looks like it's been through the wash more times than I've had my nails done. Poor cow.

I know what I'll do. I'll buy her a new hoodie for Christmas. Superdry or Hollister, something that will impress Raff, but not too expensive. And definitely not something that will make her look classy like Maxine's girl. Yes, that's a good idea, it'll put Raff off the scent of the trail I'm laying.

So what to buy Raff? We have been thinking about driving lessons, maybe a block of twenty to start with. Ed says that'll be expense enough, but I'd like to get him something else, something he can keep. A watch or something.

So.

Time to start shopping.

Rolex or Omega?

10

Enid

Friday December 18th

ABIGAIL Croxley's just given me the news. Terrible, dreadful news. It's Josie.

I can hardly say the words.

She's dead. A car crash on the way into Grantham. Late last night. Oh, God.

I've rung Peggy. I just can't believe it. We only saw her last week, only laughed and joked with her last week. I can't believe it.

I have known death before, of course, and there's always a rational explanation. This time I feel there isn't, that something's not right. It was that feeling I had as I left her house the other day, as she waved us goodbye. If only I'd realised it would be for the last time.

But she's been driving for years, knows these roads like the back of her hands, drove her kids around, then the grandkids when they came along, babysitting, taking them to the pictures or the park, out for lunch. Her car's always bobbing in and out of the village, a little red Honda Jazz it is. How on earth did it happen? And what was she doing out so late? She's usually in front of the telly with her dressing gown on by nine o'clock.

I get to thinking about the time Topper died. Distraught, I was. At sixteen, I'd already left home to join the QAs. Mum said he'd been missing me dreadfully, had been pining for weeks. But that particular morning she walked into the field to find him writhing in agony. She ran for the farmer, old Will Thomas, who sent for the vet. But it was too late. My poor Topper had to be put down. Colic, was all he said. Mum just thought he was unhappy, couldn't see any point in being here any more, not with me being away. Poor old Topper. I'd have done anything for him not to have died.

But I'd known he was ill, you know, even before I got the phone call. I was sitting in the hospital canteen, eating dinner. Steamed cod, mashed potato and peas. Not the most inviting meal, but we ate anything in those days, the result of years of rationing, even after the war had finished. And I felt Topper's pain. I really felt it, a sudden, excruciating, burning pain in the pit of my stomach. From somewhere in the distance I heard Matron calling me to the phone. And I knew.

Mum and Dad had kept Topper on, even though he was no longer needed to pull the caravan. Sam and I had both left home, they'd sold our caravan, and Topper was retired. But they refused to sell him; he'd become part of the family. I should never have left him. I felt so guilty, still feel guilty. Poor old Topper.

I remember it well, that year. 1968. Flower power was at its height, we were all 'Backing Britain', demonstrating against the war in Vietnam, and filling our larders *just in case* of anything nuclear. But at sixteen years of age all I was interested in were mini-skirts, the Beatles, and boys. I relished the freedom being away from home gave me, and the maturity expected of me as I studied for my nursing career.

What I didn't expect was being promoted to work in the geriatric wards, to seeing all those lovely people dying off, one by one, all those folks who'd told me their amazing life stories, their sad regrets, their wishes for the future. It was heart-breaking, upsetting, yet I knew in my heart of hearts they'd be coming back. I just always knew it. And the times I sat beside someone who was dying, in the last throes, and caught a glimpse of a loved one in the wings, waiting patiently to carry them off. They never, ever went alone. I knew that. Very often the person dying would reach out a hand towards them, murmuring their name. They could see them, too.

So when I became a wiccan, none of what Peggy said surprised me.

It was Peggy who converted me, you see.

At the age of twenty-four, Peter and I had been married for three years and were ready to start a family. The move to buy the house on Dunleary Lane was his idea. From the beginning, we intended doing it up to run as a bed and breakfast.

Peter had done an apprenticeship as a plumber after leaving school, so was good with his hands. He was actually helping with the carousels at the local fairground when we met. A kind of gypsy himself, a traveller, we got talking over fluffy sticks of pink candy floss. He was always a charmer, that one, with his bright blue eyes and dimples that filled his cheeks, and he was so useful when it came to the B&B. He extended the house with a new kitchen, stairs, an extra bathroom and three more bedrooms. The extension was for us to live in, leaving the original house for the guests. Lovely, it was. We made a good living out of it too, and it meant I could stay at home with the children as they came along. Carol first, then Jonathan two years later. We decided not to have any more, so we could concentrate on the business and spend precious off-duty time with the kids we did have. And they had a lovely childhood, Carol and Jonathan. We took them all over the place when we could, although the busier the B&B became the more difficult it was to get away. So I put a notice in the post office window, asking for someone to run it for a week now and then. We already had a young girl coming in, Jennifer, I think her name was. She'd clean rooms and change the beds every morning, and babysit for us on a Saturday night so we could go ballroom dancing. I do miss them, my ballroom dancing days. The glamorous frocks, my lovely gold stilettos, and just having a laugh with Sue and Terry Binns. They retired a few years ago, went back to Bournemouth for the air, but we still swap cards at Christmas-time and they're doing fine. Anyway, because Jennifer did the cleaning, it was just the checking-in and cooking breakfasts that needed looking after while we were on holiday.

Peggy Fleming applied for the job. We'd already met in the greengrocers, so knew each other a little. But she was given four weeks' holiday a year and couldn't afford to go away, being on her own. So she reckoned if she came and worked for us three weeks of the year, she'd be able to afford somewhere nice for her fourth week. Also, she admitted, she'd always quite fancied running a B&B, said it would be like a holiday in itself, meeting new people and fussing around. So she was in. I trained her up, and we became good friends.

One dark and cold winter's evening, however, we got to chatting. Peggy had popped round to discuss the following week's lettings. We were planning on taking a break to visit Mum and Dad before Christmas. Peter was out at the pub with his pals, the kids were in bed, and I was catching up with the ironing. The kitchen table was piled with freshly-aired sheets and pillowcases, and we'd got to talking about Peggy's ex-husband, how she'd discovered his sordid affair, and how she'd sensed it was going to happen even before it did.

'It's funny, though, isn't it,' I said, 'how you know something's going to happen? I get the same sometimes. A kind of sixth sense.'

'It's a gift, Enid. Don't knock it.'

'I'm not. It just fascinates me, that's all.'

'It *is* fascinating.'

She looked up at me then, watching carefully as I stood there, the steaming iron in my right hand, my left holding down the edge of a pillowcase.

'Do you believe in witchcraft, Enid?' she asked.

Well, I just burst out laughing.

'What?' she said, obviously put out.

'No, Peggy. I don't believe in witchcraft.'

'Why not?'

'That kind of thing, it's all in people's heads.'

'What, don't you ever say a prayer when something's going wrong or when you want something really important to happen?'

I thought about it. 'I suppose so. Yes, I suppose I do.'

'And don't you think that's a kind of witchcraft?'

'Possibly.' Folding the ironed pillowcase, I placed it onto the chair beside me. 'Why do you want to know, anyway?'

'Well, don't you think it would be good to be in a position to control things a bit more?'

I looked at her curiously. 'What exactly are you trying to say, Peggy?'

'What would you say if I said I was a witch?'

I laughed again. 'Sorry, Peggy, you're not making sense. Do you mean a *proper* witch, or are you in a play or something, taking after your mum at last?'

But her face was deadly serious. I remember it like it was yesterday.

'I mean a proper witch. A wiccan, to be precise. A good witch.'

'Right.' I waited for a laugh, a giggle, but nothing came. 'You mean like in *Bewitched*?'

She nodded. 'I mean like in *Bewitched*.'

'Okay.' Unplugging the iron, I filled the kettle and began to make tea. 'I think you'd better explain yourself.'

So we sat there, amidst the scent of freshly ironed bedding and Peggy's patchouli oil, and discussed the rudiments of Wicca. I found it fascinating, perplexing and, I must admit, a little exciting. Peggy described it as the science of controlling the secret forces of nature, making full use of the five senses in order to achieve results. Surprising results. The point of magic is to make the world bend to your will. But you need firm faith in your powers or you won't achieve the will and imagination needed to make it work.

And believe me, it can be done. Wiccans can cast spells to bring about real changes in the physical world. They can protect people, banish negative influences, even help with fertility problems.

That particular evening, though, I must confess to being a little concerned.

'But isn't it to do with the devil, Peggy? It all sounds a bit frightening to me.'

She shook her head vehemently. 'No, Enid, no. The devil is evil, wicked, persona non grata in the wiccan world. Nothing whatsoever to do with us. We're good witches. We believe in the Law of Three, that whatever benevolent or malevolent actions a person performs will return to that person with triple force, or with equal force on each of the three levels of body, mind and spirit. It's similar to the idea of karma. The majority of wiccans believe in reincarnation, too, where everyone gets an equal chance at living clean, honest lives. We use goodness and light, herbs and plants, Mother Nature in all her glory.' She spread out her hands, filling the cluttered room with joy.

'And if you're worried about Christianity and all that,' she continued, 'I can tell you that many wiccans see Jesus as a great prophet, although not particularly the son of God. Even some Christians today, the more progressive ones, only believe that. So the Wicca deity could still be *the one*, but with both a male and a female side.'

Despite the fact I'd had an extremely hectic day and still had a huge old pile of ironing to do, I had a sudden burst of energy, of life, of joie de vivre.

As the young say these days, I was hooked.

But look at me, sitting here reminiscing. While Josie lies dead in a morgue somewhere. Is that what death does to us – makes us relive life? Makes us appreciate what we have, what we've had?

I've gone numb, sitting here. Unable to think properly. Unable to feel, anything. No pain, or hurt, or desperation. No tears.

Genevieve is sitting behind the front door. She knows.

I'm waiting for Peggy to arrive.

I've made tea using a mixture of black tea and ginseng tea with a little honey, all of which are good for shock.

'I knew, you know. I knew there was something wrong, when we left her on Wednesday,' I say.

Peggy nods. 'Me too. When we left the house.' Sudden tears wet her cheeks and she brushes them away. 'Bloody hell. I should have done something about it. Terrible. Awful news.'

'I just can't fathom it,' I murmur. My own tears come now and I pull a tissue from the box on the side.

'I keep getting this awful feeling,' she whispers. 'What I want to know is whether or not it has anything to do with us. Is it because we were there, asking for help with Victoria?'

'You mean, is someone onto us?'

She nods quietly.

I shake my head. 'No, I don't think so. How would they know we weren't just visiting a friend?'

'I don't know. I just keep getting this awful feeling ...'

'Sixth sense?'

'Yes. It's always stood me in good stead. Usually, anyway.'

'I know the feeling. But what I can never understand is how I didn't know about my Peter's affair when it happened, how I didn't see it coming, was completely oblivious to it. Even though we'd been arguing a lot. Silly little niggling things at first, then great big explosions of anger. But the fact I never saw it coming bothers me a lot.'

'Don't let it, Enid, he ain't worth it. Some people have the ability to cloak themselves, you know. It's like an aura, an aura of innocence, of goodness and purity. If she, his lady-friend, had the ability to do that, it's quite likely she cloaked him as well. People can be fooled very easily.'

'I know,' I sigh.

'You won't have helped yourself either, I'll bet.'

'How do you mean?'

'You were in love with him. You couldn't, or didn't want to, see any bad in him. Your eyes would have been closed to any wrongdoing, even though it was staring you in the face.'

I nod, seeing the answer to what's been troubling me these past few years. I'd closed my eyes, switched off my natural instincts, even when I'd seen them in the garden that night, laughing and giggling over a glass of white wine, he with the bottle in his hand, topping her up. Huh. Just Peter being friendly with the guests, I thought.

But it puts my mind at rest, this conversation with Peggy. So I *can* trust my instincts, my inner voice. It's only that one time it had let me down, that one time I hadn't seen it coming.

I still cry over what happened, though, what we'd had, what we lost. But it's all in the past now. Qué será será and all that.

'You did manage to place the Duk Rak at Victoria's, didn't you?' I ask, anxiously.

'I did. Should have put one round at Josie's place while we were at it. For all we know, they were able to get her to go out for some reason, get her to drive into Grantham late at night when she'd normally be tucked up at home.'

I stand up. 'Right. That's it. You and me, my house and yours. And the shop. It's all we can do.'

Peggy's house is a rented property, but nice for all that. A two-up, two-down with a little cottage garden that backs onto a stream. Mallard ducks and Canada geese climb up the embankment so that, on a sunny day, we can sit and watch them for hours. But today Peggy shoos them away; we have work to do. We've spent hours loading up the car with small rocks from along the roadside and painting them with egg-white. A pentagram on each one, representing earth, air, fire, water and spirit. It's used by white witches as a religious symbol and to protect against evil. We place the rocks at the front and back of Peggy's house and the shop where she works. The front of the shop proves difficult as we have Health and Safety to consider. But eventually we decide on hiding two rocks inside the old cart that stands outside, beneath piles of potatoes. Peggy chants the relevant charm and we envisage blue light surrounding the property.

'I place you here as protection, by the elements of earth, sky, fire and water, in peace and with love.'

Satisfied, we collect the remaining rocks from Peggy's house and drive back to my place.

My next door neighbours at Lilac Cottage, Kath and Jimmy, nosey from behind their curtains as we place the Duk Rak, but who cares? They think I'm strange as it is. I would never reveal the extent of my *strangeness,* though, or they'd know who messed up their barbecue last August. Don't worry, it wasn't anything massive. I only stopped the wi-fi from streaming. Well, it *was* one o'clock in the morning, so I think I'm excused. But the music was so loud and offensive I just couldn't sleep, so I had to do something. I heard later that none of the other neighbours could sleep either. Well, apart from Lilian, who'd gone off to South Africa for three weeks. Anyway, they can think what they like. My little cottage is now protected, with Duk Rak at both the front and back. All I need do now is take care when I'm out and about.

By the time we've finished, I'm starving hungry. So I make my favourite, jacket potatoes and cheese with salad.

Peggy stuffs her mouth with food.

'Thanks, Enid. I didn't know how hungry I was 'til I sat down.'

I have a little frankincense with some sweet orange on the side, so I pour it into a burner. It's very relaxing, and we breathe in the aroma as we eat.

'I think the shock's just starting to wear off,' I say.

'Poor Josie. Such a lovely person. How old would she have been?'

'Now let me think.' I sip my tea thoughtfully. 'She was sixty the year our Carol moved down to London.

I remember, because we had to dash home for the party. Do you remember, she had this party at the Horse and Hounds? A scream, she was, had way too much to drink. And the cake, wasn't it just lovely? Chanel motifs, with tiny little shoes and handbags all over it. They'd had it specially made, I remember, because that's all she ever bought. Not Chanel, of course. But she did Paul's head in with the amount she spent on shoes.'

Peggy smiles. 'She loved her high heels, that's for sure.'

'When Paul was around, anyway. Not been quite the same since.'

'No-one to dress up for, I suppose.'

'True.'

'Here, we're getting maudlin, Enid.'

I brush away my tears. 'Sorry.'

'Her, pass me that there sherry. Let's raise a toast to her.'

I fill two small glasses and we stand up.

'To our lovely friend Josie, who died too young,' says Peggy, sighing heavily. 'And to all the memories we have of her, and to the wonderful person she was. May Bright Blessings be upon her.'

We knock it back and sit down.

'I could do with another one,' I murmur.

'The road to rack and ruin, Enid. The road to rack and ruin.'

''You know, Peggy, it only seems two minutes since I was a little girl and my dad would say that to his pals. Where on earth do the years go?'

'A good question, and one I'm not able to answer. I think we're here to learn, though. We're here to learn and to progress, and when we come back we bring what we've learned with us. People like Josie, for instance, such a good kind person. She'll come back with love and kindness already inside of her. I genuinely believe that.'

'I suppose so. I don't know what I'll bring back, though. I've had a few skirmishes along the way, what with one thing and another, but I don't know that I've learned anything.'

'Nor do I. But what I do know for definite is what I'd like to do before I go.'

'What's that then?'

'I'd like to save up and fly out to St Tropez. For a fortnight. Two whole weeks.'

My tears all forgotten, I smile at her. 'Sounds lovely, Peggy.'

'Sunshine, sea and sand. And I want to sunbathe topless, like the film stars. In a silver bikini, but only the bottom half.'

'Well, you've got the figure for it, haven't you? Now me ...'

'You could lose the weight if you wanted.'

'I know. But I'm happy as I am. Let's face it, it's not as if I've got anyone to look beautiful for, is it?'

'You never know, Enid, you never know. None of us knows what's round the corner.'

'Speaking of people that are all skin and bone,' I say, 'I forgot to tell you. I've got Tori coming round here to work. I've decided to start with a bed and breakfast again, just at weekends. She's coming over to help with breakfasts and clean the room for me. And I've got someone coming to stay already. This Monday, they're arriving.'

'I thought you said it was just weekends?'

'Well, with it being Christmas I thought it would get me off to a good start. They're only coming to visit their daughter for a few days. I thought it'd put a bit of money in Tori's pocket, maybe encourage her out of those awful clothes she wears.'

'And it gives us the opportunity to keep an eye on her. A brilliant idea, Enid. Well done.'

'The trouble is, how do we keep an eye out the rest of the time?'

'Great Uncle John's watching her as well. I'm sure he'll let me know if there's anything going on.'

'I hope so, Peggy. I really do hope so.'

'That's all we can do, isn't it – hope?'

'You sure you don't want another sherry?'

11

Tori

Saturday December 19th

NO more school until the New Year! Yes! We finished yesterday. And we totally *rocked* it. The PFTA made charity cupcakes, so we got through Maths and Chemistry, had lunch, stuffed our faces with cake (Danielle bought), then trudged off to the school disco. I hung out with Danielle, Chris and Ross all afternoon. There were balloons and hats and flashing lights, and we actually saw Mr Sadler, our deputy head, dancing to *Uptown Funk*. What a guy.

Totally owned it. Just awesome, doing all the moves and everything.

Chris is really nice. I'm so pleased for Danielle, she looks so happy.

Today is Saturday, my first day working at Mrs Phelps' B&B. I am going to buy *the* most amazing dress for Raff's New Year party.

So it's eight o'clock and I'm out of bed even before the alarm's stopped ringing. Nan's up, as per, and makes me a cuppa while I shower and dress. Red tee-shirt, jeans, trainers, hoodie. Mum's still in bed, so I eat my cereal quietly (Rice Krispies today - she buys whichever one's been reduced), clean my teeth, hug Nan goodbye, and walk over to Enid's cottage.

It's not far away, but it's a cold foggy morning and as I raise my hand to the old brass knocker I'm nervous as hell. I called over on Thursday after school, but it didn't seem quite so spooky then. Mrs Phelps was really nice, chatty, said she'd already put a note in the post office window and had got someone to book the room. There's no stopping this woman, I think, even though I still find her a bit scary. But if she wants something, she sure as hell gets it. Awesome. She said the caller was some woman in the village who's having her parents over for a few days before Christmas, but doesn't have enough room for them. They're here from Monday until Christmas Eve. Mrs Phelps says she only intends having people to stay for weekends, but seeing as it's Christmas she's making an exception.

'Come on in, my dear. Lovely to see you again,' she enthuses, opening the door for me.

It's the first time I've actually been inside the house. It's dark and a bit claustrophobic, and I nearly trip over the cat as I walk in. It just yelps and runs off to the kitchen.

'Genevieve,' Enid says. 'Don't mind her. She always waits just behind the door. But come on through,' and she ushers me into the kitchen too.

There's the scent of home baking, cinnamon and something sweet. Apples, I think. Then I see the pies on the side. Looks like she's been awake half the night. Is she mad, I wonder? Nan would never stay up half the night baking.

'Excuse my pies,' she says. 'They've been in the freezer. I'm defrosting them to sell at the Christmas Fayre. But I fancied one for myself, so I've put one in the oven to warm. But come on, sit yourself down, Victoria. Cup of tea?'

'That'd be nice.' I sit down as instructed, unsure of my role here. I assume she's going to show me where everything is. Have to find out some time, I suppose.

She chats as she makes tea. 'How are you, then? Got rid of that nasty cold yet?'

I'm totally amazed she remembers. 'It's a bit better, thanks. Still a bit sniffly, but I'm sure I'll be okay.'

The cat's sitting on a chair watching me, and I stare back. But it doesn't work, it just carries on watching.

'Good. That's good, then,' Mrs Phelps continues. 'A few drops of Echinacea, that's what you need. It's only herbs. Here, I'll put some in your tea.'

I watch her make two cups of tea. She's just like Nan. Places a teabag into the pot, pours in the boiling water, then leaves it to stew. But the smell of her apple pie is making my mouth water, even though I've only just had breakfast.

'You like apple pie, then?'

I flinch. It's as if she's read my mind.

'Yes. Yes, I do.'

'Well, we'll have a piece. It's just about ready. I'll make us some custard, or do you prefer cream?'

I swear the cat looks at her as she says the word 'cream'. Mrs Phelps sees it too.

'Don't mind Genevieve. She loves a bit of cream, don't you, Genevieve? But it's not good for her. Now then – custard or cream?'

I'm not gonna lie, I just love custard. But on this occasion I ask for cream. So I can give some to the cat. Well, why the hell not?

We drink tea and we eat apple and sultana pie with cream. It's swimming, so I manage to pour some of my cream into Genevieve's dish while Mrs Phelps pops upstairs for something. I'd noticed the dish under the table as I walked in. The table's round, with a white tablecloth, and there's a gathering of tea-lights (what's the collective noun for tea-lights, I wonder?) on one side, ready to light. The rest of the kitchen is brightly-coloured, plum red tiles and bright yellow kettle and toaster. And there's a pile of towels in the corner. Olive green, like a pile of squashed courgettes.

I finish my pie greedily while Mrs Phelps talks about her new business.

'I did run a bed and breakfast once. On Dunleary Lane, it was, not far. But I had to sell up when I got divorced, couldn't run it on my own. But now I've decided to earn a bit of extra money, just taking people in at weekends. Apart from this week, of course. But well, it'll get my little business off to a good start, won't it?'

I smile in encouragement. 'What made you get divorced?'

She looks a little embarrassed at that. 'He - my husband - ran off with a guest. I think we'd just got too used to one another. We were married a long time, and when the children left home, life got a bit boring, we didn't do much. Now, when we were courting we used to go ballroom dancing. But when I suggested we do it again, he said he was far too old for that kind of thing.'

'You like ballroom dancing then, Mrs Phelps?'

She smiles. 'Call me Enid, my dear. Mrs Phelps makes me sound so old.'

'Sorry – Enid.'

'Yes, I love dancing, always have. Now then, would you like some more?' she asks, indicating my empty bowl.

I nod gratefully, and she cuts some more.

'Are you doing anything tomorrow morning?' she asks.

Yeah, I think. I'll be lying in bed listening to shitty church bells ringing their heads off.

'Not really,' I say. 'Why?'

'I need someone to sell my pies at the Christmas Fayre. I've offered to help sell tea and coffee and suchlike, and I can't be in two places at once.'

I grin stupidly. 'What, you want *me* to sell your pies?'

'If that's alright. It is in aid of the NSPCC.'

'Yeah. Okay then. I'd like that.' The idea of helping little kids appeals.

'I'd pay you, of course. I wouldn't expect you to do it for nothing.'

They are absolutely totally delish, her pies, should sell like hotcakes. She says she did well with them at the Summer Fayre, so word will have got round. And it should be fun, selling them. I mean, some of the kids from school might be there with their mums. Danielle's mum usually goes to stuff like that, so at least I'll be able to chat.

There must be something in those pies, I decide. Or maybe it's the stuff she put into my tea. Because suddenly the old bat doesn't seem at all threatening, seems quite okay actually.

She shows me round the place. I totally love it. It's a really old cottage, not too small, and cosy and warm, with old floors that creak as soon as you put your foot down. But my fave bit is the huge rug in the lounge. It's Chinese, kind of faded pink with green dragons and flowers and coins. It makes it look so cosy in there, what with the stone fireplace and everything. The bedroom she's renting out isn't ideal, though. I mean, there's no toilet or anything, so they'll have to use the same one she does. But there is a shower fitted into a corner. It actually looks like a wardrobe until you open the door and pull down the tray. Quite clever.

She says she wants me to come over on Saturdays and Sundays, make breakfast, serve it, wash up, then sort out the bedroom and whatever else needs doing. I can see it taking up a whole morning, which is a total of eight hours for both days if I get there early enough. That makes it eighty quid per weekend. *If* she gets the punters in. Nice.

I arrive home to the scent of Nan's fruit scones in the oven and the murmur of Steve Wright's Love Songs in the background. Mum's still in her dressing gown, wandering round with a slice of toast in her hand.

'You been to that bed and breakfast place?' she asks.

'Yes,' I reply.

'Is she okay then, this woman?'

'It's Enid Phelps,' says Nan. 'She used to run the B&B on Dunleary Lane. You remember the one?'

'She's alright, actually,' I say, throwing myself onto the sofa.

'I remember,' says Mum. 'Rumour has it she's a gypsy.'

'What?' I ask. I'm astounded, imagining her sat before a crystal ball like at the fair.

'She *is* a gypsy,' Nan says, pulling out eggs and stuff to make something for lunch. 'She grew up travelling from one place to another. All over the place, she went.'

'Sounds quite romantic, actually,' Mum says, dreamily.

'Wow,' I say. 'A gypsy? Really really?'

'But don't you go letting on we were talking about her,' Nan says, shaking her finger at me. 'I know what you young things are like.'

'You shouldn't have time for tittle-tattling, anyway, young lady,' Mum warns. 'Don't you have some studying to do?'

Mum's worried I'm gonna fail my mocks, but at this rate I could pay someone to do them for me. But okay, yeah, I've promised her I'll work hard. So I will.

I've just messaged Danielle with news about my job. Six smiling emojis. Yes!

Did you know the word 'Tori' means 'bird' in Japanese? Danielle's just messaged back. I don't know why she was looking that one up. Don't you love it, though? I won't tell Mum, she already says I can't sit still for two minutes.

So I've spent all afternoon studying plant oils and their uses for Physics. Quite interesting, actually.

I'm now making myself look totally awesome for Raff. Plenty of eyeliner does it. He's just messaged me to say he's going to the Royal Oak. But there's no way I can go, they'd never let me in again. It's about time the landlord found out how old he is, I think. But no, I wouldn't tell. It's not fair on me, though. But I reckon Raff only manages to get in because he's got money to splash. And I haven't. Not yet anyway, but I'm working on it. It should be a doddle, this job.

So I manage to talk Raff out of going and we meet up outside his house. It's only six o'clock, he's got Fudge on a lead, so we go for a walk. It's been grey and misty all day, with that soft smoky scent you get on Bonfire Night. I'm still a bit sniffly, and my throat's sore, so I've actually put on my coat. I pull up my collar as we walk along and tuck my arm inside the crook of Raff's. It feels cosy, totally right, and I snuggle up. We chat about my new job and what I'm going to do with my newfound money.

'We could go to the seaside some time. In the summer,' I suggest.

He pulls a face. 'Maybe.'

'Or London? I've always wanted to go to London. I was born there, you know, lived there with my mum and dad.'

He stops walking, pulling me close with his free arm. 'You're an excitable thing, aren't you? Who's to say you'll still be seeing me in the summer? You might have met someone else, someone posh, with all this money you're getting.'

'You're posh though, aren't you?' I reply. 'What's it like being posh? Does it feel different?'

'I am *not* posh, Tori.' He frowns, not a good look. 'Just because I go to private school …'

'There you go, then. Are there any kids there who aren't posh?'

'Piss off,' he sulks.

Fudge pulls at his lead, so we begin walking again.

'Come on, don't go all sulky,' I say. 'You must know you've got things that normal people don't have.'

'That doesn't make me posh.'

'What's the definition of posh then, do you know?' I pull out my phone, looking up the word on Google. 'Elegant or luxuriously stylish. Isn't that you, then?'

'I don't know whether I am or not,' he admits. 'I've nothing to compare it with, not really.'

'But you must have. Your dad had to build up the company – you're always telling me that. So there must have been a time when you weren't posh.'

'Please stop using that word, Tori. It makes you sound so immature.'

I stop walking. Hurt fills every single space in my body.

'What did you say?' I ask.

'I said it makes you sound immature.'

His beautiful navy blue eyes look down at me, and for the first time I see myself as he sees me. Sixteen. Working class. A sixteen-year-old kid from the working classes still doing her GCSE's. And probably not brilliantly at that.

Tears run down my face.

He pulls me close. 'Tori. Don't. I'm sorry, it just came out. I'm sorry.'

As he wipes my tears away with his thumbs, I realise something. I know suddenly and completely, with a determination like the roar of a lion, exactly what's at stake here. I know I have to do well. I have to make him proud of me.

So I stand up straight, and I smile. 'It's okay. Fucking hormones. Just ignore me.'

'No, I'm really sorry, Tori. I shouldn't have said those things.'

I begin walking again, holding onto his arm.

'So what's happening over Christmas?' I ask, changing the subject ever so slightly.

'Dunno,' he shrugs.

'Want to come to mine? I could ask Mum to make us a nice meal?'

He smiles. 'Yeah, okay, that'd be good.'

That's the thing about Raff. He looks all hoity-toity, with his nice hair and perfect teeth and posh clothes. But when he smiles, his face is a total picture, he looks warm and kind and I can't get enough of him. And his eyes – well, I just love him, I suppose – they make me go completely gooey.

We walk along the Peterborough Road before turning left, past Enid's house and on, into the woods. As soon as Fudge sniffs woodland, he starts pulling, panting excitedly, and Raff has to let him off the lead.

'Go on then,' he says, releasing the clasp.

Instead, Fudge pulls himself onto his hind legs and dances. Round and round and round. He's a curiosity, is Fudge. An entertainer. He's a rescue dog and they've no idea where he came from. I can only guess it was a circus of some kind. So he waits until we laugh out loud, then runs off. Raff turns to me, puts his arms around my shoulders and kisses me. Deeply.

I melt. I turn to slush. Complete and utter, total slush.

We stand there kissing beneath the light of the streetlamp, Raff's hands massaging me all over. Until my feet, wrapped only in canvas ballet pumps, turn to ice, and I have to move.

'Where's Fudge?' asks Raff. 'I've not heard him for a while. Come on ...'

The grass is long and deep and I run carefully so as not to twist my ankles on the solid uneven clumps. It's really dark now, no streetlamps or anything. We can't even see the sky through the trees. So we pull out our phones and use them to show us the way.

We find Fudge in the clearing. It's surrounded by trees, evergreens of some kind, and a huge oak. Anyway, there he is, nose down, growling at a patch of leaves that are dark and soggy from the mist. We sneak up, attach his lead, and pull him away. He's really angry at those leaves, but we take no notice. The mist is deepening now and we need to be on our way.

'Probably a rat or something,' says Raff, tugging at him. 'Silly dog, what are you like?' and he pats the top of his head.

We reach the streetlamp and I breathe a huge sigh of relief. It's so dark in the woods. I'd have been totally scared if Raff hadn't been there. What am I like?

Hand in hand, we walk back to his place. His mum's at home and dinner's on the table, so I make myself scarce.

'Bye, Raff.'

'Bye, Tori. See you tomorrow?'

I smile. 'And I'll get Mum to have you over for dinner.'

So it is that I end up having to tidy my room. And the bathroom. And the kitchen. I mean, we all make a mess in there, but Mum insists that if I want Raff to come round, I have to clean it, cupboard doors and everything.

'But Mum, that's not fair, I thought you wanted me to do my revision,' I complain dramatically, hands on hips.

'I do, of course I do. But I think you should take some responsibility for your actions. You're the one who spills stuff down the bloody kitchen cupboards. You're the one who leaves towels all over the bloody bathroom. You're the one who completely misses the drawers in your bedroom. So you're the one who can clean it up.'

'But Mu-um ...'

It's no good, I can't talk her round. I end up doing the lot. Just so Raff can come round over Christmas. It'll be all messy again by then.

But ... result!

Much, much later, I'm stretched out on the bedroom floor. I'm supposed to be studying History, World War One (yawn), but I find myself slightly distracted by Danielle's message.

Oh, my God!

She and Chris Schofield have only gone and done it! At his house as well. And I never thought she would, not for years. I mean, she's so *innocent.*

I reply.

you on the pill?

no, working on it, we were very careful.

OMG Danielle, what were you thinking?

delete this when we've finished, don't want your mum telling mine.

you need to tell her though, or get to the doc's.

I will, promise.

what was it like?

amazing, totally amazing, just like you said.

hope you didn't do it because of me, hope you were ready.

I was, stop worrying!

I do worry, though. She's so sweet and innocent, and so lovely, the very thought of anyone taking advantage makes my blood boil. I hope she *was* ready.

I receive another message, this time from Raff. It's half past ten by now and I'm tucked up in bed with the hot water bottle Nan's made me. I'm really tired, what with having to clean up and everything, so I'm sitting up reading (a thriller Mum gave me a while back) when the message comes through.

No.

I can't believe it.

It's Megan, her parents have died, an accident in Switzerland. She and her brother are okay, but their mum and dad …

I ring Raff and he picks up straightaway.

'I know, Tori, I know,' he soothes.

'I can't believe it,' I sob. 'It's awful, Raff. Tragic. Just before Christmas, too.'

'I know,' is all he can say.

'What happened?'

'Car accident, I think. Only just heard myself. Alistair posted on Facebook.'

'Are they coming back home, then?'

'Dunno. Expect we'll find out at some point.'

I cry like crazy, I can't stop.

'Tori, don't. I'm sorry, I shouldn't have messaged you. I just needed to tell someone.'

'No, it's fine. It's just so, so sad.'

It's only later I remember my dream, the dream I had of Megan crying. Was I seeing into the future or something? That's totally, and I mean totally, weird.

12

Melissa

Sunday December 20th

I'VE done it. I've invited Maxine over for dinner on Christmas Eve. The whole family's coming. Maxine, Greg, and the kids, Charlotte and James. I've told Raff it's a family meal, so no friends round. Let's see if that doesn't set something off. I'm off to Sam's, my hairdresser, and I'll get my nails done at the same time. Got to look good ready for Christmas. Oooh, so excited, just can't wait.

Ed can be so lovely sometimes, even though most of the time he's just a grouchy old nag. Comes up to me yesterday, puts his arms around me, and says he's just ordered my Christmas present. Said he's really sorry about Bruges but he's decided to make it up to me. Goodness knows what it'll be. If he's ordered online, it'll be a piece of jewellery. Diamonds, maybe? It won't be clothing, he wouldn't dare buy me clothing, not online.

I've only just bought a new dress, actually. I drove into town late Thursday afternoon. Well, I needed something to cheer me up, didn't I? It took me ages to find, but the shops are staying open late, with it being Christmas. Cost nearly three hundred quid, but I didn't tell Ed or he'd have said it could be my Christmas present. Canny or what? It's absolutely beautiful, though. Green velvet, short sleeves, down to the knee in a kind of clingy way. Shows off my eyes beautifully.

I bought presents for Ed and Raff, too. I rang BSM about the driving lessons and bought a block of twenty. We'll just renew if he needs more. And the watch – you'll never guess. A Rolex. A bloody Rolex. That'll impress Maxine and everyone. Assuming he ends up with Charlotte, of course. Oh, he will. He's lovely, my Raff, no girl could resist him. Of course.

So I bought gold cufflinks for Ed, and a round of golf for two with dinner with a one night stay at this posh hotel in Scotland. He can take one of his golfing buddies and I can stay home for a nice girly weekend.

That's okay, isn't it? I also got a Superdry hoodie for Victoria. It's really nice actually, I hope she appreciates it.

So.

Time to wrap the pressies.

Red crinkly paper, or sparkly silver?

13

Enid

Monday December 21st

THE car park was heaving as Peggy, Victoria and I arrived at the church hall yesterday morning. I'd been up since the crack of dawn, showered, done my stretches, and eaten my breakfast. I do my stretches every morning, just like Genevieve. Both arms stretching up, down to the floor, then up, side to side and backwards. After that I spend a few minutes on deep breathing, stilling my thoughts, or trying to. I become an island, a rock, a still calm place from which to watch the rest of the world swirling around me. It sets me up for the day.

After breakfast, I set to, wrapping my pies in cellophane and placing stickers on. We were charging £3.99. I've worked out my expenses at around £1.00 per pie, so that leaves £2.99 each for charity. I made seventy pies altogether, but we've eaten two. And I've sold some in the café, alongside teas and coffees, serving it with custard at £2 a shot. So we've made nearly £250 from my pies, which isn't bad, really. Every little helps.

'If someone doesn't crash into someone else soon, I'll eat my proverbial hat,' murmured Peggy as we drove up to the entrance in her silver Polo.

Peggy couldn't help with the stall because it was Sunday, a busy time in her shop. But she'd brought the pies from her freezer the previous night, and offered to drive them round for us in the morning.

We set our stall up nicely, Victoria and me. I made some signs saying which pies were gluten-free and which weren't, and the price. Tori, as she prefers to be called, sold them for me while I helped out in the café with Nicole Brunewski, the fayre organiser, and Jenny Dawn, the church warden.

Bill Mitchell was already there, wrapped in his coat and scarf, sitting at a table with a coffee and a huge piece of chocolate fudge cake. Jenny must have given it to him, and she wouldn't have taken his money either. I know her. Well, he does live on his own, and she knows he'd rather spend money on booze down the local pub than on a plateful of decent food.

Nicole greeted me with a smile. 'Hi there, Enid. Jenny's just putting out cups and saucers, so you can concentrate on your pies, if you like.'

'Thanks,' I replied.

She's like a streak of lightening is Nicole, and she's got so much energy. She only moved here a year ago, so I don't know her that well, but she seems nice enough. Apparently her parents moved here from the Lakes after some kind of incident involving her uncle's tractor. I think it rolled over someone's foot or something. Her dad got the blame as he'd been using it the day before and hadn't left the brake on properly. Anyway, they moved here after that and he got a job working in the local garden centre.

Nicole herself has been at university for the last three years and is taking a year out. Thus the Christmas Fayre. She wants to work for the NSPCC or Oxfam, so this was to be her work experience. In fact, she's been for an interview with Oxfam. But I'm sure she'll do well, she's such a hard worker, and she'd made some lovely signs for the Christmas Fayre.

So I busied myself cutting into my pies and filling bowls. The custard was Bird's own and I made a great big panful, a yellow heap of simmering, sugary delight. We also had fresh cream in the fridge for those who wanted it.

The hall echoed with the sound of children running and mothers talking, while the bittersweet scent of coffee filled the air. There was vintage china on sale, bright wooden toys, lavender bags, home-made soaps and candles, Christmas decorations and hand-made crackers and cards. Helium-filled balloons depicting favourite cartoon characters hung in one corner of the room, and on the long stall at the end were piles of second-hand books. All in all, a nice little collection, I thought.

The fayre made a total of £1200 after expenses. Nicole was very pleased. It'll look good on her CV, that's for sure. Tori sold all my pies and had a good time, by the looks of it. She was upset by some news she'd received the day before, though. A friend of hers, Megan, is on holiday in Switzerland, and her parents have been killed in a car accident. It's in all the papers. By all accounts, they'd left their kids at their ski chalet to do some shopping when a car pushed them off the road. Killed outright, they were. Tragic. Tori isn't actually that close to her, but the girl goes to the same school as her boyfriend, Raff. She's still very upset, though.

Once the punters had gone, Tori and I helped tidy up before making our way back to my house. I offered to pay her for her time, fifty pounds in cash, but she refused it, saying she'd had such a nice time and it is for charity, after all. Such a nice girl, she is.

It's hard to believe she's low in self-esteem as Peggy suggested. I insisted she take twenty, and I'll buy her a box of chocolates as well. Looks like she could do with a bit of fattening up.

I stood watching her and Nicole chatting together yesterday. Tori seems to have taken a shine to her, despite the age difference. So I'm hoping Nicole will be a good influence.

I spent the rest of Sunday afternoon cleaning the house. Tori couldn't help as she had revision to do for her mock exams and had promised her mum. But I have guests arriving today, so it needed to be spick and span. I also bought sausage, bacon, eggs and tinned tomatoes from Spar, ensured there was enough bread and milk in the freezer, and used lavender wax to polish the furniture. A rare treat these days. Well, it's so expensive, but I knew it would be welcoming and they are paying me good money.

But by six o'clock I was completely exhausted. And, what with the news of Josie, and Megan's parents, and with getting up early, I began to feel quite tearful. So I burned some frankincense and flopped onto the sofa with a cup of tea and a cheese and tomato sandwich. But an hour later I woke up, my tea cold and the bread stale. Genevieve, stretched across my feet, purred as I opened my eyes.

'Sorry, Genevieve, I've forgotten to feed you, haven't I? Come on, let's have a butchers in that there

kitchen and see what we've got. No cream today, though – Tori's not coming.'
My new guests are very nice, a lady in her fifties, and her husband, who's a bit older. They've come all the way from Birmingham to spend a few days with their daughter, who lives just outside of Pepingham.

'Their house is a bit small, you know, and she has the four kids, the husband and a spaniel to see to, so it's easier for us to stay somewhere nearby. I do like it here, though, it's cosy and warm and friendly.' says Mrs Taylor, loquaciously.

She likes to chat, does Mrs Taylor, while Mr Taylor sits there, silent and morose. I get the feeling he'd much rather be at home in his own bed, so he can watch the football. They arrived just before twelve this morning, parked their cases, and went straight out for something to eat. I recommended Ellie's Café along the road, but they've no doubt ended up at the Royal Oak. They're selling two for one and there's a great big banner outside, so you can't exactly miss it. Decent food it is, too, by all accounts, but not quite the home-made stuff Ellie dishes out.

Josie. Josie. I can't believe we'll never see her again. Such a kind, gentle woman. How her poor children must be feeling. Oh, I don't even want to think about it.

So after lunch I sit here reminiscing. And as I do, my thoughts turn to my own children, to Carol and

Jonathan. They flew the nest many years ago, and quite rightly, of course. I do get to see Carol and her kids occasionally, although it's difficult, now she and Richard are both working and little Rosie's at school. I do miss them, of course I do, but I keep myself going, using my oils and my herbs. Jonathan comes home when he can, when he's worn out from travelling the world and working in all temperatures. It must be in the genes, the travelling. We made sure to have a permanent address while they were growing up, so it's not as if he's used to it or anything.

The phone rings, making me jump, so deeply am I entrenched in my thoughts. I dash to answer it.

'Hallo?'

'Mum …'

'Carol! I was just thinking about you. Are you okay? I texted last night, but you didn't get back.'

'Sorry, Mum, it's been really busy, it's like a madhouse down here. It was Rosie's nativity on Friday, school fayre on Saturday, and we went to see Father Christmas yesterday. It's been completely manic. Sorry.'

'Don't worry, love. I knew you'd be busy this time of year, so it's not like I was worried.'

'Anyway, Mum, we've got a really nice surprise for you. We're coming up to see you for Christmas. That's if it's okay?'

My heart begins to race. Panic, get thee behind me.

'But I've got no food in, Carol, and I'll never get a turkey now, not unless the butcher can find me one, and ...'

'Mum, stop,' she interrupts. 'I've got everything. I'll bring it all, don't worry. You just have to provide somewhere for us to sleep and we'll be fine.'

'But where will you sleep, now Rosie's bigger?'

'I'll bring the travel cot for Adam, and Rosie can sleep on the floor. We'll bring a carry-mat. Stop worrying, we'll be fine.'

'When are you arriving, then? I've got guests here until lunchtime Thursday.'

'Oh. Who's that?'

'It's for Bed and Breakfast, if you must know. It's a bit of a long story, but I'll fill you in when I see you.'

'We were planning on coming over Christmas Eve.'

'I can do a quick turnaround, I'm sure. It's fine, it'll be fine. It'll be wonderful to see you.'

'You're sure?'

I nod at the phone, grinning like the Cheshire Cat. 'Of course I'm sure. It'll be lovely.'

So I put on my coat and boots and call to see Abigail Croxley. I need to buy a tree and hope against hope they've got some left. Well, I can't use my dusty old plastic one, can I, not when the grandchildren are visiting?

But the only ones they have left are six foot high, and cost an arm and a leg.

'Look, I'll let you have it at cost, seeing as it's nearly Christmas Day,' says Abigail, winking.

'Oh, thank you,' I sigh. 'They are a bit pricey, aren't they?'

'You got someone special coming round, then?'

'Carol and her two. She's only just rung to let me know.'

'Oh, lovely ...'

I drag the tree home as best I can, leather gloves protecting my fingers. But two hours later it looks beautiful standing there in the corner of the room. I've only put a few decorations on, baubles and lights, and the two Father Christmases I've kept from the children's baby days. But the smell is divine, it fills the entire house.

By six o'clock my guests have returned briefly, then left to visit their daughter. So I nip round to Frank Johnson's place. He lives in one of the apartments I nearly bought. He' s an old pal of mine, and ran the local garage in the days when Peter and I had a car. He's retired now, so volunteers at the Arts Centre in Grantham, showing people to their seats and that kind of thing. They're showing *Aladdin* this year, and I know they give him free tickets for volunteering, but he sells them on if he can. I don't blame him for that, of course. Anyway, I manage to buy five tickets from him. They cost me a fiver each, so I hope the children enjoy it.

Frank offers me a cup of tea, but I decline. For some reason I'm feeling a bit fragile, being out in the dark, and want to get home to Genevieve.

'Thanks, Enid,' he calls as I leave the house. 'Have a good time with your family, and Merry Christmas!'

I've had my dinner and have just settled down to watch the telly with Genevieve on my knee, when the phone rings again.

This time it's Peggy.

'I've just had Julia on the phone. The funeral's tomorrow at Pepingham Parish.'

'That was quick.'

'They've rushed it through before Christmas.'

'How is Julia?'

'That poor girl. Honestly, she doesn't know which way to turn. She and Sam have been making all the arrangements, bless them.'

'Do they know what happened yet?'

'No. No details, not yet. All they do know is she ran off the road on the A1 coming out of Grantham, and hit a tree. Why she'd been there at all they don't know, unless she'd been Christmas shopping or something. The police are still trying to fit the pieces together.'

I feel sick. It's hitting me again, the shock of it. I think Carol coming over has been taking my mind off it.

'What a thing, and just before Christmas.'

'I know. But Enid, it's Yuletide tomorrow. We'll need to fit it all in.'

Yuletide is celebrated by wiccans on the day of the Winter Solstice every year. It's a pagan festival marking the death of the Sun-God and his rebirth from the Earth Goddess, basically when the dark half of the year gives way to the light half. It's the sun's rebirth, I suppose, because from this time forwards the days become longer. In the olden days, people would place holly and ivy around their homes, inside and out, in the hope that nature sprites would arrive. In fact, if you go to Peggy's house now you'll see a sprig of holly just inside her front door. It's supposed to bring good fortune.

'Damn,' I murmur. 'I'd forgotten. What time's the funeral?'

'Two o'clock. We're supposed to be meeting at half eight, so it should be okay.'

'Yes, we should be home well before that.'

'We won't quite be in the mood for celebrating, though.'

'I know.'

'We could celebrate Josie's life, I suppose.'

'That's a lovely idea. Yes, we'll do that. I'll bring some food, as usual.'

'Thanks, Enid.'

But then I hesitate. 'You don't think we should cancel? It is going to be a very sad day.'

'No. We shouldn't. She's always believed she'll come back, so we need to celebrate that, and her life, and everything we believe in.'

Josie was a wiccan in Lincoln for many years, so when she upped sticks and came to Pepingham she agreed to go part-time, to be someone we could turn to if we needed extra help. And she was always there for us. Always.

Tears fill my eyes. 'You're right. I just feel bad. I wish we'd set the Duk Rak before it all happened.'

'Don't cry, Enid. It's natural to feel like that, but there's nothing we can do. It's not like we knew it was going to happen, is it? And who's to say it wasn't just an accident, after all?'

'I don't think it was. Genuinely. I'm sure there's something not right. I really wish there was something we could do.'

'We will do something. We're going to find out exactly what happened. And if it is anything to do with Victoria ...'

'That's another thing. Tori's friend's just lost her parents too. Another car crash.'

The phone goes quiet. Peggy's struggling with the news.

'No. No, Enid. Let's hope it's just coincidence.'

'It probably is. It was hundreds of miles away, in Switzerland. But what if it isn't, Peggy? What if it isn't?'

'Then we'll get them. We'll bloody well get them. I promise.'

'Thanks, Peggy.'

'Now – about tomorrow. Wendy Broome's picking you up, if that's okay?'

My guests are still out. I check the guest room before turning in for the night. It's neat and tidy. A clean white duvet rests beneath the mauve satin bedspread. Pillows to match are piled at the head of the bed, while the small chest of drawers holds a vase of fresh freesias. I've sprinkled a few drops of essential oil of rose on the sheets. It's uplifting, welcoming, but can also act as an aphrodisiac, so I must be careful not to use it for Carol and Richard, not with the kids in here. There are clean towels on the rail beside the shower, fresh soap and shampoo inside. Not perfect, but a damn sight better than the washing facilities we had when I was a girl.

No, we had to wash in an old tin bath when I was a youngster. It used to hang beneath our small caravan on hooks, making it swish and sway while we were moving. But what a godsend it was when we finally arrived at our destination. Mum would fill it with hot water boiled over a huge log fire, then we'd all take it in turns to wash ourselves in the privacy of our caravan. Once a week it was. I remember Mum's luxury would be a small bar of Pear's soap. It's brown, but becomes see-through once you've used it.

It had a kind of herby scent at the time. I can smell it even now. I've bought it since and it doesn't smell the same at all. Mum used to love it, though.

The alternative to our weekly bath would be the occasional farmer's wife who'd let us use their bathroom or the outside shower they'd have set up for farmhands. I loved the bathrooms the best, when I'd climb out of a warm soapy bath onto a real tiled floor and dry myself on a soft, clean towel. Then, wrapped inside my nightie and Mum's thick warm blanket, I'd stumble across the field to our caravan and climb into bed. Pure luxury to a little gypsy girl.

Our small caravan, the one Sam and I slept in, consisted of two beds and a long table. The table was for our studies and we'd sit either side of it, books out, while Mum made dinner. The worst bit about sharing a caravan with Sam was his morbid collection of empty snail shells. He'd keep them in a shoebox beneath his bed, right under our noses, and I'd forget about them until I dropped something on the floor and had to go searching, or when Mum asked me to tidy up. It was never Sam who had to tidy up. No, he had to do *boys* stuff. Which consisted of cleaning the outsides of both caravans, a job that was more fun than anything. Dad would pull a hosepipe all the way from the farmhouse and they'd squirt water at the caravans, then all over each other, and sometimes me if I got in the way. Which I did. Boys stuff, my foot.

The guest room looks inviting. I plump up the pillows and go to draw the curtains together, keeping out the cold. But Genevieve's behind me as I do so. She's warning me, telling me. My hands still holding the curtains, I look out, over to the woodland at the rear of my house. It's very quiet out there. Eerily quiet. I see a green haze emerging, a misty green cloud that obscures my vision of the oak tree standing there. I blink, but the cloud remains. It begins to flicker, and I wonder if there's a fire burning. My eyes follow the grey-green smoke as it rises to the stars, the bright moonlight forming a shadow beneath it. I know we're four days off a full moon because it's set to be on Christmas Day this year. Then I recall the pagan Yuletide tomorrow and a sudden fear grips me.

Is something going on out there, something we should be aware of? No, I convince myself. No, don't be silly, Enid. You're tired, girl. Get yourself to bed.

14

Tori

Tuesday December 22nd

OKAY. So I've done my revision, as promised. I've also helped out at the Christmas Fayre. All Sunday morning. So what does she expect - blood? Just because I met up with Raff afterwards she went off on one. Okay, so I didn't get home 'til five in the morning, but I did let her know where I was, didn't I? I mean, I texted her, yeah?

It's not like *she* doesn't have sex, is it? I mean, that Mike somebody she's seeing, she stays out half the night with him sometimes, and you're not telling me they don't do it. He's a bit of a loser, to be fair, thinks he's the bee's knees. She could do better, my mum. Loads better. But she's smitten. So now it's *Mike this* and *Mike that*. He's not even cute.

We went to this party at Tom's house last night. Fab, it was. Alright, yeah, they were smoking weed, and that's one of Mum's big bugbears. Doesn't mean I smoked it, though. I didn't. I stuck to drinking alcohol, and yeah, I did have a bit much. Well, they were all drinking vodka shots and coke when we arrived, so we had to join in. Obvs. Actually, I think I did alright, didn't get sick or anything.

Jade from school was there, too, with Jermaine, her bloke. Another J. We were completely pissed, laughing and singing, when Raff pulled me away, upstairs, so we could be on our own. Nice bed. Big house. Nearly as big as Raff's, though not as posh, no sleek cupboards or fancy radiators climbing the walls. But nice.

To be fair, it wasn't the greatest idea we've ever had. We must have been up there for over an hour when Tom started banging like mad on the door. I thought he was going to come crashing in, the way he was banging.

'Raff! Come on, come out!'

Raff was lying there smoking, one arm around me as if he hadn't a care in the world.

'What is it, dickhead?'

'It's Mum and Dad! Quick! They're getting out the car!'

Oh, my God. We were in his parents' room, too. I've never seen Raff move so fast, never seen a bed made so quickly, and by a bloke. We were dressed and downstairs before they set foot through the door. God knows what would have happened if Tom hadn't been listening out.

Seriously, though, Mum doesn't half go on. I mean, she knows we're sleeping together, doesn't she? So what's the big deal?

She hasn't asked me about the Christmas Fayre yet, hasn't asked how much work I put in, or how much money we made. Enid is really nice, by the way. I like her, even if she is old. And that other one, Nicole somebody. Cool. I mean really, really cool. And her clothes are awesome. Leggings, oversized red and blue shirt, and the coolest white trainers. She's even asked me to her place on Christmas Eve. There's a party on and she wants me to go. Says I can take Raff too. Go girl, yeah? Two parties in one week. But I need to decide what to wear. I've seen a fab dress online. Black, off-the- shoulder. But there's no way I'd get it in time, not for Christmas, and anyway I haven't got enough money together yet. I could get it for New Year's Eve, I suppose, but by the time I've earned enough money it'll be too late to order it. So, never to be outdone, I've asked Nan.

Yesterday afternoon, it was. She was in the kitchen, cup of tea and a biscuit on the table, opening the post. They all seemed to be Christmas cards with notes folded inside. But then I saw her wipe a tear from her eye.

'What's wrong, Nan?' I asked.

'Oh, nothing, love. Just memories. Someone's died. They're all dying off now, one after the other. Soon there'll only be me left.'

'Oh, Nan.' I hugged her, and she put an arm around me.

'Sorry, love, I'm being silly. Just ignore me.'

'Who is it, Nan? Someone special?'

'They're all special when you've known them all your life. You don't realise it at the time, until they're taken away.'

'Who is it?'

'Someone I used to work with. From back when I first started work. Sixteen I was, same age as you are now. Bright-eyed and bushy-tailed. You think you own the world at that age. Sheila, her name was. We had a right old laugh when she was around, she was a scream.'

Pulling her arm away, she smiled at me, her teeth crooked and yellow, her skin grey and wrinkled. But it was still a beautiful smile.

I sat down beside her. 'What exactly did you get up to in those days, Nan? I mean, you didn't have the telly or anything for entertainment, did you?'

'You put me the kettle on, Tori love, and I'll tell you a little story.'

Nan took a whole hour telling me that little story, what with one thing and another. Good job Mum was at work because she'd have gone mad, I was supposed to be studying. But no amount of studying would help awaken my soul to the life my nan has led, or help me understand the workings of her mind. I mean, from talking to my Nan I now understand why she doesn't want to buy ripped jeans. Everything she owned as a teenager had to be mended, patched up, stitched together, after it wore out. There was no Primark or H&M then, selling cheap clothing from some tatty little sweatshop in India.

'Sheila started at Woolworths before me. Well, she was a few years older. We worked on the cosmetics counter, helping women choose lipsticks and rouge, and face powder. A right good job, it was.'

I remember Woolies from my childhood. Nan used to take me there for drawing things, paper and pens, and books, and sometimes she'd buy me a dressing-up outfit. Snow White was my favourite. Awesome, that dress was.

'Didn't you get bored though, Nan? Just standing around behind a shop counter?'

'Ooh, no. No. We never had a dull moment with Sheila. Besides, you got to know about them, your customers, you got to know about their lives. A bit of gossip now and then never does anyone any harm.'

'Right. Yeah, Nan. So what was she like, this Sheila?'

'A scream. She'd be putting lipstick onto the back of someone's hand, you know, so they could test it. And her hand would slip so the lipstick went everywhere, and she'd be apologising like nobody's business and get really upset with herself. What we didn't know was she did it on purpose, so the punters would feel sorry for her and buy it.'

'Really?' I was astounded, didn't think people Nan's age did things like that.

'Then there was the time she put salt into the branch manager's sugar bowl instead of sugar. No-one ever found out who'd done it, but I knew. And she never admitted it, even to me. But I knew he'd not given her a pay-rise because she'd had too much sick leave, so I think it was her way of repaying him.'

'Oh, my God, Nan. I'd never do a thing like that.'

'No, you wouldn't. You're a good girl, Tori, that's why. But she came to a sad end, did Sheila. Well, sad to me, anyway.'

Now I *was* intrigued. 'Why? What happened?'

'She went to Spain for a week's holiday. You have to remember it was back in the days when it was really expensive to go abroad, so not many people got to do it, and it was a big thing for her. But her dad had come into some money, so they decided to splash out.'

'What happened? Did the plane crash or something?'

She shook her head. 'No, Tori, no. She got pregnant to some Spanish boy. Only found out when she came home, of course. By then, it was too late to do anything about it.'

'But Nan, she could still have had an abortion, couldn't she?'

'Not as easy as it sounds that, especially in those days. They'd only just changed the law and you had to have a really good reason, so it wasn't available to just anyone. Anyway, I doubt she'd have wanted to do it, and I can't say I blame her. No, she had a long-time boyfriend back home and he offered to marry her, to make the child legitimate.'

'That was nice of him. So she didn't come to a sad end after all.'

Nan started giggling, small silly giggles that shook her tiny shoulders.

'What's wrong?' I asked.

'Nothing.' She took a deep breath, calming herself. 'Except, she bought the dress, they arranged the day, the bridesmaids, and the reception. But two weeks before the wedding, the woman who'd been making her dress walked in and marched straight over to Cosmetics. Had a right face on her, she did.'

'Bloody hell. What had she done?'

'Language, Tori.'

'Sorry.'

'Poor old Sheila ran off like nobody's business, before the woman could catch her. Told me to say she was at home, poorly, then hid behind the stationery counter. I've never seen anything like it in my entire life.'

'But why would she do that?'

'She'd called off the wedding and hadn't told anyone, not even the woman making the dress. She just couldn't go through with it.'

'No, Nan! What happened to the baby, then?'

'It was put up for adoption,' she sighed. 'She was never the same girl again. Never as happy-go-lucky. She moved away the following year, down to Hastings, got work in a hotel.'

'Nan, that's so sad. Did you stay in touch with her?'

She shook her head sadly. 'I managed to, through a cousin of hers. It's her daughter who's just written to me about her death. Sheila did settle down in the end, had three more children, so she had a decent enough life, I suppose.'

'It does sound like it, Nan.'

'But there's a moral in there somewhere, Tori.'

'What's that?'

'You don't go getting yourself pregnant to anyone, not anyone, you hear me, not until you've a ring on your finger.'

'Didn't do Mum much good,' I retorted.

'You leave your mum alone. She's done her very best for you. And at least she tried. At least she tried to be good, to do the right thing.'

I felt really bad then. 'Sorry, Nan.'

'Time for another cuppa, I think. Haven't you got revision to do, young lady?'

'I'll do it in a minute. I'd just like to ask a favour, though.'

She went to fill the kettle. 'What's that, then?'

I smiled. My very best smile. It always works with Nan.

'Well - you know I'm working now, don't you?'

'Of course I know you're working now. What do you think I am - senile?'

I grinned. 'Not ever, Nan. It's just, there's this dress I've seen, but I need it for New Year's Eve? And I just wondered …'

'You wondered if I'd lend you the money until you get paid.'

'Yes. Please.'

'Seeing as it's Christmas ...'

So today I've been doing my revision, as promised. See, Mum, I do keep my promises. I've done a report in French about this boy called Maurice who goes shopping with his little sister and gets lost. To be fair, it was really easy, didn't take long at all. But then I did a Physics paper which was really, really hard. I didn't time it or anything, just needed to get to the end. But it's taken hours, with Nan making me food and coffee so I didn't have to stop. And I was supposed to be meeting Danielle at five.

I made it, though. Just. We went to McDonald's in Sleaford, then the cinema. It's really good having some money in my pocket at last. Thanks, Enid. We watched *Sisters*, a film about two sisters sent home to tidy their rooms before their parents sell up, and they decide to throw a party. It was really funny, although a bit rude for Danielle, I think. But we did enjoy it.

I've lost my hoodie, can't find it anywhere. I've left it somewhere, obviously, but can't think where the hell it can be. It's either at McDonald's or the cinema. I've messaged both Danielle and Raff, but they've not seen it. Someone else will have picked it up by now, I think. Not that it was anything special. Shit, it's the warmest thing I've got. I'm having to wear my old blue sweatshirt, which I absolutely hate, but it's the only thing that fits. I need to check Enid's place, although why I'd come home without it I've no idea.

Nan's in bed, Mum's out with that Mike bloke, and I'm on Facebook, one eye on the telly. But I've also got an eye on the clock. It's always after midnight, you see, when I get that feeling, that weird sensation. So I've decided to get to bed before twelve if I can. It's ten to, so I've got ten minutes in which to wash and clean my teeth.

It's funny, I think, how well I get on with older people. I mean, you'd think we'd have nothing in common, yeah? But I so love my Nan, and I get on well with Enid, and I even got chatting to Bill Mitchell at the Christmas Fayre thing. Turns out he was the managing director of an electronics company that went bust in the nineties. His wife and kids left him after that, he lost his home and couldn't find another job, and that's how he's ended up where he is. Bless him. He lives just around the corner from Enid, in a scruffy old cottage with a massive garden, full of plants and pots and things. He says he only drinks whisky because there's nothing else to do. He certainly doesn't look well, a bit grey and grizzly. But he's so nice, there must be something he could do for a living. Probs a bit old now, though, to be taking on another job. Poor chap. I'll take some chocolates round some time, see if there's anything I can do.

I've just messaged Raff about Nicole's party, but he can't make it. His mum's having some friends round for dinner and he has to be there. And I'm not invited. He says it's an annual tradition, but I don't believe him, he's never mentioned it before. Well, I'll just go to Nicole's and have a good time without him. Or maybe Danielle can come.

Bugger Raff's mum. Why can't she let her precious son do what he wants on Christmas Eve? I'm sure he'd much rather be with me than her fucking friends.

Just noticed the time. Five minutes to midnight. Bedtime.

So I'm in bed, trying to sleep. But instead I've begun to worry. I mean, surely Raff could come out on Christmas Eve if he really wanted. His mum's not that much of a witch, is she? I hope he's not going off me. I haven't seen the signs or anything. And it's not like I've never been dumped before. I mean, like, twice.

Okay, so the first bloke to dump me was Andy. He lives over in Grantham, so I don't see him at all nowadays. He's a lot older than me, anyway. Twenty-five he'll be now. Worked in the chicken factory. He dumped me for this blonde. I saw them together afterwards, arms round each other's waists like they were madly in love or something. But he's probably got someone else by now. Bastard. I'm better off without him, although I didn't think so at the time. I nearly topped myself, but don't tell Mum. No, I had some of Nan's painkillers in my drawer, all ready. I was going to take them with the bottle of vodka I'd managed to sneak from a party. Lethal combination, yeah? In the end I couldn't do it, don't know what stopped me, except the bedroom door wouldn't shut properly, kept coming unlocked and swinging open, and I had the weirdest feeling I was being watched. Yeah, as per.

Then I met Luke. It was his mum who ended up telling my mum about our quick shag in the back of his dad's van. I actually dumped him because of his mum telling my mum. It was all *so* embarrassing.

But then I met Olly. Gorgeous, he was. I don't mean cute, I mean gorgeous inside, where it counts. He'd just finished his first year of Politics at Edinburgh Uni. I mean, now I look back I can see it was just one of those summer romances, it was never going to last. But when he dumped me to go back to Edinburgh, I was devastated. I nearly did it again, only this time I planned on walking into the sea, dramatically, and never looking back. I had it all planned. I was going to catch the bus into Grantham and then the train out to Skeggie. But that plan was totally scuppered when I got off the train and saw it was pissing it down. I had no coat, it was blowing a gale, and I just couldn't bring myself to do it, couldn't bear the thought of getting all wet and freezing cold. So I sat inside an amusement arcade with a cup of tea all afternoon, feeling sorry for myself and watching the rain lash down outside. It was kind of cathartic in a way (big word, yeah?), all that rain pouring down, as if the day was in sympathy with me, almost as if it had actually prevented me from topping myself. Good job I didn't, though, or I'd never have met up with Raff again.

We knew each other years ago, you know. At the youth club. They don't run it now, too many drug dealers hanging round. They think we're all rich kids, for some reason. Just because we're a village with cute little cottages and wooden windows (conservation area - no UPVC) painted in Farrow and

Ball green. It's not true, of course, but they'd try it on anyway. So if Raff went along on a Monday night, I'd chat with him. I was only eleven, but Mum would let me go with Danielle and Jessie, my friend from school who left to go to Canada. She was great, Jessie. I've looked for her on Facebook, but I don't think her parents let her on. They were quite strict. Anyway, we'd gulp down Fruit Shoots and salt 'n' vinegar crisps while the youth club leaders got us to play silly games. It was okay for a while, I suppose, we enjoyed it, but then school got in the way, so we stopped going.

So when I met up with Raff again, last year at the local Spar, we just sparkled. Like stars in the sky, we were. I'd only popped in for some bread for Mum. That very same night, Raff took me to see *Insurgent*, a science fiction film starring the gorgeous Theo James. Had no-one else to go with, he said. Like yeah. But then we just kept on seeing each other.

I mean, it was totally meant to be.

15

Melissa

Wednesday December 23rd

JUST a few more touches, then we're all ready. There's poinsettia in all the downstairs rooms, including the cloakroom, would you believe. Ed's outside now, hanging icicle lights along the front of the house and fairy lights across the pine trees at the back. I doubt whether anyone will want to go out there, except to smoke maybe, but it'll look pretty. The Christmas tree looks just amazing, too, and smells divine. We bought it last week from Philip at the local garden centre. It's just perfect, so symmetrical. I've told the new cleaners not to hoover near it, though. I know from past experience the bloody thing blows the needles off. But no, they're good, professional, have cleaned around it with the dustpan and brush. I only know that because I noticed a few needles in the dustpan. I don't hang around when the cleaners are here, you see. Oh, no. No, I stay out of the way, book my nails in or something. I have to say, though, they're a good bunch, know what they're doing. The house looked spotless when I walked back in at five o'clock yesterday.

So we've got Maxine, Greg, Charlotte and James to feed. Charlotte's such a lovely girl. I've practically watched her grow up. It would be so lovely if she ended up as my daughter in law. She's mature, sophisticated, not like that little toe-rag Victoria. How on earth she and Raff met up is a puzzle to me. They don't even move in the same circles, surely. Raff *says* they knew each other at the youth club years ago, and then got chatting in Spar last year. That's when he asked her out, took her to the pictures. He even remembers the bloody film. Well, we'll soon sort that out. It can't last forever, after all. They're hardly a match made in Heaven.

So.

The Christmas Eve menu.

Poached salmon and asparagus to start with, then beef wellington, followed by lightly blushed meringues. Well, a girl's got to watch her figure. Must be careful not to burn them this time, though. Oh, I'm so looking forward to it. Must decide on the seating. Raff next to Charlotte, of course. Or Raff opposite Charlotte?

16

Enid

Thursday December 24th

THEY played Bing Crosby at the funeral.

For you and I have a guardian angel
On high, with nothin' to do
But to give to you and to give to me
Love forever true
Love forever true.

Josie asked for it to be played at her funeral, had merely mentioned it in passing, thinking it wouldn't be for years. But how like her those words are. Full of love and life and faith. Never a bad word about anyone. Bless her.

The church was full, chock-a-block, crammed from side to side, front to back. I've never seen anything like it. And so many tears. Bill Mitchell was there, handkerchief at the ready. To be honest, I felt like giving the thing a good old bleach in Domestos. But I mustn't be harsh on him, the poor bloke. There was a police constable in church as well, right at the back. Peggy chatted to her for a couple of minutes as we left, but didn't glean much information. The burial itself was just for family, so we headed straight over to Julia's house in Folksbury. We just paid our condolences as the family arrived, didn't feel much like eating. A glass of sherry and a cup of tea did me just fine.

'Lovely song, that. Bing Crosby, wasn't it?' said Peggy, sitting beside me on the sofa.

'It was lovely, yes. Do you think we all have a guardian angel, Peggy?'

'Of course I do. The times I've been asked to help out through the years …'

'I don't think mine does a very good job of it.'

She smiled. 'You're not doing so badly. We have some laughs, don't we? And look, you're still walking around, fit as a fiddle.'

'At my age as well,' I volunteered.

'At your age as well.'

'But it would be nice to have someone to come home to sometimes, don't you think?'

'Enid, if fate has decreed you should live on your own for a bit, then that's what you must do. There's a purpose to everything.' She patted my knee. 'Besides, you don't know what's around the corner yet, do you?'

Wendy took me home after the funeral, then picked me up again at eight to drive back to Folksbury for the Solstice Night celebrations. Very good of her, it was. Wendy Broome's the wiccan for Beckington, a small village on the way into Sleaford. She has a new, shiny black Ford Fiesta with heated seats, so we drove there in considerable comfort.

Peggy's shop is part of an old row of cottages, a bit ramshackle but serviceable, with an old cart outside for display purposes. It's kept inside at night, so we have to push past it to get into the shop, but other than that there's just enough room for us all. Ian, Peggy's boss, had brought round an old table for us to use. He's alright about our meetings, says as long as we're not putting spells on him, we're okay doing whatever we do. And well, let's face it, he and Peggy go back a long way.

Peggy, wrapped in a long purple cloak, was just opening a bottle of chilled white wine as we arrived. I carried a basket containing two quiches, a rice salad, a carrot and bean salad, and some warm baguettes. The table was laid out with all our goodies, food, drink, plates and cutlery. There were tall white candles too, but where they're normally aglow with celebration, that night they were alight with grief. Peggy passed us each a glass of wine and we stood in a circle, all eight of us. Myself, Peggy, Wendy, Heather, Susie, Joan, Katie and Marie. There should have been nine, but of course Josie wasn't there. The number nine represents faithfulness, gentleness, goodness, joy, kindness, long-suffering, love, peace and self-control, and we in the Sleaford coven agree to use it for our number.

'May Bright Blessings be upon you, and welcome to the forty-eighth Solstice Night celebration of the Sleaford Coven,' said Peggy in her huge theatrical voice, the aroma of patchouli heralding her every word. 'Tonight should be an evening of celebration, of rebirth, of joy. But we know in our heart of hearts that this year we're unable to fulfil these … these … yardsticks.' Her voice wobbled and she had to cough to regain her composure. 'One of our number is missing. One of our number has died tragically and we shall miss her forever more. So tonight is to be a remembrance of her memory, a thanksgiving for her life.'

We murmured in agreement, lifting our glasses into the air and drinking.

'Let us begin.'

We broke the circle and helped ourselves to food. Peggy made tea using a small kettle and we stood eating and drinking, chatting to each other quietly.

We always meet at the back of Peggy's shop on Solstice Night, then spend an hour meditating afterwards, sitting around a lit fire in the woods near her house. Which is all well and good if you're a youngster like Wendy and Heather. But me and my old back. And if it's snowed, well, you can imagine. I wear my thermals as a general rule.

After the food, we gave thanks for Josie's life. Susie read a piece she'd written about Josie and the kind of person she was. It was so beautiful, we cried bitter tears and sobbed and sobbed. Even Peggy, who's usually hard as nails.

'Bright blessings,' we said to one another.

Even though we all believe in reincarnation and know Josie will be coming back, we'll still miss her terribly. She was such a character. The way she'd stir sugar into her tea, first one way three times then the other way three times. The way she'd wink at you cheekily for no reason whatsoever. And the way she'd always wait for the waning moon before uttering spells of healing. Even if the children were ill under a waxing moon, she would never recite her spell, said it was a waste of time.

Sickness, vanish and be gone
Fly into the air and go
Do not darken this being again
Let her/him be well and whole.

We'd usually be in a party mood, laughing and joking, as we encircled the fire. But tonight we were solemn, whispering in hushed tones. Peggy had set it alight earlier, but now she threw rosemary and lavender oil onto the burning embers to help us relax. The scent was delicious and we breathed in deeply.

Holding up the pentacle she always brings, Peggy walked around our circle, pausing at each quarter, her words filling the air, her soft footsteps calming us.

'I call upon the element of earth to bless this circle. May it protect us with its grounding force as we perform our works tonight.'

We each had a letter we'd written to Josie, saying how much we valued her time in this incarnation, how much we loved her, how we'll miss her, and to ask for white light to carry her up and away to the place she needs to be. It's to help her move on. But it's also to help us let go.

We threw the letters into the fire to release our words to the sky.

It was eleven thirty by the time I arrived home. Wendy dropped me off, and I stood waving until her car disappeared round the corner of the cul-de-sac.

But as I moved towards my gate, a shadow caught my eye. A shadow, there, beneath Lilian's cherry blossom. I thought I recognised the shape at first. A man, I thought, then realised it might actually be a woman, slim and smallish. I knew it wasn't Lilian because she was on holiday again, off skiing with her new beau. Then the shadow moved out of sight, and I wondered if it was actually a burglar. I pressed my thumb into the centre of my right palm automatically. As I've said before, the minor chakras at the centre of each palm are quite useful for energy healing, so they help when suffering stress or illness.

Freezing cold already, I stood there shivering, deciding whether or not to investigate. Suddenly Peggy's voice seemed to wrap itself around me.

The Duk Rak, Enid, the bloody Duk Rak!

I moved quickly into the safety of my garden and unlocked the door. Genevieve was in the hallway, awake and alert. Her eyes watched approvingly as I turned the key and fastened the chain.

'That's it, Genevieve,' I whispered. 'Safe and sound now. Come on, a nice hot drink, then we'll get ourselves to bed.'

I rang the police while the kettle boiled. But I had the distinct feeling they weren't interested. The girl's voice was drowsy, and my guess was she was ready for bed like me. So I made soothing camomile tea and crawled upstairs with it, Genevieve at my heels. My guests were fast asleep, no sound whatsoever coming from their room.

I ran a hot bath, right to the top, sprinkled Epsom salts and a few drops of lavender oil, and soaked my cold, aching limbs.

Ah, she was a sight to behold, was Josie. She'd warm her oils in a burner, chanting as she did so, it didn't matter who was there. And they'd just accept her for who she was, clever and witty and loving. I think the thing I'll miss most about her is the way she'd wink at you, her brown eyes sparkling with mischief. It was her way of saying *Don't ever take anything too seriously, girl.*

Tori had come over the morning before the funeral to make breakfast and clean the guestroom. I supervised the cooking as it was her first time, and she took to it like a duck to water, said she's been watching her Nan cook fry-ups for years. The cleaning wasn't quite so spot-on, however, but she'll soon learn. A messy lot Mr and Mrs Taylor are, as it happens. Towels on the floor, toothpaste on the sink. You'd think they'd know better at their age. Anyway, Tori was a big help and I know I can rely on her, once she knows what's what.

There is something that's troubling me, though. Even though I can't quite put my finger on it. We were in the kitchen after breakfast the next day, the

Wednesday, me washing and Tori drying. Mr and Mrs Taylor had gone upstairs with a cup of tea.

'How long have you lived here, Enid?' Tori asked.

'In Pepingham, do you mean?'

'Yes?'

'Ooh, let me think now.' I added it up. 'All in all, it's been thirty-nine years. A long time.'

'It's really nice, isn't it, though? I mean, there are some lovely people here. I got talking to that old chap, Bill Mitchell, on Sunday, at the Christmas Fayre. He looks like a complete soak, but he's actually really nice, isn't he?'

I nodded. 'He is. He's lovely. Life's been hard on him, he's had a rough time of it and that's why he's like he is. So we mustn't judge too harshly. We don't know what the future will bring to us yet.'

Tori pointed to some dried-up egg on the frying pan. 'Enid, you've missed a bit.'

'Sorry. My eyes again. I really should wear reading glasses when I'm washing up.'

She grinned. 'I'll remind you next time. That Nicole, though, isn't she just awesome? I love her clothes. And she's asked me to a party at her place on Christmas Eve. It sounds amazing.'

I just think it sounds a little strange, that's all. Why would someone like Nicole, who must surely have plenty of friends of her own, invite Tori, a complete stranger and just a kid, to her house? Especially at Christmas when people only really want to see family and close friends? Is it because she feels sorry for her? And if that is the case, what would that do to Tori once she found out?

But I didn't want to hurt her feelings.

'Well, you must have impressed her, you know. She probably wants to make friends.'

Her smile lit the kitchen. 'You think so? That would be so cool, wouldn't it?'

Rinsing the sink with the cloth, I smiled back. 'Yes. Yes, it would.'

'She's been to university, you know,' she continued. 'Studied geology. Though why she did that I don't know, not when she wants to work for charity.'

'I suppose it was probably something that interested her at the time, but now she's changed her mind.'

'But geology? Yurk!'

'Some places just like you to have a degree, no matter what the subject is. I think they like to know you can stick at something.'

She hung the tea towel behind the kitchen door. 'I wonder what I'll do at uni ...'

'You're thinking of going, then?'

'Too right. I'm going to get a top job, company director or something, make loads of money, buy a great big house with a massive garden, then me and Raff can live there forever.'

'So you're really keen on Raff?'

'Of course.'

'Does he live in Pepingham?'

'He lives in that old white house on Peterborough Road. You know the one? Gorgeous, it is.'

'Nice,' I murmured. I knew the house, of course, but not the family. 'How long's he lived there, then?'

'Ten years. They used to live in Sleaford, but when his dad got going with his car business they moved here. Raff goes to Abbey Hill School, the private one?'

I nodded. 'Oh, yes. A good school, by all accounts.'

'The uniform's gross, though. I mean, have you seen it?'

'Purple, isn't it?'

We burst out laughing at the same time. She really is a very pretty girl. Pity about the ripped jeans.

This morning, Christmas Eve, I awoke to bright sunshine and frost, a beautiful and sparkling winter's day. Tori's breakfasts are also a sight to behold. Cooked to perfection, they are, crisp bacon, soft eggs, and sausages that are just the right shade of brown, heading towards black. That's what brings out the flavour, you know. And Mr and Mrs Taylor obviously slept well, he wasn't as sullen as he was and she wasn't quite so talkative. Rested, I think the correct phrase is. The lavender and rosemary I placed inside their pillowcases had nothing to do with it, of course. So they left this morning to head home ready for Christmas Day.

Yes, I'm very impressed with Tori. She's an intelligent girl. She's upstairs now, cleaning the room, changing the beds and putting out fresh towels for when Carol and Richard arrive. And she seems determined to do well at school. I am hoping she'll buy herself some new clothes, though. No-one would employ her looking like that. And why on earth do kids these days walk round with rips in their jeans? They'll end up with bloody arthritis in their knees. To my mind, anyway.

I hear a knock at the door.

'Who's that at this time in a morning?' I ask Genevieve, hanging up the tea towel I've been using.

She rushes ahead, tail held high. In charge as usual. She knows who it is alright.

Then I know too. It's Mattie, I think, pulling open the door.

'Mattie!' I exclaim. 'What a lovely surprise.'

'Happy Christmas, Enid.'

'And a Happy Christmas to you too, my dear.'

'We thought we'd pop round to see you. Hope you don't mind.'

She's like a second daughter to me, is Mattie. And her two children – so lovely. There's Lily, who's five, and Thomas, who's nine. Lily's a little tomboy, all pigtails and legs, with a huge smile for everyone. And Thomas – well, considering he's nine years old he's growing into a wonderful young man. Thoughtful, intelligent, caring. Just like his mum, I suppose. But no, Mattie had a hard time of it a few years ago. I was glad Peggy and I were able to help. And now she's happily married with two gorgeous children and a beautiful old farmhouse in Bamborough. She and Andrew bought it at auction three years ago, been doing it up ever since. They're nearly there now, and lovely it is, all high ceilings and big windows downstairs, cosy little bedrooms upstairs. I've been to visit a couple of times. She's doing well with her decorating business, too. It's been just the job since she had Lily; much easier to work round a baby when you can decide on your own hours.

Today they've brought presents. I have some too, all ready beneath the tree. I won't be caught out again. Twice they've turned up with presents and twice I haven't bought them one in time. So now I'm prepared. A *Frozen* necklace and card game for Lily, and a glow in the dark solar system for Thomas's bedroom. And a nice box of chocolates for Mattie and Andrew, of course. I don't spend a lot, it's the thought that counts.

I cut the stems from the pink roses Mattie's brought. Beautiful, they are, and they smell wonderful. Placing them inside my largest glass vase, I display them on the kitchen table for now. I'll be putting them in the sitting room later.

'They're beautiful, Mattie. Thank you so much.'

I make tea and chocolate milkshake and we sit in the kitchen drinking and chatting. I've some gingerbread men in the freezer, too. They've always been Thomas's favourite, and the children tuck in eagerly as we chat. A little later, Lily climbs onto my knee, her arms around my neck.

'Enid?'

'Yes, Lily?'

'I want to play outside. Can I?'

'Of course you can. Come on, I'll unlock the back door for you.'

My back garden is lovely, just a strip of lawn and a small patio filled with pots. This is where I grow my marigolds, pansies, poppies and stinging nettles. My herbs, my mint, rosemary, lemon balm, chamomile and suchlike, all of which I use in my *concoctions* as Peter would say, I grow in the conservatory. My garden gets the sun nearly all day, and I do love to sit here with a glass of Pinot Grigio on a warm summer's evening.

Both children run outside and immediately find the swing in the far corner. So Mattie and I have time to ourselves. We get to talking about Tori. Mattie's son is also a special child. He's been here before, but he remembered it, used to talk about it. Or did until he was five years old. They lose the memories as they get older, you see, which is a good thing to my mind. Otherwise it'd drive people crazy.

It's an interesting story, actually. Mattie has a grandma called Beattie, on her mother's side. She's dead now, but after she died her house was rented out. When it was eventually put up for sale, they found a diary in the attic. Beattie wrote it as a child in 1941, and it's actually proven that Thomas is the reincarnation of Mattie's great grandad. Fascinating it is, absolutely fascinating.

What happened was that when Thomas was very young, he'd make up stories about a pink house. Mattie thought it was just his imagination, of course. But when her grandma's diary showed she'd lived in a pink house as a child and had broken her arm after falling from a window there, we realised Thomas was actually talking about real-life events, that he'd actually lived as Benny Baxter, his great, great grandad. Benny died during the war, of course, after a terrible mining accident.

'You will keep this information about Tori to yourself, won't you?' I whisper. 'She's upstairs now, so we need to be quiet.'

'Of course, Enid,' she replies. 'I wouldn't want to scare her. I never say anything to Thomas, you know. He needs to lead a normal life, and anyway he's completely forgotten about his pink house now. Anyway, this Tori – how do you know she's lived before? They forget those memories while they're still young, don't they?'

'Oh, she doesn't remember anything. Might be better if she did. But Peggy Fleming, she gets visitors, you know, spirits who look after us. That's how I knew about you, if you remember, after your Grandma Beattie contacted her. No, Tori's deceased great uncle has asked Peggy to keep an eye on her. She's in great danger, has committed suicide twice before, looks like she might do it again.'

She looks distraught. 'Oh, Enid, that's awful …'

'Although I have to say, she seems a bright young thing. I've started her working here, just to give her some money really and so I can keep an eye out. And they're not very well off, so I thought it would help out a bit.'

'What's she doing, then – cleaning?'

'Actually, I've started up a bit of a bed and breakfast. Just at weekends, you know. Now I don't need the money, and I certainly don't need the hassle, but it's a way of allowing me to get to know Tori.'

'Is there anything I can do to help, Enid? I would like to.'

I smile. 'I'd love it if you could, Mattie. But at the moment we just have to sit and watch, I'm afraid.'

'Benjamin Bradstock's coming to visit us over the New Year, if that would help. He might be able to do something, do you think?'

Benjamin Bradstock is a hypnotherapist. Folks can sometimes regress to their previous lives under hypnosis, you know, and it often helps them with problems in this lifetime.

'Now that *is* an idea,' I say. 'I'll discuss it with Peggy, have a think about it. Thank you, Mattie.'

Just then, Tori appears at the door, duster and polish in hand, so I stand up to introduce her.

'Come on in, Tori, sit down. I've just been telling Mattie here what a marvellous job you're doing. Would you like a cup of tea after all that hard work?'

I watch her carefully. Did she hear us talking about her? But no, I see nothing in her eyes, just a little shyness at Mattie's presence. She comes in and sits onto the chair I've just vacated.

'Now then, cup of tea, yes?' I busy myself putting on the kettle. 'Mattie here lives out at Bamborough. She's an old and very special friend.'

'Thanks, Enid,' Mattie says.

'I'm only telling it like it is.' I place cups onto the worktop. 'And this is Tori, who will also become an old and very special friend. I hope.'

Tori blushes, right from the top of her head right down to the edge of her navy sweatshirt. It's in a better state than that grey hoodie she always wears, I must confess.

'Now then, gingerbread man or cinnamon shortbread?'

I offer the plate and Tori takes a gingerbread man. 'Thank you,' she says politely.

Mattie takes some shortbread. 'Thanks, Enid. Are you still at school then, Tori?'

Her mouth full, she merely nods.

'And what's your favourite subject?'

She swallows quickly. 'French.'

'French? My, you must be clever. I was always useless at languages. I'm a bit better now I've been abroad a few times, I must confess. It makes much more sense when you actually need to use it.'

I stand there, leaning against the sink. 'Where do you go to on holiday, Tori? Do you get chance to use your French?'

She shakes her head. 'We don't really go on holiday, to be fair.'

Mattie offers her the cinnamon shortbread. 'Here, try one of these, they're delicious.'

But Tori shakes her head. 'No. I'm okay, thanks.'

'Another gingerbread man?'

'Thanks.' She takes one.

'Going on holiday's not all it's cracked up to be, anyway,' I murmur sympathetically. 'Nothing but packing your case before you go, trying to fit it all in, then a load of washing when you get back. You end up more worn out than before you've started.'

'It's my Nan,' Tori hastens to explain. 'She's not very good on her feet, likes to be at home.'

I smile. 'Well, once you've left home, who knows what you'll be able to do, where you'll be able to go?'

'I just want to go to university, then come back here and buy a nice house.'

'Well, it's an ambitious young lady you've got there, Enid,' says Mattie. 'More than I had. I left uni after one year to go and get married. And look where that got me.'

'Where?' Tori asks innocently.

'Mattie married a man who wasn't quite right for her, but she's met the right one now, haven't you, love?' I reply.

'Slight understatement there,' Mattie mutters under her breath, her eyebrows raised as she remembers the cheating, lying thug she married first time round.

'When I get married, I'll make really sure he's the right one. I'll know straightaway,' says Tori, her eyes sparkling.

'Well, just make sure you do,' I reply. 'You just make sure you do.'

17

Tori

Friday December 25th

IT'S Christmas Day! Yes!

I've been awake since five o'clock. To be fair, one of my weird dreams woke me up. It was really strange. I was holding this rifle, up over my shoulder as if I was marching or something. But it was really heavy, and I think that's what woke me up because I'd had enough of carrying it, couldn't carry on any longer. Me and my totally weird imagination.

So I'm sitting here on the floor beside the Christmas tree as wide awake as anything. Mum and

Nan are up too, but they're just drinking tea. As per. I'm being allowed to open one pressie and I've chosen the one from Nan, because she's just so excited about it. It's small, a box of some kind. Oh, my God. I can't wait.

I pull off the shiny red wrapping. Inside is an empty box from Aldi that once held teabags. But it's not empty, there's some sticky tape holding the lid down. I pull it away and peer inside. There's a piece of paper inside. I pull it out. It's a gift voucher from River Island. And when I see the amount I can't believe it. One hundred and fifty pounds!

'For me? Seriously?' Tears fill my eyes.

Nan smiles and I rush over, hugging her as if she's going to run away.

'Thank you, thank you, thank you!'

'Hey, don't go strangling me. That's not how you get favours,' she laughs, her arms around me.

'It's awesome, Nan, I love it. Thank you so, so much.' I kiss her soft cheek.

'And you can keep the money for the Asos dress. It's alright, I've had a little nest-egg come through.'

'No! That's amazing! Thank you!'

'Just do me a favour,' she says, quietly.

'What?'

'No ripped jeans.'

'Okay,' I agree.

I really, honestly, can't believe it. My Nan is just totally amazing. I am going to buy so many new things.

We have to wait five minutes, then Mum says I can open her present too. But I want to wait a little longer, have some breakfast, spread it out a bit.

So we eat home-made porridge, Nan-style. It has squashed bananas and sultanas with a little cinnamon and is totally yummy.

Another cup of tea, then I'm ready.

Mum's pressie is a pair of boots, black leather ankle boots with a kitten heel. From River Island, again. They must have been shopping together. But they're awesome, perfect, I love them, and they fit just right.

'Thank you, Mum, they're awesome, I love them,' and I rush to kiss her too.

I make Nan and Mum open my presents to them. I bought them weeks ago while I was still working at the Coffee House. Calvin Klein perfume for Mum, bubble bath and hand cream for Nan, and a massive box of Thorntons between them. They love them.

'There's some other little things under the tree, just chocolates and stuff,' says Nan.

I smile. A huge, great smile. 'This is the best Christmas ever.'

We spend the morning in our PJs watching telly and eating chocolate. Mum and Nan keep dashing through to the kitchen, messing with the turkey and veg. The smell is making my mouth water. I decide at twelve o'clock to get washed and dressed. Raff's meeting me outside Spar after dinner and I think we're taking Fudge for a walk, so I won't be wearing my new boots just yet. But we'll be swapping presents, too, and I'm just so excited. It is turning out to be the best day ever. I hope he likes my present to him. It's not much, but I do like it. It's a VANS shirt, a checked one in different shades of blue. Cost me twenty-five quid in the sale. Me and Danielle chose it weeks ago, the day we went to Lincoln with her mum. I got him Lindor chocolates too. I hope he likes them, because I *love* them.

This will be our first Christmas as a couple. We've been dating six months now and I can't believe it, because it's the longest time I've ever been out with anyone. And he's coming over on Sunday for dinner, too, so I can introduce him to Mum and Nan properly. I hope they like him. I think Mum's avoided him so far because she doesn't quite approve of us sleeping together. Well, okay, she doesn't approve of us enough to say, *I'm so pleased to meet you, and I hope you're going to look after my little girl,* which is what she'd really like to be saying.

So I'm out of the shower, hair all wet and dressing gown on, and it's my hairdryer that reminds me. I found a letter yesterday, just beside the hairdryer in Enid's guest room, next to an empty box of Mrs Taylor's prescription pills. The envelope wasn't stuck down or anything. It was just lying on the side ready to post, by the looks of it, although there was no address on, it just said *'Dear Sirs',* and I know I shouldn't have opened it, but something made me. I just had to. I was right to as well, because she'd written about me. Fucking guests writing fucking letters about me. I mean, what's that all about? But as I read it, I got really, really upset and angry. She talks about Enid's house, how small it is, how noisy at night with dogs barking and floors creaking. Then she goes on about me. And I quote. *"This silly little girl who's never so much as seen a frying pan, let alone cooked a full English,"* and *"a dowdy schoolgirl, ugly as sin, dresses in the same clothes every day, scruffy top and jeans, looks like she could do with a good wash."* I mean, the cheek of it! I didn't say anything to Enid, it would have upset her. I just shoved it inside a drawer. And anyway, I don't want her to know I was noseying, do I? But I can't believe it, they seemed so nice, especially him, even though he didn't say much. And I thought my cooking was alright, actually. I mean, I know Enid's been helping a bit, but that's only because I'm new. I thought I was doing alright.

So why am I sitting here on my bed, all morose? Why am I taking it so much to heart? To be fair, I don't wear the most brilliant clothes in the world, but she's not exactly Kim Kardashian herself. Big flowery shirts and cheap trousers with an old overwashed sweatshirt on top. I mean. And her choice of nightwear? Stripey PJs. Like a prisoner of war or something. No wonder her husband's the meek and mild sort. Probably has nightmares, sleeping next to that.

Yeah, okay, I might be exaggerating slightly. But honestly, she has no need to talk about me like that. Anyway, I'm going to sort out my clothes, what with Nan's brilliant voucher and Mum's new boots.

And last night didn't make me feel any better. I decided to go to Nicole's party on my own in the end. Well, I asked Danielle, but she was going out with Chris. So I asked Nicky from school, who said she couldn't go because she was going to a nightclub with friends. Get her. Then I rang Beth, who sits next to me in Maths, but she lives in Grantham and couldn't have got here as her parents were going out. So, it was just me and Mr Nobody.

Now I've got to be honest here. I didn't think the party would be up to much, and I didn't want to let Nicole down by not turning up when she'd been so kind as to invite me. So when I did turn up, well, I couldn't believe it. I mean, her dad works at the garden centre, so I thought it would be a little two-up, two down kind of a place, not being snobby or anything. But, oh my God, it was totally amazing. Now I don't know what Nicole's mum does, but she sure brings home the bacon. It's totally fab, and I swear it's bigger than Raff's house. Three floors, a room with a jacuzzi downstairs, and a massive garden that had a band playing inside a white marquee, open to the garden so we could hear it through the French doors. Totally. Amazing.

But I felt really nervous as I approached the house. I mean, there are only small cottages and bungalows on that road, so to come across a house like that at the end, with actual streetlamps *in the garden* - well, I nearly turned round and came back home. But Nicole saw me. I think she was waiting for someone else, to be fair, but she saw me so I couldn't turn back. But I really, really wish I had now. I felt so out of it, what with the heavily-perfumed blonde woman who came up to admire my dress, but was in fact peering down her nose like it was a piece of shit, and the bloke who offered me a drink but made sure not to touch my fingers when he gave it to me. And the little woman with long grey hair who was sat in the corner, and who followed me with her eyes. Totally weird, she was.

I mean, on the outside everyone was really nice and friendly, smiling and nodding as I walked past them with Nicole, but I could tell there was something not quite right, that I didn't fit in, like a crude brown weed poking out from a vase of gorgeous red roses. Nicole's mum and dad greeted me like I was her long-lost sister, which I found really weird too, then introduced me to other people's kids, who were kind of the same age as me. They were all tall and slim and perfect, with mouths that smiled, but eyes that didn't.

I didn't know any of them, so I guess they must go to a different school. So I said hello and smiled, and drank red wine, and prayed for the roof to lift off and a big hand to come and pull me out.

I so wanted Raff to be there. If he'd been with me, they'd never have dared look at me like that.

I felt like a real loser. Even though I was wearing Danielle's gorgeous dress and had felt like a million dollars when I left home. Compared to them, though, with their sleek hair and posh frocks and high heels, I *was* a loser. In fact, by the time I left, I was ready to burst into tears. I actually began planning my exit as soon as I arrived, so I said Mum wanted me home for ten. Couldn't wait to get out.

Fucking stupid. I shouldn't let people get to me like that.

Dinner is delicious. I so love Christmas dinner. And there are crackers and party hats, all courtesy of Nan. Mum's disappointed yet again that we haven't heard from my dad, that he's not bothered to send me anything. I'm not, though. He never has before, so why would he now? He's probably got another kid, or kids, and another wife and mother-in-law. Let him get on with it, I think. We're quite happy as we are, just the three of us.

'Let's raise a toast,' says Nan, lifting her glass of Prosecco. 'To a splendid Christmas and a very happy New Year.'

'I'll drink to that,' says Mum, and we lift our glasses in the air.

'And another toast to my Ron. It would have been his birthday today. Eighty-seven, he would have been. May he rest in peace.'

'May he rest in peace,' Mum and I said.

Grandad died many years ago, before I was born. He was quite a bit older than Nan, by about eighteen years. She's always saying how much in love they were. *Better an old man's darling than a young man's slave,* she says. I think it's really sweet, the way she talks about him, the way he'd take her to the park for a walk after work, even though he was dog-tired from working in builder's yards. And the way he'd help with the children sometimes, giving Nan time off for herself. They had two daughters, my mum and Auntie Cath, who lives down in Bournemouth now. We don't see so much of her since she moved down there, and they've got no kids anyway. Mum says they're not having much luck on that score, but that she and Uncle Mark keep trying. Nan's sad at only having the one grandchild, but I'm not. It means I have her all to myself. Which is ace.

Mum's done us proud with the turkey and roast veg, and Nan's Yorkshires are the best ever. Despite this, I just can't wait for pudding, because then I'll be one hour nearer meeting up with Raff.

Raff's standing outside looking totally gorgeous. There's the scent of snow in the air, the sky is heavy with it. I just can't wait to go sledging with him. Last time it snowed it was just me and Danielle, and we used the back hill at Pepingham Farm to sledge down on black bin liners. There aren't many other hills around here, and the farmer's fine about it as long as we don't hurt ourselves. His kids go to our school, all three of them, so he's okay, actually.

Fudge is sniffing at the ground, as per, and I take the lead so Raff can put his arms around me. But he doesn't, even though I snuggle in, making it pretty obvious that's what I want. He seems a bit down for some reason, and I wonder what the hell's happened.

'You okay?' I ask, tucking my arm into his.

'Sorry, a bit tired, I think. Probably coming down with something.'

I smile. 'Too much wine last night?'

He nods mournfully. 'Something like that.'

'A good dinner party, was it?'

'It was okay.'

'What did you have?'

'Nothing interesting.'

'What? Your mum did a spread and you can't remember what you had?'

'Tori – don't.' He looks so miserable I could cry.

'Come on,' I call, running off with Fudge. I make sure to keep tight hold of Raff's present, tucked carefully inside the top of my jeans. 'It's Christmas Day, you can't be miserable.'

He catches up with me at the edge of the woods, slightly out of breath. 'You're fucking crackers, Tori Seaborne, do you know that?'

I stand beneath the streetlamp and let Fudge off the lead so I can place my arms around Raff's neck. I notice he's wearing a rucksack, but I don't say anything.

'I know,' I say. 'Fucking crackers, that's what I am.'

He kisses me gently, and I feel a real sorrow gnawing inside of him. There *is* something wrong.

I pull away. 'What is it, Raff? What's wrong?'

'There's nothing wrong, stupid, nothing at all. Here, for you. Happy Christmas,' and he produces a parcel from his rucksack. It's wrapped in shiny silver paper, with tiny bells fastened to the broad red ribbon. I love it already.

'Thank you.'

He's smiling now. 'Open it then.'

I sigh with relief. There's nothing wrong after all. I pull the ribbon away. It's a top, Ted Baker, black and sleeveless with huge white flowers across the front. It is beautiful.

I hug him close. 'It's gorgeous, Raff. I totally love it. Thank you so much.'

But he pulls out yet another parcel, this one small and square. Jewellery, I think?

'But you haven't opened mine yet,' I protest, embarrassed at the amount he must have spent on the Ted Baker top alone. I fish out my present and give it to him.

'No. I want you to open mine first. It's special.'

He looks so sad I've changed my mind. There is something very wrong.

I pull off the paper and open the box. It's a necklace, silver with tiny white pearls tied into a knot. 'Oh, Raff. It's beautiful.' It's the first necklace I've ever owned. And it matches one of Nan's rings. I have to swallow hard to stop the tears. 'I love it. Thank you.'

'Come here, let me put it on you.' His fingers are gentle as he stands behind me, pulls the chain around my neck and fastens it, turning me to face him. 'There. Beautiful. Just like you.'

We kiss, long and hard. I love him so much.

'Here,' he says, another present in his hand. 'A pressie from Mum and Dad.'

I unwrap it. It's a Superdry hoodie, still in its bright orange bag. I've seen girls walking around school with these bags, have always wanted one. But the hoodie is just right. Perfect. Pale blue and soft and warm.

'Thank you, Raff, it's really lovely.'

'Mum thought you'd like it,' he replies, smiling. 'I told her you've lost your other one, and she said she'd already bought this one. She must have had a premonition, aye?'

Then he opens my present. I've wrapped the chocolates inside the shirt to save on paper, but am suddenly worried it might have creased. It hasn't, it's fine.

'VANS. I love their stuff. Thank you, Tori, it's perfect, just right.' He hugs me. 'Come on, let's open the chocolates.'

So we walk along, catching up with Fudge, until all the chocolates have gone. Once we reach the clearing, we fasten on Fudge's lead and walk him back to the road. Raff's very quiet, he won't tell me what's wrong, and I begin to worry. But I'm not about to let him know that.

'So, what did you get for Christmas then?' I ask.

He shrugs. 'Nothing very exciting, really.'

'What then? Tell me.'

'A watch.'

'Oh. Let me see.'

I pull at his sleeve and find *the* most expensive-looking watch you have ever seen in your entire life.

'Wow. Raff.' I look closer. It's black and silver. It's made by Rolex. 'Is it real, then, genuine?'

He doesn't answer, looks slightly embarrassed. But I'm not. I think it's amazing.

'Wow. Raff,' I repeat.

He shrugs. 'It's a watch.'

'Must have cost thousands.'

'They bought me driving lessons as well. Much more useful.'

'Oh, my God. Driving lessons *and* a Rolex watch? What, have they won the fucking lottery or something?'

'Dad's business is doing well, that's all. And they do like to splash their money, I suppose.'

'Can't blame them for that. I bet if we had that kind of money, we'd do the same, spoil our kids something rotten.'

'Tori …' he murmurs.

'What?'

'Nothing.'

'What? What is it, Raff?'

Taking hold of my hand, he pulls me along. 'Come on, let's walk.'

Back home, I show off my presents to Mum and Nan. But I'm not as excited as I'm making out. I know there's something wrong, but no way have I been able to make Raff tell me. As long as there's nothing wrong with *him*, I think. I can cope with anything, but not that.

We have tea, basically leftover turkey with bread and cranberry sauce, then watch more telly. Danielle rings for a chat and we swap tales of 'what we got for Christmas'. Her parents got her an Apple laptop to help with her GCSE's. Lucky thing. All I've got to work on is that old Acer of Mum's. And *then* I have to ask her to put the password in. Danielle's also got some earrings and a massive heart-shaped box of Thorntons from Chris Schofield. She totally loves them.

I tell her about the mood Raff is in. It's so unlike him and it's really upsetting me, but I don't know what to do about it.

'Maybe he has a conscience.'

'How do you mean?' I ask.

'Well, maybe he doesn't approve of his parents splashing all their cash on him when there's so much poverty in the world.'

'Yeah. Like that would bother him.'

'It might.'

'I suppose so,' I agree half-heartedly.

'Well, I can't think of anything else.'

'No.'

She hears the doubt in my voice. 'What is it, Tori?'

'It's just, when he gave me my necklace he said, *It's special*. Why did he say that? What did he mean by that?'

'He means it's bloody special, that's what he means. It is though, isn't it? I mean, it's something you can keep. Forever, if you want.'

'Do you think that's it? He wants me to keep it forever? Does that mean he wants *me* forever?'

'Zut alors, mon ami! I don't know, Tori, I really don't.'

'I hope it does, Danielle. It just has to ...'

It's nearly midnight and I'm still awake. We've left the kitchen curtains open as it's a full moon outside and Mum thinks it's beautiful. And I know the ghost thing will be here soon, but I'm much too awake to go to bed. Anyway, Mum's here, so I feel safe. We're watching an old film and she's getting all soppy, talking about her and Dad, who was the *love of her life,* apparently. Yeah, you've guessed it. Mum's had the best part of a bottle of Cabernet Sauvignon. And that's after the bottle of Prosecco we drank over dinner. Oh, and the two brandies she and Nan had before Nan went to bed.

The ghost is there now, I can feel him. He doesn't feel malevolent or sinister or anything like that. I think he's just here to watch, I don't know why. A bit creepy, you've got to admit, but I don't think he'll harm us. And I can finally see the footprints Nan was on about. They're fairly small, around size eight, and are invisible, except around the edge there's a white line, like it's made from ice particles or something. And there's that strange alcohol smell again. It's defo a bloke.

It's the bathroom door thing that worries me now, though. I mean, is he some kind of paedophilic ghost? And is that an actual word, anyway? Maybe I should get undressed in the dark, just to be sure, and only switch on the light just before I climb into the bath, and draw the shower curtain across quickly. I should just about manage it.

Oh my God, listen to me. Scared of showing my bits to a ghost.

Obviously had a long day. Obviously worried about me and Raff.

18

Melissa

Saturday December 26th

I have had *the* most amazing Christmas. You will never guess, not in a million years, what Ed's bought me. *Only* a bloody car! A bloody real, beautiful, bloody car! An Alfa Romeo Giulietta, in gorgeous shiny red. Grey leather seats and everything. Can you believe it! It pulled up outside our house at nine o'clock yesterday morning with a great big navy blue ribbon fastened round it. I wasn't even dressed, still in my dressing gown, stuffing my face with Thorntons, would you believe, when it pulled up.

Johnnie from the garage drove it here. He left his wife and family on Christmas morning, just to do that for me. I couldn't believe it. In fact, it made me cry. And yes, I know Ed's got it at cost price and all that, but it's still a wonderful, amazing present. And *so* beautiful, so much classier than that tired old thing I've been driving round, that blue Hyundai Comfort. A misnomer if ever I heard one. Ed's scrapping it, he says. And not before time, I say.

Our Christmas Eve dinner was just as predicted. Raff and Charlotte looked amazing together. Chatted all evening, went for a walk in the garden, then a longer one up the street. Like two young lovebirds, they were. She's *exactly* the right kind of girl for him. All it needs now is for him to finish with that little toe-rag Victoria. Or Tori, as she prefers to be called. What a name. Sounds like some kind of bland food. Or am I thinking of tofu? Anyway, Charlotte's a much prettier name. I understand Maxine chose it after some princess or other. Greg has tried shortening it to Charlie, but gets short shrift from his wife. And when Maxine's not happy, Maxine's not happy.

The food went down a treat, as well. Even though it took me all afternoon slaving in the kitchen. I had a couple of G and T's, admittedly, to help with the old concentration, and the radio was blaring out like an idiotic vuvuzela-thing let loose. But it was worth it. The poached salmon just melted in the mouth, and the meringues – oh – to die for. Everything was cooked to perfection and the timing was just immaculate. A great big pat on the back for me.

So.

Time for a little chat with my very handsome son.

Would you describe her as a nasty little gold-digger, or just a tramp?

19

Enid

Sunday December 27th

CAROL, Richard and the kids arrived around teatime on Christmas Eve, as promised. I was so excited at seeing them, and the children have grown so much since July, when I last visited. I had cooked a chicken stew, all ready to warm up when they arrived, but they rang before they set off, telling me not to cook anything. So I nipped it round to Bill Mitchell's and stuffed it into his fridge. Well, didn't want it going to waste, did I?

'Here you go, Bill. Happy Christmas!' I said as he opened the door.

'Thank you, Enid, and a Happy Christmas to you too.' He smiled softly, his clothes smelling of beer.

He waved me into his house, a mess of old magazines, newspapers and dirty plates. The only thing that gets looked after is his vast display of books. They always seem to be looked after, always neat and tidy, which constantly surprises me for some reason.

'How are you today?' he continued, taking me through to the kitchen whilst pushing a mint into his mouth. The edges of his white shirt were grimy with age, I noticed, need a really good bleach.

I smiled. 'I'm fine, thank you. I've got my Carol and her family coming over later, so that'll be nice.'

'How lovely. They're staying for Christmas, then?

'I've made this casserole for when they arrive, but they have other plans. So you may as well use it up.'

I placed the casserole inside his fridge, completely empty apart from milk, beer, bread, margarine and a lonely pack of pork sausages.

'That's really good of you, thank you. I'm sure it will taste delicious. Do you want some money for it?'

'Of course not. Don't be silly. Call it a Christmas present.'

'How is your daughter, then?'

'Busy. She works for a firm of accountants now, you know, company secretary. A good job, by all accounts.'

'Lovely. And what about your son – what's his name, I can't remember? How's he doing?'

'Jonathan's out in Dubai at the moment, working for a firm of structural engineers. Been out there a couple of years now.'

He grins. 'Doing all right for himself, then. I bet you miss him.'

'I do. Very much. It's about time he got himself settled down and married, though. He'll be thirty-six in August.'

'Can't say I blame him for that. You need to find the right one, don't you? And there's no rush when you're a bloke, is there? Not like women with their body-clocks and all that.'

'I suppose so. But it would be nice to see him settled, and to have some more grandchildren.'

'You'd never see them, Enid, not if he's off all over the place. You wouldn't get a flaming look-in.'

'I suppose not.'

'You want to stay for a cuppa?' he asked, indicating the kettle.

'No - thank you, Bill. I've got a few more bits to get from Spar before our Carol arrives.'

'Oh, well then, another time. Thank you for the casserole. It's very good of you. You're sure you won't need it, you've got a lot of mouths to be feeding?'

I shook my head. 'I'm sure. She's bringing a load of stuff with her, so we'll be fine. Looks like you need something to fill your fridge, anyway, Bill. Are you looking after yourself properly?'

'Why wouldn't I be? And anyway, if I don't look after myself, someone else will. I've no doubt about that.'

I smiled at that. He was right. There are some lovely people in this village, and they do look after each other.

'Okay then, I'll leave you to it. Just take what you need and pop it into the microwave, but make sure it's hot – it's chicken.'

His kind face wrinkled with pleasure. 'I will. It looks delicious, Enid. Thank you.'

'Right then, I'll be off. Have a lovely Christmas, won't you?'

'You too.'

The front door burst open as four tiny feet ran through to my kitchen.

'Nannie! Nannie! We're here!'

'I can tell,' I laughed, greeting them with hugs.

The peace shattered, Genevieve ran beneath the table to hide.

Carol loaded my fridge with food, a turkey, home-made Yorkshires, veges already prepared, home-made

Christmas pudding, gravy, stuffing, the works. She and Richard busied themselves placing presents around the tree, and then we set off for the Drunken Duck in Folksbury. A lovely meal, it was. I don't just mean the food, but to be able to sit there and relax with my family around me was delightful, just what I was needing. The place itself was really friendly as well, with a big log fire and waitresses in frilly aprons. And so Christmassy, with a lovely tree in the corner, and smelling of Yorkshire pudding, cinnamon and oranges.

'This is lovely, Carol. Thank you,' I beamed.

'It's what you deserve, Mum.'

'You mean for putting up with you lot over Christmas?' I joked.

'You know what I mean.'

'So what made you come up last minute like this? I'd have thought you'd have had Christmas all planned weeks ago.'

'Us? Never. No, it was when you texted me about your friend. I just couldn't bear the thought of you up here on your own over Christmas, feeling all sad. And anyway, the kids haven't seen you since the summer holidays …'

The children were in bed for ten o'clock, which is late for them, so I was hoping for a lie-in on Christmas morning.

Not much chance of that, then. My bed practically collapsed in their excitement.

'Nannie, wake up! Look what we got!' cried Rosie.

Rosie is five years old, so the big sister of the two. Adam's only two, so he tends to follow her lead. Thus the two of them jumping up and down on my bed.

I sat up, my throat dry and ready for a cuppa. Genevieve had escaped to sit beneath the window, away from bouncing feet. My alarm clock showed six forty-five. Not too early, it could have been worse.

'Here, sit down nicely, let me see what you've got,' I said.

'Father Christmas has been,' Rosie explained, displaying a lovely smile with two teeth missing.

'Has he? Well, I wonder how he knew where you were?'

'We sent him a letter. On Monday. I wrote it,' she said proudly, sitting cross-legged onto the bed beside me.

'Well, that was very clever of you. He must be very organised to have changed it all at the last minute, though.'

'Mummy says he gets a lot of help,' said Adam, sliding down to the carpet, his eyes shining brightly.

'Just what *I* could do with – some help.'

Rosie smiled. 'I can help you, Nannie.'

'I just need your mum to make me a nice cup of tea.'

Immediately, Carol appeared at the door with a mug of lovely hot tea.

'Sorry about these two,' she said. 'I hope they didn't wake you up.'

My Carol's a lovely girl. Woman, I should say, she's all of thirty-eight. She has my red hair and lovely brown eyes, but she is a tad on the heavy side these days. Gets that from me too, I suppose, although I do my best. But I noticed she was out of breath just from climbing the stairs.

'Are you alright, Carol?' I asked, anxiously.

'I'm fine, Mum. Stop worrying all the time.'

'I'm not worrying all the time. Just *this* time. You seem a little out of breath, that's all. Are you getting enough exercise?'

'Like I have time for exercise. By the time I've picked the kids up, taken them home, made dinner, eaten it, and got them to bed – I'm knackered.'

'Can't Richard help sometimes?'

'He doesn't get home til seven, and he gets knackered too, you know.'

'Are you sure you did the right thing, going back to work so soon after having Adam?'

'I am. We need the money. Have you seen the amount we spend on the mortgage and rates every month?'

'There's more to life than money.'

'I know. But the kids need a nice area to grow up in, don't they?'

'I suppose so. Well, that's why your father and I moved up here, isn't it? But it meant I could be at home with you two as well, you know.'

'Adam starts school in a couple of years. By that time I'll be forty, and then where would I be if I didn't have a job to go to? Gossiping with the ladies who lunch? I don't think so.' She pulled a face.

'Look – I'll give you some herbs. Give you more energy so you can at least get a walk in once they're in bed.'

So after breakfast I mixed together a blend of grated ginger, a few nettles from the garden, boiled them with some green tea, and made her drink the liquid that very morning.

'What is it, Mum?' she moaned.

'I'll give you the recipe. It's not expensive. If you drink it in a morning instead of your usual tea or coffee, it'll fill you with energy. And if you manage to get out for a walk in the evening, get the blood circulating, you'll have even more.'

'If you say so.'

'I do say so. You're not getting any younger, and you need to keep fit and active for those kids.'

She drank it.

'In fact, I'll collect some nettles when we go for a walk and make some of my nettlespud soup for you to take home.'

Jonathan rang at eleven o'clock, just as we were having a coffee. He doesn't ring often enough, to my mind, but I suppose he has his own life to lead.

'We're heading down to the beach with some friends, and there's a party later. Sara's made a load of food, and I'm the one having to carry it all. God knows how I'm going to manage.'

'Oh?' I queried, thoughts of the maternity ward filling my head.

'Yeah, she's pulled her back. Stupid, really. It was only a little thing, just picked up a suitcase and it went. Too tall, that's the trouble.'

I could picture them together. Both tall, bronzed, laughing, her long blonde hair blowing in the breeze. He sends me pictures now and again, then texts me to check I've received them. He has a wonderful life over there, and plenty of money. Well, he works hard, he deserves it. But I do miss him.

'Carol's here with the children. Do you want a word?' I asked.

'Yeah, that'd be cool. Thanks.'

'I'll just put you on, then.'

'Happy Christmas, Mum. Love you.'

'Happy Christmas. I love you too.'

I went to fetch Carol and left them to it, her laughs echoing through the house. Peggy arrived not long afterwards, just in time for lunch. I always invite her for Christmas dinner, ever since Peter left. Well, it's silly us both being on our own over Christmas. And she's met Carol and Richard before, so it's all okay.

And there was more than enough food for everyone, even with Peggy there. In fact, it was the biggest turkey I've ever seen.

We were just watching the Queen's Speech when Sam rang. He lives in Snowdonia now, on one of these residential caravan sites. It's beautiful, he says, with a lake and trees and a golf course nearby. He and Jackie sold their house a few years ago after they retired from teaching. They bought the caravan so they could use their money to travel, see the world. They've been everywhere, even out to visit Jonathan. Loved Dubai, they did.

But Rosie got to the phone before me, smiling as she handed me the receiver.

'It's Uncle Sam.'

'Hi, Sam,' I said as she ran into the sitting room, curls flowing. 'How are you?'

'Fine, thank you, we're all fine. I'm just ringing to wish you a Merry Christmas.'

The sound of his voice was like birdsong to my ears. Memories came flooding back. Sam riding Sonny like a madman along the beach; Sam falling off his bike and fracturing his wrist; Sam bringing home his first girlfriend, an older American woman; Sam going off to college, me in tears, me missing him like crazy and running away from home. Until Dad found me, hiding in a barn ...

'I'm fine, just fine. Merry Christmas to you too, Sam. I've got Carol visiting, as you can tell. She only rang me last week to say they were coming over.'

'Well now, that is a lovely surprise. We've done the same, we're going over to our Samantha's tomorrow. Her three will be going as well, so it's quite a family get-together.'

'Any of them got married yet?'

It's a standing joke. None of his grandchildren are married yet, even though Jackie is dying to be Grandmother of the bride. One of their girls, Amanda, has a little boy, and is living with the father, but that's about it.'

'Jackie keeps dropping hints, but kids these days aren't interested. It's so expensive.'

'As long as they're happy, I suppose.'

After the Queen's Speech we settled down to watch the telly. There'd been a good film advertised, The Muppets Christmas Carol, a real family film, and I thought the kids would enjoy it. But one after the other they sneaked out to play in the hall, running up and down the stairs. As kids do.

'So what have you been up to lately?' asked Richard, settling down with a beer in his hand.

'Not a lot, really,' I replied, sipping my sherry. 'I've spent ages making apple pies for the Christmas Fayre, but that's about it.'

'Well done, though. Did you make much money?'

'Two hundred and fifty. Which is alright, I suppose.'

'That's very good. So you've not been away anywhere, then?'

'No.' I shook my head remorsefully. 'It's not the same when you're on your own.'

'You need to find that there millionaire,' laughed Carol, sitting down beside him, legs tucked beneath her.

'You know you're always welcome at our place,' said Richard.

Carol pulled a face. 'A bit boring. You should be visiting Jonathan out in Dubai.'

'Ooh, no. He's busy with his new girlfriend, so what would I do with myself all day?'

At that moment Rosie ran in, a small brown envelope clutched in her hand.

'Mummy, Mummy, look what we found in the drawer.'

Carol reprimanded her. 'Rosie, you shouldn't be taking things out of Nannie's drawers. It's not nice.' She passed the envelope to me. 'Here you go, Mum. Sorry about that.'

Puzzled, fumbling for my reading glasses, I stared at it. Nothing was written on the envelope, so I guessed it was an old letter I'd mistakenly left in the guest room. I had cleared it out before Mr and Mrs Taylor arrived, but I honestly couldn't remember seeing this. So I looked inside.

Pulling out a letter, written on soft-blue writing paper, I read it. Then I read it again. Shaking, outraged, unable to believe what I was seeing, I stood up and staggered through to the kitchen. Genevieve jumped onto my lap as I sat down. Stroking her soft fur, I read the words again.

Carol followed me through. 'You alright, Mum?'

'Not really, no. This was left by my guest, the one who's just rented the room from me. It's just … it's … I can't believe what she's put.'

She read it. 'Oh, my God! The cheek of it! How dare she?'

I grabbed the sherry bottle from the worktop and poured myself a glass. I needed to show Peggy the letter, but she was upstairs in the bathroom.

'Fetch Peggy, will you, please.'

'Mum – what is it?'

'I've got a strange feeling about this. Something's not right.'

'You and your strange feelings. It'll be nothing. Just a stupid, spiteful woman with nothing better to do. I shouldn't let *her* stay again, that's for sure.'

'I wonder if Tori's read it,' I replied.

'Who's Tori?'

Peggy and I pondered over that letter for hours, all through the film, all through teatime and into the evening. Quietly, in our heads. She was of the same opinion as me, that Mr and Mrs Taylor had somehow infiltrated, had managed to get on the inside of the Duk Rak. But why? And how? And had they actually wanted Tori to find that letter while she was cleaning? They'd obviously not succeeded, or she'd have said something. What was the point of it, anyway? After all, sticks and stones etc.

So as Peggy left to drive home that evening we were none the wiser. But I still had that strange feeling, that feeling that says something's not right.

We went to see the panto yesterday. All thoughts of the letter pushed to the backs of our minds, we wrapped up warm and climbed into Richard's black Volvo. They'd forecast snow on the radio and the sky was full of it, gloomy and grey and depressing. We needed headlights all the way to Grantham. I sat in the back with Rosie and Adam, who were so excited at seeing their first panto their lovely smiles were infectious, so by the time we arrived at the theatre I was feeling like a child myself.

There was no-one famous in the panto, just local performers. Which I really like, to be honest. I always feel sorry for them otherwise, and it spoils my enjoyment a bit. Well, it can't be fun being so far away from home at Christmastime. Yes, I know - I'm too empathic for my own good. Carol's always telling me. Peter too, when he was around. He'd say, *They're guests, Enid, let them be, let them live their own lives.*

I just want everyone to be happy.

But the children loved the panto, and fond memories of taking Carol and Jonathan to the theatre in the old Mazda came flooding back. Where does the time go?

The girl who played Aladdin was both beautiful and talented, had us eating out of her hands. Widow Twanky, too. In fact, the whole production was excellent, especially for such a small theatre. Apart from the incident with the box where something was supposed to appear and didn't. But that's what local pantos are all about, I suppose, and no-one minded a jot.

We drove home through the dark winding lanes, me thinking about what we'd seen, Rosie and Adam fast asleep in the back beside me. We'd just pulled up at the traffic lights heading into Sleaford when something caught my eye.

A shadow. There was a shadow at the side of the car.

I screamed out. 'Lock the doors, Richard, lock the doors!'

I leaned over Rosie to get to Adam's door, holding onto the handle.

'They're locked, Enid,' replied Richard. 'What's wrong?'

Sitting upright as the lights changed, I watched the shadow disappear smoothly into the woods behind us. My heart racing, I sat back and sighed fearfully.

'What was all that about?' asked Richard.

'What's wrong, Mum?' asked Carol, anxiously.

Tears threatened, but I shook my head. I didn't want to alarm them.

'It's nothing. I just thought someone was outside the door, that's all.'

'I didn't see anyone,' she replied.

'Probably imagined it, then. Sorry.'

To be honest, I wasn't sure if I had actually imagined it; it all happened so quickly. But my mood at the time, what with the panto and the laughter and all the smiling faces, was fine, I felt happy. I'd not been thinking about Josie or Tori or anything. So why *would* I imagine such a thing?

We've woken up to the aroma of bacon and eggs. Richard's making breakfast, the children are awake and running round the place, and Carol's brought me up a nice cup of tea.

Today we're going for a walk. So after our delicious cooked breakfast, we don our walking boots and go, Adam tucked snugly inside his buggy.

Outside, there's a biting wind and the sky is still threatening snow, but we've had no snowfall yet.

'It'll be saving itself for some special occasion, then it's going to come down all at once and block everything out,' Carol jokes.

I shiver with a premonition I don't want to acknowledge.

'As long as it stays away for your journey home tomorrow,' I reply.

'It'd be a good excuse not to go into work on Tuesday.'

'It is a pity you couldn't get time off to stay a bit longer.'

'Richard needs to be back anyway, they've got a big project going on.'

Richard's a software developer for a well-known architectural firm in London. He earns plenty of money by all accounts, so why Carol has to go out to work and leave the kids with a childminder I've no idea. I know. It's none of my business. But I do worry about them all.

We turn right, out of the gate and into the woods. It's been a while since I've been here, what with the sun coming up so late and setting so early. But this morning it's light and fresh and I'm looking forward to walking along the rough tracks and smelling that earthy smell you get from rotting leaves.

So we carry on, through the long grass, the shivering nettles, and the scent of wild garlic. Richard and Carol have to sometimes carry the buggy between them, but they don't mind.

I pull on plastic gloves and fill a carrier bag with nettles for my soup. Then Rosie takes hold of my hand and we walk on. She so reminds me of Carol as a child, the way she skips along, pulling on me to walk faster, chatting away, pointing at everything and enthusing about the world around her. Oh, to be five years old again and know what I know now.

'Nannie?' she asks.

'Yes, Rosie?'

'Do you ever get to climb trees?'

'I did when I was younger, a bit older than you are now. We used to climb them all the time, me and Uncle Sam.'

'You lived in a caravan, didn't you?'

'I did.'

'That must have been so cool, Nannie.'

I smile at her enthusiasm, at my memories.

'It *was* cool. We travelled all over the place.'

'Does that mean you didn't have to go to school?'

'Of course not. I went to school all the time, just like you. But I went to lots of different schools, that's all.'

'It must have been so weird. Did you take all your friends with you, then?'

I laugh out loud at that one, at the vision that appears in my head of Mum and Dad bundling up my friends and pushing them into our caravan.

'No. I had to say goodbye to them, then make new friends at my new school.'

'Didn't that make you really sad?'

I think about it for a moment. Yes, it did make me sad. It made me emotional. Is that what's made me into the person I am today, the kind who understands, who always wants to help people?

I look down at Rosie. Carol and Richard are ahead of us with the buggy.

'Yes, it did make me sad. But think of all the different people I was able to make friends with. That's an awful lot of friends to have, isn't it?'

We've reached the old oak tree by this time. There's a clearing here and we pause to decide which way to go. There are two paths, one leading towards the main road into Boston, one leading to an old disused quarry.

'Shall we show the kids the quarry?' asks Richard. 'They can see where we get our limestone from, for building houses and stuff.'

'Okay,' Carol replies, turning the buggy to the right.

For some reason, I balk at the idea. I actually feel a little sick. But I can't say anything, it would sound melodramatic.

'What's this?' asks Richard, kicking at a pile of leaves.

There's been a fire here, a pile of small animal bones at the centre.

'A squirrel,' says Richard, picking out its tail with his foot. 'Looks like someone's been eating squirrel for dinner.'

'Ooh, Mummy!' screams Rosie, letting go of my hand and running up to Carol.

I'm standing there, all alone. Or feel as if I am. I'm sinking, swaying. I feel faint. I lean against the oak tree to steady myself.

'Mum, are you alright?' asks Carol, anxiously. She lets go of the buggy to come over to me.

I scream out. 'No, don't leave the buggy! Richard, get it!'

A sudden squall of wind whips around us, pulling at our coats and scarves. Screwing up my eyes, I hang on tight to my woollen beret. Rosie sits down cross-legged in order to steady herself.

I watch as the wind pushes the buggy away, carrying it down the hill and towards the quarry.

'Richard!' I scream.

He sprints after it, one arm stretched out, his legs long and loping.

Terrified, I can only stand and watch.

But he catches it.

I am shaking with relief.

He turns the buggy round and brings it back.

'Oh, my God!' screams Carol. 'Did you see that?'

'It nearly took him,' says Richard, his face grim.

I check little Adam. He's safe, still fastened in, his expression slightly shocked but smiling at all the fuss.

My heart pounding, I can hardly breathe. 'Come one, let's get away from here.'

The storm stops then, as quickly as it began.

Safe within the aura of the Duk Rak, I make coffee and dig out the box of sultana scones I have in the freezer. We watch The Polar Express, a DVD Carol's brought along. We need to take our minds off what just happened.

But I can't.

I'm convinced that fire I saw out of the guestroom window the Monday before Christmas is the one we've just seen the remains of. So someone sacrificed a squirrel, did they? The squirrel represents fire to wiccans and witches. So, a fire and a dead squirrel. A double element of fire. That means a change is coming, according to Wicca belief. But what change? And why?

20

Tori

Monday December 28th

NO!

I don't believe it! He's having me on. He must be. It's some kind of sick joke.

It's Raff. He's just messaged. Says he's dumping me, we're finished, I'm no good for him any more.

He can't. He loves me. He said so.

What have I done? Is it the present I bought him? Not expensive enough? Not intellectual enough? Not fucking posh enough?

I've just messaged back, telling him not to joke about such things, that I love him, he loves me, that he must be on something.

But no.

He says he means it.

Every single word.

So I'm lying here in bed, sobbing. My world is over, my plans destroyed, all of them little bits of paper screwed up into tiny balls and thrown across the room.

What do I do now?

He came round yesterday, the very day Mum was planning on feeding him. I was so excited, so nervous, so looking forward to it. She was doing chicken and stuffing and everything, the works. She was feeling quite nervous herself. I mean, she'd only met him a couple of times. Once when we were out walking Fudge and she'd dashed over to Spar for something. And once when Raff went to the post office to get a letter weighed.

I knew they'd get on really well, though. I knew he'd love Nan too, because everyone loves Nan.

But he came round early, half past ten, before she'd even had chance to put the chicken in the oven. I introduced him to Mum, then Nan. They were both very excited, smiling at everything and being really polite. I mean, he's so lovely and handsome and tall, who wouldn't? Then he said he was really sorry, he couldn't stay for dinner, his mum had arranged something and had forgotten to tell him. Mum and Nan were disappointed, of course, but *I* felt like my whole world was splitting in two, then falling to pieces. Tiny, tiny crumbs of pain. Mum offered him a cuppa, but he refused, looked at me pointedly and said he wanted to go for a walk. He looked really sad the whole time, just like on Christmas Day.

'But Raff, you said you were coming for dinner. Mum's bought the stuff in and everything,' I complained as we walked along.

'I … I need to visit this friend of Mum's. She agreed it all weeks ago, but forgot to tell me about it. I'm really sorry, Tori.'

'But it's not good enough, Raff. And since when did your mum tell you what to do?'

'Look – Tori …'

'What?' I rounded on him then. I was really, really upset. 'So you'd rather upset me than your mum? Is that it? Don't I mean anything to you?'

'Tori, when I go off to uni next year …'

'When you go off to fucking uni, we won't see each other, is that what you're saying?'

He nodded grimly.

I was panicking by now, my heart pounding like mad, and there was a sick feeling in the pit of my stomach.

'But what if I work really, really hard, and end up at the same uni? Like we said we would? I could, you know. I'm clever, I can do it if I really want to.'

'I know you can, Tori.'

'So, come on, Raff. What exactly are you trying to say here?'

'Tori, can we talk about this another time? Please? It's just, Mum's waiting for me. We're driving out to Boston.'

'Okay. Fine. I'll just go home and eat the delicious dinner Mum's cooking for us, shall I?'

I flounced off, not looking back once, tears streaming down my face. I actually felt like hitting him.

So what do I do *now*?

I knew there was something wrong on Christmas Day, didn't I? But he just kept saying he wasn't feeling well, coming down with something. But I knew it for certain. I always know things. And I'm always right.

We need to talk, I need to know what's gone wrong. I mean, is it because I only live in a rented apartment and he lives in a great swanky house that his parents actually own? I can't believe that's the reason though, or he wouldn't have gone out with me all this time. Would he? I mean, he's not like that. Is he?

Or am I just some slapper he's been practising on until the right one comes along? Is that it? Is it?

No. He wouldn't have said he loves me. Would he?

No. He wouldn't have made me feel a million dollars if he'd been having me on. I'd have known.

Wouldn't I?

Oh my God, I just can't stop crying. Danielle keeps messaging me, asking why I'm not getting back. But I can't tell anyone, I'm so ashamed. I mean, I thought we were going somewhere, I'm always telling everyone we're going somewhere, will probably get married one day, will go to the same uni, live together. What's the point of all that now? What's the point of studying hard like Mum says if all I'm going to do is be lonely in some scruffy little hall of residence?

There must be someone else.

I wake up, my eyes red and sore, my throat dry and aching for a drink. It's nearly one o'clock, midday. Mum's left me a mug of tea by the bed. It's cold, but I drink it anyway. I'm hungry too, but there's no way I can eat. I feel sick. Mum must have taken the tissues I'd piled up, they've gone. Poor Mum. She was amazing last night. If she and Nan hadn't been here, I'd have probably done something stupid, I know I would.

There must be someone else. There has to be. Otherwise, why? Why all this? Why dump me when all I've ever done is pander to him, worship him, love him?

It must be someone he's met in the pub. That's it. He said he'd be going there tonight.

That's what I'll do. I'll get myself all dressed up and wait outside. And watch.

Nan makes me a bowl of Corn Flakes, says I'll be able to eat that. She knows what it's like being without someone, she says. I force it down as I know I have work to do.

I have to win him back.

Mum tries to talk me out of going. 'You'll catch your death of cold out there in that dress.'

'I'll put my new hoodie on top,' I lie, knowing full well I'll take it off when I get there.

'And what are you going to the Royal Oak for, anyway? You know they're really strict, won't accept kids after seven o'clock.'

I shrug and force down the second bowl of Corn Flakes Nan puts in front of me.

Mum knows she's lost the battle before it's begun. She never can win with me. She only wants me to stay home because she thinks I'll do something stupid, she says. I promise I won't.

So I get under the shower and make myself look fucking *awesome*. Danielle's black dress, leggings, and boots, my new ones. Just right, they are, perfect. My makeup's perfect, too. Mountains of eyeliner and mascara, pale lips. Raff always says the prettiest thing about me is my eyes. So I totally make the most of them. Then I hang my new necklace around my neck, and I admire.

I hang around watching telly until nine o'clock, all thoughts of studying gone out the window, and Mum knows better than to nag me right now. At nine, I wander round to the Royal Oak. It's only two streets away, on the main road. There's another pub along the way that would have let me in, so trust it to be the Royal Oak that's awkward. And trust Raff to prefer the Royal Oak. I mean, why can't he go to the Ship instead, like normal people? They let kids in any time. I don't feel like a kid, anyway. I'm not a kid. Kids hang around street corners with bottles of Coke in their hands, or sit outside Spar eating cheese 'n' onion crisps. I'm no more a kid than Raff is.

I wonder what he's doing right now.

So here I am, waiting. There's no sign of him or his friends, but plenty of noise leaves the place every time someone walks in or out. Music playing, people laughing and talking. Having fun.

Bitch. I wonder who the hell she is? It must be someone we know, he can't have met someone new that quickly, he never *goes* anywhere.

Okay, it's ten o'clock and I can't feel a thing. Except for my heart racing like mad. But my fingers and toes are dead. My face, dead. I've already put my hoodie back on, complete with hood up. I can always take it off again when he comes out. I am starting to have second thoughts, though, I must admit. Maybe this is a really bad idea.

Right. I'm going in. Can't stand out here any longer. Off with the hoodie, which I throw over my arm.

Three girls push their way through the door as I reach it. They ignore me and I brush past quickly, hoping to sneak in before the landlord sees me. I know he'll remember me from last time.

I spot Raff in the corner, downing a pint with some friends. There's no girl around that I can see. That's a relief then. Maybe there isn't a girl. Maybe I was wrong.

I sidle up to him, smiling.

'Hi, Raff.'

Embarrassed, he puts down his pint and scowls. 'Tori. What are you doing here? You know they'll throw you out.'

'I don't care. I just wanted to see you,' and I burst into silly, girly tears.

'Tori – don't.'

He pulls on his thick tweed coat, takes my arm, apologises to his pals and drags me outside.

'What's all this about?' he asks angrily. 'We're finished, Tori, I've told you.'

'Yeah, a PM on Facebook,' I retort. 'What kind of message is that, after we've been together six months?'

He looks shamefaced. 'Sorry.'

'Sorry? For what? For dumping me, or for doing it like that?'

'Sorry for being a coward.' He sees a couple of blokes hanging around the pub entrance. 'Come on, let's move away from here.'

We walk towards the woods, our favourite haunt, and stand beneath the streetlamp. I'm the first to speak.

'So come on then. Out with it. Why?'

'Because …' he falters.

'Don't you love me any more, is that it?' I ask the question, but I don't want to know the answer.

'I do love you, Tori. You know that.'

I suddenly realise something. He's crying, too. Soft tears rolling down his cheeks.

'Then why …?' I begin. But my own tears choke me, and I can't continue.

He takes my hands into his. 'Tori, I've always loved you, ever since …' he shakes his head, he's said all this before, 'but you're not right for me, not for the lifestyle I'm going to have. I need someone more - more …'

I fill the gap for him. 'More marriageable, is that it? You need someone more marriageable, more upper class, more hoity-toity, not as *cheap* as me. That's it, isn't it?'

Releasing a huge sob, I pull away and run into the woods, even though it's dark and scary and I can't see a thing. But I know my way around, and head towards the clearing. Sobbing and sobbing and sobbing, I sit down on the wet grass.

Minutes later, Raff joins me, holding up his phone as a torch.

No words are said.

Instead, he lays down his coat, pulls me towards him, and kisses me. He kisses me as if he would never let me go.

He pulls away my new boots and my old leggings. The cold embraces me like a warm friend.

I ache for him. I sigh his name with each and every kiss.

We make love beneath the huge oak tree. It's for the last time, and I know it.

It begins to snow as Raff walks me home. I swear the sky is crying with me, thick flakes of misery falling through the air.

We've been sharing one of his fags, and he leaves me at the door so he can throw the butt to the ground, away from the house.

I call after him. 'I love you, Raff. I'll always love you.'

He just carries on walking. Not a word.

never used after Andy dumped me. That'll help me get to sleep. Climbing out of bed, I pull down the old Napolina tomatoes box carefully. It's full of stuff from years ago, from when I was at Pepingham C of E. There are certificates from teachers for stuff I did that was good, some bright breezy pictures I drew once upon a time, blu-tac still stuck to the back, collages all dried up and falling apart, and childish Get Well Soon cards from when I caught chicken pox. But hidden at the bottom is my bottle of Smirnoff. I remember now, it was a birthday party at Josh's house, his sixteenth. Danielle's dad gave us both a lift because Josh lives in the middle of nowhere. Good party, it was. Josh got absolutely rat-arsed. Me and Danielle weren't in such a state, but we'd had enough to make us sneak away the vodka for later on. Then forgot about it.

There's something tucked beneath the bottle. I pull at it. It's the blister pack of Nan's painkillers, also saved from when Andy dumped me. Bastard. All men are bastards, I decide, and take a long, hard swig of vodka.

Bastards, the lot of them. Total bastards.

I take one of the pills, and wash it down with more vodka.

Then another pill, then more vodka.

The bedroom door swings open. Wide open. I can smell the alcohol again. It's really strong this time. And footprints appear on the floor, white and shiny and still.

It scares me, really scares me, freaks me out.

Is it waiting for me? Is that it? Is it waiting for me to die?

But I ignore it. Nothing's as painful as the way I'm feeling now. Here, deep inside. Nothing. Total, utter pain that's killing me already.

I take some more.

21

Melissa

Tuesday December 29th

I got to show off my new car on Sunday. And my new velvet dress. It looked lovely, Ed said. But it's a good job we went out when we did, because it snowed last night and I wouldn't want to be driving my lovely new Alfa Romeo in all that. No, we drove out to meet Ade and Imogen. Lovely name, that is, Imogen. Irish, you know. She's from Kilkenny. Actually, Ade had left hospital on Christmas Eve, but we decided not to disturb them too soon. Best to let him get a bit better first. And anyway, they had their kids to see to, to enjoy Christmas with. Two girls, they have. Grownups now, both at uni, one studying nursing, the other chemistry. Clever girls.

Ade and Imogen absolutely adored my car. We met up in the Royal Oak, just for a quick drink really, and to get Ade out of the house. And I made sure not to park too close to anyone. In fact, I made sure to take up two parking spaces, if I'm honest. *And quite right too,* said Ade when he saw it, *don't want someone bashing into that until you've had it a month.* I pulled a face, not my best look, so he laughed and said, *Only joking.* He looked really well, better than he has in months. Imogen didn't, though. She's probably not slept properly in days. But she's promised us another weekend in Bruges, says she was really looking forward to it and wants to get back to feeling normal again. Imogen's nice, caring and motherly, but not over-protective. Actually, if you think about it, Ade should be the last bloke to have a heart attack.

My Raff's doing ever so well for himself now. He's finished with that Tori and been out with Charlotte twice. She has a car, a little VW Beetle in orange, and they've been to an afternoon drinks party at this posh house in Lincoln and to an art gallery preview on Bailgate, would you believe. More to the point, he's really enjoying himself. I've told him we'll buy him a car too, once he's passed his test. I'm thinking maybe a Citroen C3?

He takes his first driving lesson next Saturday. Quietly confident, I would say. Well, he should be. If a private education can't buy you confidence, then nothing can.

So.

Time to organise our New Year's Eve party.

Do you think fancy dress or not?

22

Enid

Wednesday December 30th

IT was Peggy who rang me. Four o'clock yesterday morning, it was.

A vision of Great Uncle John had woken her up, come to her in a dream. He showed her a vision of Tori, then the empty pill packet and the vodka bottle beside her bed. Said she had to be *bloody quick*.

Peggy rang for the ambulance straightaway, of course, but the roads were treacherous, thick with snow, the girl said they could be quite a while. So she rang me in a blind panic.

'Get yourself round there, Enid, see if there's anything you can do. For God's sake.'

My heart racing, I felt sick to the stomach, wondering if we were already too late. I pulled some clothes over my nightie, put my winter boots and coat on, and trudged round there as fast as I could, using an old walking pole to help me through the snow.

I banged on the door again and again, like a madman, but there was no answer. And the bell didn't work. So I marched through the garden to the back door, found it unlocked and pelted upstairs to Tori's apartment. Then it was just a matter of banging on their front door and ringing the bell. Frantically.

It was Christine, her Nan, who opened the door, peering through the gap suspiciously. But I pushed my way in.

'Where's Tori?'

Tori's bedroom door was wide open, so I rushed through and switched on the light. She was completely out, deathly white, an empty vodka bottle and a blister pack of pills on the bed beside her. I checked her neck for a pulse. It was very slow, but still beating.

'Oh, my God!' Christine cried, her hands to her face.

'Come on, help me get her upright,' I said.

We managed it, tucking our arms beneath hers and yanking. I tucked the pillows behind her, but her head lolled forward.

'Tori! Wake up! Come on, wake up!' I shouted, slapping her face with both hands.

There was no response.

'Get some coffee. Strong!' I ordered.

Christine ran off and I pulled Tori more upright, placing her left arm around my neck. With some difficulty, I might add. She's a slim girl, but she's solid.

Lizzie suddenly appeared, running up and screaming, slapping the poor girl's face even harder that I had. Then she burst into tears.

'No, Tori, no ...'

'Come on, help me pull her up,' I cried, in tears myself now.

So together we pulled her up to standing, her arms around our necks.

'Come on, Tori, wake up,' prayed her mother as we walked her up and down the room, to get her blood flowing, to clear out her system. Up and down, up and down, up and down.

'We've called an ambulance,' I said. 'It should be on its way, but the roads are treacherous, so I've no idea how long it'll be.'

'Oh, my God. I should never have left her, I knew she was in a state. Oh, my God. Tori, Tori, my darling, don't die. Stay with me. Please don't die.'

Christine appeared with the coffee, nicely cooled so Tori could drink it. We sat her against the bedhead and forced it down her, Lizzie pulling her head back and me tipping it in. And Tori swallowed it, thank God, which showed she was beginning to come round. It splashed all over the place, but we managed to get most of it down her.

'More,' I said, passing the mug back to Christine. 'Loads of the stuff. Really strong.'

So we did it again, walking her from one end of the room to the other and back. There were a few moans from her this time, complaining at our intrusion, and she seemed to be more in control of her legs.

Christine and Lizzie poured more coffee down her throat, while I patted her hands, trying to wake her up.

'Come on, Tori. Please, just wake up.'

She groaned slightly, pulling her hand away.

'Wake up, darling,' cried Lizzie.

'Come on,' I cried. 'We need to get her walking again.'

But Lizzie just couldn't do it. She broke down, sobbing uncontrollably.

'Sorry. Sorry, she's all I've got.'

'I know,' I sympathised. 'But she needs to be moving ...'

We were saved by the bell. The ambulance had arrived, and two strong paramedics came charging in, took over completely, made Tori sick in the bathroom and then whisked her off to hospital, Lizzie with them.

That poor, poor girl. But they did get her to hospital in time. The gritters had been working all through the night, thank God.

After they'd gone, Christine and I cleaned up the bathroom and tidied Tori's room. There were coffee stains all over the white duvet, so I put it and the cover straight into the washer. The empty vodka bottle and pill pack had been taken away by the paramedics. Goodness knows how many she'd taken.

'You want to stay here for a few hours, Enid, get your head down?' asked Christine.

'I'm fine, thanks, I'll get off home. You look all in yourself. Go on, get back to bed.'

'I'm okay, I won't sleep anyway. I just thank God we got to her in time.' She looked at me oddly. 'But how did you know? How did you know what she'd done?'

So I accepted her second offer of the morning. A nice hot cup of tea. We sat in the kitchen, a couple of Digestives on the side, and I told her. About Peggy, and the wiccans, and about Great Uncle John.

'Are you sure about this?' she asked. 'I mean, you're not having me on or anything?'

I shook my head. 'I know it sounds far-fetched and all that. But no, I'm not having you on. Besides, what other explanation could there be?'

'There has been some kind of presence here, if I'm honest. Tori's been going on about it, says it's been scaring her. It only appears after midnight, though.

So that must be him, Great Uncle John. I must look him up. I can't remember an Uncle John on our side. I wonder if he's on her dad's side, then?'

'So why did she do it, do you know?'

'Bloody boyfriend. Finished with her yesterday. She was distraught, poor child. We should never have left her, should have taken more notice.'

'You weren't to know, were you, so don't go blaming yourself.' I shook my head. 'I don't know. The things we do over men …'

It was nearly six o'clock by the time I arrived home to Genevieve yesterday morning. Never have I been so glad to climb into my own bed.

Today, the house feels empty. Our Carol and the children have gone, half the neighbours are missing, and Genevieve's curled up beside the radiator, still sulking over my not greeting her when I got back from Tori's.

I need to get out. So I ring Peggy. I have rung her with the good news about Tori, and she said she wasn't working today, so I hope she's still around. She is.

'Hi, Peggy. You doing anything today?'

'Why? Is that old house rattling without them kids running about and driving you ragged?'

'I suppose,' I admitted.

'Well, I was thinking of calling in at the garden centre later. I can pick you up, if you fancy it.'

'It's hardly gardening weather, is it?'

'I just need some new secateurs. Thought I'd have a look at some new cloches as well. Mine are on their last legs and I need to keep the ducks out.'

'Okay, that'd be nice. We can have a coffee while we're there.'

'That's that, then. I'll call round at two, shall I?'

I ring off, then dial Mattie's number.

'Mattie?' I say when she picks up.

'Hi Enid, how are you?'

'Fine, thank you. I just wondered if Benjamin's still there? It's just …'

'Of course. You want a word?'

She hands me over to him immediately. She's already told him about Tori, but I fill him in on all the details, and he agrees to come over. I need to discuss it with Tori first, though.

So I make lunch, and fill in time baking chocolate muffins and freezing them. They always come in handy for guests and my usual supply has been used up by Carol's two. I make some of my cinnamon shortbread too, but that's just for me.

The garden centre's on the main road going out towards Boston. Peggy drives carefully, there's still some ice on the roads, although most of the snow has gone.

There's not exactly a lot going on when we arrive. The place is empty, save a couple of bored assistants standing by the tills. Well, it is Christmas, and everyone's staying home where it's warm.

'Come on, let's grab a coffee first,' says Peggy.

We order coffee and carrot cake. The cake's not as good as mine, of course, but then I'm always slightly biased.

'Probably had it on the shelf the best part of a week,' murmurs Peggy.

'Probably,' I reply, suddenly struck by the way the week has whizzed by. 'My God, we were burying Josie a week ago yesterday. I still can't believe she's gone.'

'I keep meaning to pop over to Julia's, see how she is.'

'What a shock. I wonder if the police have found anything out yet.'

'Well, they're not going to tell us, now are they? Julia will know if anybody will.'

'I rang the police, you know, on Solstice Night, after I got back from your place.'

'Did you?'

'I thought there was someone watching me, along the road, just as I got out of Wendy's car, so I reported it.'

'Really? You didn't mention it.'

'I've not heard anything from them, though. To be honest, I didn't think they were that interested at the time.'

'So what happened?'

'I got inside the house as fast as I could and locked the door. Tight.'

She smiles. 'This coffee's good, even if the cake's crap. Any idea who it might have been?'

'No. Unfortunately. But we've got Duk Rak in place, that's the main thing.'

'We need to find out what happened to Josie. I mean, if it was a genuine accident, then all well and good, but ... '

'There's something else that's very odd, Peggy. Tori was invited to this party, Christmas Eve, it was. Nicole, the girl who organised the NSPCC Christmas Fayre, invited her. I thought it was strange before, but the more I think about it ... the thing is, she doesn't really know Tori, she'd only just met her. So why would she invite a young schoolgirl to her house on Christmas Eve, someone she's only met the once? I'm surprised Tori's mum even allowed her to go.'

'Maybe she didn't know. Maybe Tori just said it was a friend's party and that was that. She didn't go on her own, did she?'

I shake my head. 'No idea. She'll have taken the boyfriend, I guess.'

Her eyes narrow. 'Oh? Who's that then? Anyone we know?'

'I know the family - well, I've heard of them. They live in that old white house on Peterborough Road.'

'Okay, are they?'

'I've no idea. Why?'

'You don't think we should check them out?'

'It's probably too late for that. That's why she did what she did – he's finished with her.'

'When was that, then?'

'Monday night, according to her Nan. Poor kid.'

'I suppose we could still check them out. If he has got something to do with her attempted suicide, then he's not quite finished the job, has he?'

We wander round the garden centre after that. There are half-price decorations for sale, fresh bowls of hyacinths scenting the air, and tables and chairs with parasols, all ready to infiltrate our New Year gardens. Peggy buys a pair of red secateurs and a couple of cloches for her tomatoes. She grows some lovely stuff, does Peggy, even though she works in a veg shop and gets discount. She says she prefers to know where it's from, often brings a nice salad round for us to eat on her day off.

It's just as we're heading back to the car that I spot him. A chap walking across the path to the staff entrance. A chap who is slim, smallish, with a round head. A chap who reminds me distinctly of the chap in Lilian's garden.

'Peggy – it's him,' I whisper, nudging her arm.

'Who?'

'The chap I saw in Lilian's garden. I think it's him. Over there.'

I try to point discreetly, but he's seen me. He's recognised me.

'Oh, my God,' I cry, running towards the car.

'He's heading this way,' calls Peggy, running after me.

He climbs into his car, a black Megane, rather new and shiny for someone who works in a garden centre, and starts the engine.

Her gout suddenly forgotten, Peggy scrambles into the driving seat and starts the car.

'No smoke without fire,' she mutters, her long legs letting out the clutch.

I hold onto the dashboard for dear life as she swings the car round and exits the car park, the secateurs and cloches sliding along on the back seat.

The chap drives like a madman. He swerves round the roundabout and heads towards Spalding. Peggy tails him, trying to match his speed, her tongue sticking out in concentration.

We drive and drive and drive. But we're doing over sixty miles an hour on small country roads now, and I'm starting to worry. Is he trying to make us crash?

There's a sign for Pepingham. He turns at the next roundabout, back the way he's come, then sharp right and left, speeding away into the distance.

'He's trying to lose us,' says Peggy, changing down and following.

I grip the door handle. 'Peggy …'

'Mm?' Her tongue's sticking out again.

'Why are we doing this?'

'To see where he lives, of course.'

'I mean, what good will it do? We can't prove it was him, can we?'

She presses hard on the accelerator. 'No, but it'll help find out what he's up to.'

'Can't we just follow him more discreetly, another time?'

She slows down. 'You're right. We can find out where he lives from the garden centre.'

'What?'

'I know the chap who owns it. Mickey, he's called.'

'Why would he give you that kind of information?'

'He owes me a favour or two. I helped get his business going. Enough said.'

She stops, does a three point turn, and heads back to the garden centre.

'Another cup of tea, Enid. That's what we need.'

I'm thinking more along the lines of a gin and tonic.

Mickey comes up trumps and we find out exactly who this chap is. He's called Philip Brunewski, and he lives on Pumpkin Drive, Pepingham.

'Well, that is a turn-up for the books,' I murmur as we return to the car. 'I reckon he must be Nicole's dad. I don't know of any other Brunewskis in Pepingham.'

'I wonder why he'd be sneaking round Lilian's house, then?'

I shudder at the recollection. 'He was just keeping an eye on me.'

'I wonder why, though?'

'I don't know. But I'm going to find out.'

We drive back to my house and I get my much-needed G&T. Afterwards, we sit down to a cuppa, and cogitate.

'If he was watching me, there must be a reason,' I begin.

'But you have nothing he wants.'

Then it hits me. 'So *that's* why Nicole asked Tori to her party. They must be in it together.'

'You're joking!'

'I said it sounded strange, didn't I?'

'Oh, my God! We definitely need to pay that man a visit.'

'No,' I say. 'Not now. We need to pay Tori a visit. If that's alright?'

'You're right,' she sighs, checking her watch. 'Do you know when visiting time is?'

'Seven o'clock. I rang this morning to see how she was, but they wouldn't tell me because I'm not family. And I've been worried.'

'You've taken a real shine to her, haven't you?' Peggy says softly.

'Mm,' I nod.

'Come on then, grab your coat.'

Grantham and Kesteven Hospital dates back to 1874, obviously with some additions along the way. It takes us half an hour to get there, and then we have to find a parking space. But eventually, breathless with rushing, we get to see Tori. Her ward's just on the ground floor, easy to find.

She's sitting up in bed, pale and dreamy, with soft white pillows framing her dark hair. She smiles as we enter the room.

But we're not the only visitors. Lizzie is there, pale and thin, looking older than her years, having spent the night. And there's a girl.

'Nicole,' I say, greeting her warmly.

She stands up to hug me. 'Hi, Enid. Thought I'd drop by, see how the patient's doing.'

'That's kind of you.'

But I'm confused, my mind searching for answers. Why would Nicole ask Tori to a party, then visit her in hospital, when they've only known each other two minutes? It's not what I would have expected. Alright, I've only just befriended her too, I realise. But no, there's definitely something not quite right here. But can I hell as like put my finger on it.

I introduce Peggy. 'My very good friend, Peggy. She's given me a lift, bless her.'

Lizzie beams. 'It's good to see you both. And thank you so, so much for what you did, Enid. I can't imagine what would have happened …' She blinks back her tears.

'It was nothing. I only did what needed to be done. I'm just glad it did the trick.'

'She's on the mend, thank goodness. They're letting her out tomorrow, aren't they, love, all being well?'

Tori smiles, her whole face lighting up. 'They are, Mum, yes.'

I turn to Lizzie. 'Is there anything I can get you? A cup of tea from the machine or anything?'

'Actually, I need the loo, and then I'll get a decent drink from the caff. You want me to bring you one?'

I shake my head. 'I'm fine, thanks. We won't stay long.'

'I'll come with you,' Nicole says to her.

Peggy grins. 'Me too. I'm dying for a wee.'

So I sit down at the side of the bed and come straight to the point. No beating about the bush, as far as I'm concerned.

'So what made you do it, Tori?' I place my hand onto hers. 'Why, when you've got so many people who love you?'

She begins to cry, warm tears running down her face.

'I'm sorry, love,' I say gently, pushing a clean tissue into her hand.

'Thanks,' she mumbles.

'I'm just concerned, Tori. I mean, why did you do it? Was it just the boyfriend?'

Shaking her head, she wipes her face unsuccessfully. Because the tears keep coming and her sobs become stronger, so much so that she's gulping in air.

'I … I just can't see any way out, can't see which way to go.'

'It is the boyfriend, then?'

'It's Raff. He's dumped me. We're over. Totally over.'

'You know,' I say, 'there's more to life than boys. I mean, they're nice to have and all that, but we shouldn't put them above everything else. There's so much more out there.'

'I know,' she sobs, her face red and shiny with tears.

'Think about what else you could do with your life. You could get a really good job – I don't know, teaching, or helping other people like these lovely nurses in here. And while you're doing that and getting on with your life, who knows who you might meet?'

'But I want Raff!' she squeals.

I feel dreadful. After all, I'm only trying to help, to make her feel optimistic. But there's a time and a place, I suppose.

Peggy appears then, carrying two teas in foam cups. 'Here you go. Got it from the machine.' She gives one to me and one to Tori.

'Thanks, Peggy.'

Embarrassed, Tori stops crying and wipes her face.

Peggy sits onto the armchair beside the bed. 'Oh, dear, has Enid been upsetting you all over again?'

'I'm sorry,' I say. 'Come on, dry your eyes, and let's have a smile before your mum and Nicole get back.'

'I don't want Nicole back,' she cries.

I'm shocked. 'Why ever not?'

'She keeps going on about that stupid, idiotic party I went to. I hated it, I hated it all, all those awful people. Totally weird, they were.'

'What?' I gasp.

'They were, they were like vultures, staring at me like I was the scum of the earth. Little Miss Nowhere To Go, no posh clothes, no nice shoes …'

I stop her, squeezing her hand tight and shaking my head. 'But Tori, I'm sure it wasn't like that …'

She pulls away, the tears coming again, thick and fast. 'No-one believes anything I say any more. What's wrong with you all? They were, they were like fucking vultures, the lot of 'em!'

I've never heard her swear before and, to be honest, I wonder what I've got myself into. But then, I realise, we hear that word all over the place these days, so why would she be any different?

'Tori. Please don't.'

She stops as suddenly as she began, and I see a veil of perception fall across her face.

'I'm sorry, Enid, I'm really sorry. I'm just upset, I can't believe he doesn't want to see me any more.'

I smile gently. 'Listen, when you're out of this place, we're going to get you working, at my place and at school. You're going to work so flaming hard you won't have time for boys. But you'll be able to be the person you were meant to be, make a good future for yourself.'

She looks at me questioningly.

'You could get some nice new clothes, get a bit of self-confidence, push some important knowledge into that head of yours. You're not stupid, Tori, not by any means. And if you work hard enough, who knows what you could become?'

'Yeah. A lollipop lady,' she smirks.

'Someone important. Someone who can help others. That's my opinion, anyway,' I insist. 'But you're welcome to prove me wrong, if you like.'

'What do you mean?' she puzzles.

'I mean, if you're determined you're not going to do something with your life, then that's what will happen.'

'She's right, you know,' says Peggy.

'Okay,' says Tori.

'But if you're determined to do something useful, be someone, then that's what will happen too. *"We know what we are, but not what we may be"*.

'Shakespeare,' she says.

I nod. 'You see? Clever girl.'

'Mrs Baker quotes it. She's our English teacher.'

Later, as we leave the hospital, Peggy has a huge smile on her face.

'Quite a useful cup of tea, that.'

'What?'

'I've only gone and got us an invite to the New Year's Eve party at Raff Slater's place.'

'Oh, Peggy, I don't want to go gallivanting. I'd much rather sit at home with a nice bottle of wine.'

'Oh, you won't be gallivanting, Enid. You'll be gleaning information.'

'What?'

'Know thine enemy.'

'How did you manage that, then?'

'Nicole. I knew she'd fall for it if I made out we'd be all alone on New Year's Eve. Says she'll have a word with her mum and it'll be fine. They'll both be there.'

'Okay,' I sigh.

'I've put a protective spell on those rings Tori wears, by the way. I just hope she's the type that never takes them off.'

'She doesn't. She said so. Thank you, Peggy.'

I arrive home to find not only Genevieve behind the door, but a small note on lined paper pushed through the letterbox.

nurses for looking after me, picks up my things, and we trundle out to the car.

But I feel so miserable. I want to cry. It's Raff's party tonight. His New Year's Eve party, and I won't be going.

I wonder who will be.

I wipe my eyes before anyone sees my tears.

We pile into the car, all four of us. It smells of some musky hippy scent, the kind you get when you go into these shops that sell crystals and stuff. We call at Enid's on the way home, and she comes out of the house with a massive bouquet of flowers for me.

'Well, no good leaving them at the hospital for the nurses to enjoy,' she says, handing them to me.

They're so beautiful. Reds and oranges and yellows. They make me cry, again.

Once we arrive home, Mum puts them into water. They really are lovely, the biggest bunch of flowers I've ever been given.

Nan makes tea for us all.

'Oh love, we've been so worried about you,' she says.

But her eyes question me, saying *why did you do it, my little dumpling?*

'Sorry, Nan.'

'We love you so much. You could just have come and talked to me, you know. Any time, I wouldn't have minded. I'm up with the lark as it is.'

I smile my thanks, but I feel awful. Part guilt for putting her through it, part sorrow for having to do it in the first place.

Enid and Peggy sit in our kitchen with cups of tea. Peggy has to leave soon to go back to work. She runs a shop, says they want her to lock up for the night. But I think she and Enid look kind of right here, as if they belong. Not that they shouldn't, but usually when people come and visit they look out of place. I mean, it's not the most salubrious place in the world.

Nan fusses round, making toast and crumpets for whoever wants them.

Enid looks at me. 'Tori?' she says.

I look up from studying the white name tag that's still on my left wrist. 'Yes?'

'I have a friend, someone I've known for years. I think he might be able to help you, and I'd like you to meet him.'

I fear some kind of psychotherapist person, like the woman at the hospital, the psychiatrist. I'm supposed to be seeing her on Friday for a *chat*. More like an inquisition, I should think.

'What kind of friend? What does he do?'

'He's actually a hypnotherapist. He's really nice, and I think he could help you.'

'What will he do?' I ask, my stomach churning.

But she doesn't answer, which makes me even more terrified. Instead, she takes hold of my hand.

'Do you believe in reincarnation?'

I laugh out loud at that. 'What? You're joking me.'

'No. I'm not.' She looks deadly, totally, serious.

'There's no such thing.'

'Well, not everyone believes in it. But there are many who do.'

'Right, yeah.'

Peggy interrupts her. 'She's right, Tori. It is possible we've all lived before, and many studies have been done on the subject. I mean, as a child did you ever have flashbacks, strange dreams?'

Now this is getting scary. Like for real.

'Sometimes,' I confess.

'And did they seem really *in the moment*, as if you were really there?'

'Yeah.' I nod my head furiously, nearly knocking Nan's hand as she pushes toast and strawberry jam in front of me. I pick it up and eat. Suddenly I'm hungry.

Enid smiles. 'That's what Benjamin does. He hypnotises you, puts you into a trance and takes you back to your previous lives. If you have any.'

'But only if you allow it. He wouldn't do anything to harm you,' says Peggy.

'Would you agree to see him, do you think? I could be there with you if you like. Or Mattie, the lady you met at my house the other day?'

I remember her. She seemed nice. 'Does she know him, then? Has he hypnotised her as well?'

'No. No, he hasn't. But he has been very good to her and she trusts him completely. It's Mattie who introduced me to Benjamin.'

I nod. 'Okay. But only if you're there as well.'

Nan gives me my dress after everyone's gone. It's the one I ordered from ASOS. She says it arrived yesterday. It is *so* beautiful. But Raff will never see me in it now. The thought makes me cry.

Nan pulls me to her and wraps me in her soft arms. I close my eyes and breathe her in. I want to stay there forever.

'You just cry, Tori. You cry as much as you want. Let it all out, dumpling.'

I cry and cry and cry. I can't stop.

'I'm here,' she soothes. 'I'm always here.'

After I've had a shower to wipe off the smell of hospital, Nan makes another cuppa. We sit down to watch telly and Mum fusses around me like it's going out of fashion. She was supposed to be going out with her bloke tonight. It's New Year's Eve and they were supposed to be going to his local for a few drinks. But she's cancelled now, says she doesn't want to leave me. He'd better be understanding about it, I think.

But she's saved by the bell, because the next minute there's Danielle at the door with a bouquet of flowers, even bigger than Enid's, and the most massive box of Thornton's I've ever seen. Her mum's standing behind her, but she smiles and waves goodbye as soon as I open the door. Just making sure I'm home, I suppose.

So we sit in my room, all cleaned and vacuumed by Mum while I've been in hospital, and eat chocolates. I've defo regained my appetite. And Danielle fusses round me as if I'm bone china, too scared to actually come out with Raff's name, yet anxious to know I'm okay.

I admire the earrings Chris bought her, a pair of sparkly danglers (they *are* beautiful), then I sort her out good and proper.

'So yeah, he's dumped me, but I'll find someone else really easily, you know?'

She smiles gently. 'You don't have to pretend with me. I'm your bestest, remember?'

'I know that, Danielle.' I pick out a Turkish Delight, my favourite, and chomp on it. It is totally delish. 'But I'm so over him. I don't need the hassle any more.'

'What went wrong?' she asks. 'I mean, why did he do it? It was all so sudden?'

'I don't know, Danielle, I really don't. He said something about me not being right for him.'

I can actually recall his exact words, the exact fucking words. But I don't tell her that.

Tori, I've always loved you, ever since - but you're not right for me, not for the lifestyle I'm going to have. I need someone more - more …

Covering my face with my hands, I burst into heart-rending tears. I sob and sob and sob. Danielle holds me, her quiet perfume invading my senses, until I manage to stop and pull myself upright.

I grab the tissue box. 'Sorry.'

She's crying too, so I pass her one.

'What are you crying for?' I ask.

'Bloody idiot.'

'Excuse me? Who's a bloody idiot?'

'Raff.'

'What?'

'He doesn't know what he's done, what he's lost.' She bursts into tears again.

I hug her, but I can't take any more. 'Don't, Danielle. Please.'

'Sorry.'

She wipes the tissue around her eyes with delicate fingers, so as not to smudge her makeup.

'I'm sorry, too. I've just had enough of talking about it, that's all. It's not helping.'

Then she looks up, all excited. 'Listen, why don't you come to our party tonight? Mum's doing a big bowl of punch and everything. You could get absolutely smashed if you wanted to.'

'Yeah, like that's a good idea.'

'I'd look after you, Tori, you know I would.'

'You'd be snogging Chris's face off, that's what you'd be doing.'

'Oh, please come,' she begs. 'I'd love you to come. I'll lend you something to wear, if you want.'

'I've got something.' I go to my chest of drawers and pull my new dress from the box it arrived in. I hang it in front of me, admiring myself in the mirror.

'Try it on,' Danielle says from behind.

But I suddenly hate the idea. 'No. No, I don't want to.'

'Why not?'

'It was meant for Raff. For his party tonight.'

'Oh, you silly. Come on, try it on,' and she begins to tug at my tee-shirt.

'Danielle!' I scream, pulling away. But my tee-shirt rips suddenly, and I'm standing there with ripped jeans *and* a ripped tee-shirt. I look like one of the kids from *Oliver*.

Danielle bursts out laughing, so I thump her playfully, but she just keels over and carries on.

'Not funny!' I shout. But then I start laughing too, and we both end up in fits of giggles.

Mum comes in, wondering what the hell's going on, but we can't talk. Not one word.

My new dress looks totally awesome. My shoulders are bare, and the tiny freckles on them look really cute.

Danielle smiles, her head tilted to one side. 'I knew it. You look beautiful, Tori. I just knew it.'

Okay, so she's talked me into going to her party, even though I totally know I'll be miserable. It starts at eight o'clock, so by midnight I should be so rat-arsed nothing will bother me anyway.

Satisfied, Danielle leaves to go home and get ready. Mum's cooked a chicken and red wine casserole, and the apartment smells divine as I walk back in from waving Danielle off. And Nan's made my favourite, apple sponge pudding. I know, because the apartment has been filled with the noise of her old mixer going, so I've asked her. Are they making a fuss because it's New Year's Eve, I wonder, or because I've tried ending it all and they want to make me feel special?

Mum hugs me, running her fingers through my hair. 'Danielle says you're off to her house tonight.'

'I am. So you can go out if you like.'

'No, it's fine. I'll stay home with Nan. We can have a glass of bubbly together. What time are you out?'

'It starts at eight, but there's something I've got to do first.'

'What's that? Where are you going?' She looks terrified, as if I might do something *stupid* again.

'I'm paying a visit to the Royal Oak.'

'Oh no, Tori, not that again. You can't go chasing him forever, you know. Don't belittle yourself. Have some pride, some self-respect.'

'I'm not chasing him, I'm not, Mum. It's just something I've got to do.'

The landlord at the Royal Oak is a big guy, with a dark beard and a balding head. He sees me walk in, but it's not yet seven o'clock, so he can't throw me out. There are banners everywhere, and a mike stand set up for a karaoke or something. The atmosphere is charged with excitement. The punters are all dressed up, obviously looking forward to singing Auld Lang Syne at midnight. I'm not. I can't wait for New Year's Eve to be over. Trying to smile at everyone and look happy? It's a joke. I mean, what's the point? A new year. Since when did everything change overnight? It doesn't. It just stays the same. The same old schoolwork, the same old routine of getting up in a morning, of going to bed at night. By myself. Okay, so I've not exactly managed to sleep with Raff the whole night through, but I was planning on it. Just had to get Mum's say-so. But I was able to snuggle up for a few hours at least, to feel his arms around me, run my fingers through the soft dark hair on his chest, feel the scrape of his stubble on my cheek. I was able to smell him. Oh, the scent of him. Like fresh air at the seaside, warm and invigorating. Makes you kind of want to climb inside and stay there, safe and sound and snug.

I go up to the landlord (Tom Beckett his name is, it's over the door) with my heart in my mouth. But

I'm determined to say something. I check first, to make sure none of Raff's friends are around. They're not. There are just a few couples eating in the corner near the fire and some old blokes at the bar.

'You okay, Tori?' asks Tom, wiping a cloth along the bar.

'Mm,' I nod. 'I just … I just wanted to say … you shouldn't be serving Raff Slater. He's only seventeen, you know.'

'Raff Slater?'

He tilts his head as if he's never heard the name. Total liar. So I raise my voice, make it more insistent. I'm not giving up that easily.

'He comes in here a lot. He's a friend of Jack Thornley's, and Jacob Meakin. Do you know them?'

He nods, pretending to suddenly remember. 'Oh yes. Tall lads, aren't they? Stand over by the snooker table?'

'That's right,' I nod. 'Well, you shouldn't be serving them, any of them. They're seventeen and it's against the law.'

'This isn't anything to do with the new girl he's been hanging around with, is it?'

My heart sinks.

My stomach churns like it's just been squeezed and emptied out all over again.

I feel totally sick.

I stare at him, at the cloth he's holding in his hand.

I blink.

'Sorry? What? What did you say?'

'That girl from over Sleaford way. Pretty, she is. I doubt *she's* only seventeen.'

He's moving away, his eyes mocking me over the hand pumps, the names of the beers on sale displayed enticingly. The word *Poachers* springs out at me. It's a small brewery based in a local village, one of these cottage-industry types. But it's the right word. Because that's what she's done, she's poached him. She's fucking well poached him from me.

I run out, hardly able to breathe, tears streaming down my face.

Danielle's house is warm and inviting. The scent of garlic bread makes my mouth water. Her mum welcomes me, but I can sense she's a little concerned her daughter is best friends with a girl who's just attempted suicide.

'Come on in, Tori. Let me take your coat. Danielle's just in the lounge.'

I follow her through and she waves to Danielle in the corner. It's a big room, but tonight it feels small, there are so many people. Danielle rushes over, takes my arm and leads me through to the kitchen.

'Oh my God, Tori. You look totally amazing. I just love that dress. And I'm so glad you could make it. I thought you might change your mind after I'd gone.'

I smile. 'I nearly did.'

'Come on, let's get you a drink. Mum's bought some low alc lager for us, but there's punch as well. I hope that's okay.'

'It's fine. Thanks.'

'Actually, I did say you'd be able to get smashed if you wanted, so I've hidden some beers behind the bin outside. If you want them.'

'Thanks,' I grin, helping myself to some punch from the huge glass bowl. 'I'll try not to get totally smashed, though. It wouldn't do to upset your mum. She's really nice.'

'Thanks, Tori.'

'Sorry I thought about not coming. It's just, I went to the Royal Oak, and …' I begin to cry.

She pulls at my arm. 'Come on, let's head upstairs. We can talk there.'

Wiping my tears away, I follow her, the noisy chatter receding into the background as we enter her bedroom and close the door.

Bouncing onto the huge bed, she pats the mattress.

'Come on, sit down.' I do, and she puts an arm around me. 'Come on, tell Auntie Danielle all about it.'

'No,' I reply, 'it's not funny. It's fucking horrendous, Danielle.'

The tears come now, thick and fast. I've spent ages making my eyes look awesome, but it's all been for nothing. I lay face down on the bed. I am practically drowning in my own tears.

Danielle hugs me, shushing me, telling me it's going to be alright, it will all work itself out, it's not the end of the world.

Not for one second do I believe her.

'He's got someone else, Danielle. Tom Beckett told me. You know - the landlord?' I sob.

'Oh God, Tori.'

'And she's really pretty.'

'Who is she?'

'From Sleaford,' I manage to say.

She reaches over for the box of tissues on the bedside table.

'Here. Sit up,' she coaxes gently.

I obey, wiping my eyes with my fingers. 'Oh God, I must look a sight.'

'You could say that,' she laughs. 'But we'll soon sort you out.'

It takes a full quarter of an hour before I look okay. But I don't feel like facing anyone just yet.

'You go downstairs,' I insist. 'You've got guests to see to.'

'Mum'll see to them. I'm fine.'

'Where's Chris?' I ask, suddenly realising he wasn't there when I arrived.

'He's coming over at ten. He's meeting up with a cousin of his first. So no rush.'

She's busy on her phone. I'm checking my eyes in the mirror. Slightly swollen, but not as red as they were.

'Right,' she says, her tongue sticking out in concentration. 'I've got Gigi on the job.'

'Who?'

'Gigi. From Sleaford, Wateringham Lane. Her mum's a teacher, so they know people.'

'Sorry? I don't understand.'

'They'll know if someone's going out with Raff Slater. Silly.'

It's ten o'clock, my eyes are no longer swollen and red, and my makeup looks totally awesome. Danielle has some amazing stuff. She even uses her GHDs on my hair, twirling it round so it looks like giant corkscrews. It looks amazing. I *feel* amazing.

Chris is in the kitchen chatting to his cousin, a beer in his hand, grownup all of a sudden. His cousin has his back to us as we walk in, but as he turns to greet us I see who it is. I recognise him.

'Tori!' he exclaims. 'Look at you! You look amazing!' and he hugs me.

Olly. The bloke I nearly drowned myself for, that rainy day in Skeggie.

'Looks like you two know each other,' says Danielle, happily. 'We'll leave you to it, then.'

As she and Chris walk off, hand in hand, I smile up at Olly. My gorgeous, lovely Olly.

'So how are you?' I ask.

He smiles back. 'I'm fine, thank you. Having an awesome time at uni. Just love it. Think I'm definitely headed for the political scene in London.'

'That's fantastic,' I say. 'Amazing.'

'You used to live in London, didn't you?'

I nod. 'Many years ago.'

'Come on then, let's find a spot where we can chat.'

And he takes my hand.

24

Melissa

Friday January 1st

I'VE only just heard about that silly little girl and her ridiculous attempted suicide. Just a cry for help, of course. Just wanted my Raff to go running round there. As if.

He doesn't know about it yet, been much too busy. But he and Charlotte looked fabulous last night. They're such a beautiful couple. We decided not to have fancy dress, after all. No, I wanted to get all dressed up, so I wore my long black evening gown with the feathery bits around the neckline. Absolutely gorgeous, it is. Maxine's friend, Eva Brunewski, was there too, kind of invited herself along, would you believe. She brought some friends with her that I wasn't too sure about, to be honest. A bit weird. I met her yesterday at the garden centre (her husband works there - the shame of it!) and she just invited herself along, didn't say anything about bringing any friends. So I wasn't too pleased, as you can imagine. Actually, now I think about it, she's the one who put the idea into my head of getting Raff to finish with Tori. That time we met up for lunch with Maxine. Said Tori's got a reputation and isn't good enough, not with us having our own business and everything. I mean, she is right, of course. My Raff's definitely going places now, certainly doesn't want that little toe-rag dragging him back.

Gosh, my head does hurt today. Much too much champagne. But it was worth it. Just think, New Year's Eve, a brand new year. So I need to start making plans. There's the weekend in Bruges, and maybe another trip to Florida. Or maybe the Seychelles. We could take Charlotte with us. I'm fancying New York this year, too.

Must renew my gym membership. I'm just dying to get into that gorgeous black bikini I bought in Selfridge's.

I suppose I should buy Victoria some flowers, get them delivered. Well, there's no-one else with enough money to spoil her, is there? Poor cow. Why would anyone want to kill themselves, end it all like that? A tragedy. No, I'll drive out to Lincoln this afternoon and choose some, get a little retail therapy at the same time, get rid of this headache. I can show off my new car, too. I love it, I really do. Ed is so good to me. We've started having sex again, too. Poor Ed. I'd begun to think I was going off him, haven't fancied it in ages.

So.

I'll ring Maxine, see if she wants to meet up.

Lilies or a bouquet?

25

Enid

Saturday January 2nd

SO there we were, eight o'clock New Year's Eve, stepping out in all our finery. I'd pulled an old dress out of the wardrobe, one Peter and I bought many years ago and which still fits, thank goodness. It's got a satin slip, with a black lace bodice and skirt over the top. Long-sleeved it is, just right for this time of year. We bought it for a charity do Jonathan's school were putting on. My Peter was a good dancer, I'll say that for him. Still is, I imagine. Unless his gout's finally caught up with him.

Anyway, there we were, up to our eyes in makeup and hairspray, stepping very gingerly into the house of Rafferty Slater.

A tall slim woman in a flowery kaftan welcomed us in.

'Mrs Slater?' I asked, smiling and holding out my hand.

'Oh no, she's with her guests in the drawing room. I'm just showing people round. So if you need anything ...'

Outside, cars were pulling up, women were walking in on tiptoe to protect their heels from the gravel drive, and bottles of booze were being held aloft in fancy paper bags.

The flowery woman guided us through the spacious hall towards the kitchen, where the rumble of sound indicated a gathering of people eating and drinking. But as we walked along, my hands began to tremble, my arms and shoulders stiffening in response. Whether it was with cold or fear, I don't know, but I quickly pressed my thumb into the palm of my right hand.

'That old trick,' Peggy whispered. 'You okay, Enid?'

'Fine,' I replied, following on behind the flowery woman, my bottle of Beaujolais in a Tesco carrier bag. It was a bottle someone once bought me that had been sitting in my cupboard. I'm not a fan of red wine.

'I'll make us something to eat, shall I? A snack or something? Cheese on toast?' I pulled open the fridge door just as Genevieve appeared from beneath the table. 'Or I've a couple of cold chicken legs?'

'Chicken legs would be lovely. And a bit of mayo would be nice.'

'No, Genevieve, you've had your dinner,' I soothed, pushing her away. I pulled out the chicken legs and mayonnaise. 'Here we go, then.'

I buttered some bread and we ate the chicken with baby tomatoes and spinach, sipping chilled Pinot Grigio.

'So come on then, what did this woman look like?' asked Peggy.

I shivered at the recollection. I was still shaking, still felt a bit sick. I was terrified, truth be told. But more for Tori than myself. The way I figured it - if she could do that to me, what could she do to Tori?

'She was quite tall, about your height,' I said. 'With very long, black hair. A handsome face, I suppose. Not beautiful, but good-looking. I'm sure she's Nicole's mother, they looked very much alike, apart from the colouring.'

'She probably takes after her father. He's got fair hair. Not that there's much of it to see.'

I laughed out loud at that. 'Very true. I wonder what the connection is, though, if there is one?'

'How do you mean?'

'Well, Philp Brunewski must have something to hide or he wouldn't have been noseying around Lilian's front garden, or driving off like an idiot when we spotted him at the garden centre.'

'But it's his wife who tried to harm you tonight.'

'I know that. So what's the connection – I mean, why are they involved in all this?'

'You're protecting Tori, that's why.'

'That's what I'm getting at. What's their connection with Tori? They don't even know her. Well, they do now, through Nicole. But they didn't, not before I introduced her to Nicole at the Christmas Fayre.'

'Maybe they arranged the introduction?' she ventured.

'No. I mean, I only took Tori along so I could help with teas and coffees. I needed someone to sell my pies for me, and she agreed, bless her.'

Peggy's eyes narrowed. 'So no-one else could have helped sell teas and coffees? There was no-one hanging around doing nothing?'

I thought about it, and yes. Yes, there was. Nicole didn't do a lot, just hung around supervising. Not that anyone needed it. And now I thought about it, she could have sold her own teas and coffees, left me to sell my pies. Did she know I'd invite Tori along to help?

'Oh my God, Peggy. What have I done?' I cried.

'What?'

'I just handed her to them, didn't I?'

'How do you mean?'

'I can see it all now. If I hadn't introduced Tori to Nicole, she wouldn't have been invited to that awful party, everyone looking down their noses at her and making her feel inferior. So if she hadn't gone to that party, she probably wouldn't have felt so bad when Raff finished with her, would have felt more able to go out there and find someone else, bounce back ...'

'And not taken an overdose,' Peggy concluded.

'It all seemed to happen at the same time, didn't it? As if it was planned?'

'So why did Raff finish with her? I mean, why now? Is there some kind of connection between him and Nicole?'

'Well, Nicole's parents must know Raff's, or they wouldn't have been there tonight, would they?'

'Yes, but how?'

Tired, confused, I shook my head. 'No idea.'

'Enid, is there a coven around here, do you know?'

A long shiver ran through me, clinging and cold.

'I did see a strange fire recently, just before Christmas. In the woods, out the back, just before the Pagan Yuletide. I remember it was quite late and it was really cold, not the kind of evening for a bonfire. I did think it odd at the time.'

'And you didn't think to mention it?' she snapped.

'I was so busy, it was nearly Christmas, and ...'

'Sorry, Enid, I'm sorry. It's just, we could have done with investigating. At the time, while there was still evidence.'

We sat in silence then, our food finished, our minds in turmoil.

What had I done?

Genevieve jumped onto my lap, purring, her soft fur finding its way to the palms of my hands.

'Well, this is no good,' said Peggy, quietly. 'We need to take a look. Come on, let's get our coats.'

The darkness seeped through my coat and scarf. A soft drizzle caught the light from our torches as we shone them along the pavements. Peggy carried the heavy torch from the boot of her car, while I carried a smaller one from my conservatory.

'This way,' I whispered sleepily, turning down the path towards the streetlamp.

A bat swooped low as we entered the woods.

'Don't bats hibernate?' I asked, anxiously.

'Some do, some don't. It's fine, don't worry so much. '

I led the way. 'Come on, along here. This path leads down to the oak tree. There's a clearing there, that's where I think the fire was.'

The ground was solid, hardened. Clumps of grass caught the beam of my torch. Wide awake now, I made sure to tread carefully.

'Are we sure about this?' asked Peggy.

'It was your idea!' I retorted, playfully.

But she was right. It was a bloody stupid idea.

Before we knew it, we were standing beside the pile of leaves Carol, Richard and I had found on our Boxing Day walk. But now there was a cauldron hanging above them, the tripod hewn from old bamboo sticks. Peggy used a stick to delve through the rotting remains.

There were no squirrel bones this time. No. There was ash, and leaves, and twigs. And a sleeve.

'What's this?' Peggy pulled at it with the end of her stick.

Screwing up my eyes, I investigated it with the beam of my torch. It had a cuff, an elasticated cuff, the kind you'd find on a sweatshirt.

Or a hoodie.

'Oh, God,' I cried, my stomach churning. 'Oh, God.'

'What? What is it?'

'It's Tori's. It's Tori's hoodie.'

'What? Are you sure?' She picked it up, shining her torch right through it.

A grey over-washed hoodie sleeve. It was definitely Tori's.

'I'm sure.'

A sudden wind whipped the sleeve from Peggy's hand, carrying it far away, down towards the quarry.

'Enid!' she cried. 'Hold onto my hand! Don't let go!'

I forced my hand into hers, catching hold just in time. We tried to run, but our legs felt like lead. All we could do was stand and watch.

A storm began to build around us, echoing and flapping like huge birds' wings, deafening, screeching, wailing, the squall of wind twisting and rolling its way through the woods.

We were terrified. It was just us. Us against the elements.

Our torches stopped working, both at the same time. The streetlamp we had just passed flew towards us at speed, crashing and disintegrating against the oak tree. The tree responded by crashing down upon us, its huge branches heavy and solid and frightening. Luckily, we were standing at a distance, so the main part of the tree, the trunk and the branches, missed us by inches. But as it fell, its harsh long twigs snapped against me and I screamed out as the skin on my face and arms ripped open, blood spurting everywhere. Other trees leered at us through the darkness, and black owls swooped down and swayed above me as I fell to the ground.

'Peggy!' I screamed.

'Enid!' Her voice came at me from somewhere far, far away, even though I could have sworn I was still holding her hand. 'Don't let go!'

An owl landed its long scary claws upon my head, and I managed to knock it away with my free hand. Terrified, my scream ricocheting through the air, I tried to stand, to struggle through the branches, to lean against Peggy. But the ground had begun to heave around us, up and down and round and round. Like a roller-coaster destined to never, ever stop.

Then Peggy called out, her huge theatrical voice filling the air.

'Away with you! Be away! Away, and let us live!'

I began to vomit, great gulps of thick, warm vomit.

'Let harmony descend! Let peace remain! Away, I tell you. Away!'

She pulled off the ring she always wears, the huge gold ring on her left hand, and threw it high into the air with long, scarlet-tipped fingers.

'Away!'

It stopped. The storm stopped.

All was quiet. Calm was restored. Our torches switched themselves on and light flooded the air around us. The streetlamp had returned to its rightful place, the oak tree was upright, and the bats had completely disappeared.

Leaning against the oak tree, I wiped my mouth with my coat sleeve and began to cry. Soft, warm tears of relief.

Peggy put her arms around me. 'They've gone, Enid. It's okay. They've gone.'

Back home, within the safety of the Duk Rak, we took stock. My face and arms had survived. There was no damage, no blood, nothing.

'How can that be?' I asked, peering at myself in the kitchen mirror.

'Magic. Black magic. It makes you believe things. Terrible things.'

'But it was real, Peggy. I was there. I felt it. I saw the blood.'

'You were made to think it was real. That's what they do.'

'I wonder if they put something in our drinks? At the party?'

'It wasn't a drug, Enid. They'd put some kind of spell on Tori's hoodie. So when we disturbed it ...'

I shivered, right down to the ends of my toes.

'Bloody hell, Peggy. I need a drink.'

So there we were on New Year's Eve, in my sitting room, a second bottle of wine on the go, with our thinking caps on. Jools Holland and his guests were on the telly and we were waiting for Big Ben, for the New Year. For inspiration.

'How about this,' Peggy said, scribbling at an A4 pad of paper. 'We've got Mr and Mrs Brunewski with Nicole. Then Mr and Mrs Taylor, the ghoulish guests, with a possible daughter. Did we ever get to know her name?'

I shook my head sadly. 'No, but I do know Tori read that letter. She told me. Finally. Someone was out to really upset her.'

She nodded grimly. 'Okay. So there's Mr and Mrs Slater, with Raff.' She'd drawn matchstick men and named them all. 'Then we've got Josie – oh, and Megan and her parents. What's their surname?'

'Harvey, I think.'

'Mr and Mrs Harvey. And Tori, her mum and her nan.' She drew more pictures.

'What about me?'

'That's true. You're another one like Josie, here to help Tori.' She drew another matchstick man and named it. 'You need to be especially careful, Enid. You're doing it openly, you've offered her work, you've made friends with her. Thank goodness we've placed a Duk Rak outside.'

I went cold. 'Bill Mitchell's dead, too. You know, the chap who brings me his rhubarb?'

Peggy sat up straight, every sense on fire, her fingers taut, her red nails gripping at the pencil.

'What?'

'They think it was natural causes, but we can't be too sure, not with everything that's been going on.'

'What natural cause?'

'Heart attack. Well, he did drink a lot. He was an alcoholic, truth be told.'

'When was this?'

'Some time between Monday and Wednesday – they're not quite sure yet.'

'My God. Any connection to Tori, do you think?'

'Only that she was chatting to him at the Christmas Fayre. They did seem to get on well.'

'Right.' She drew another matchstick man and named him Bill.

'Such a lovely man, Peggy. He had a very sad life, though. His wife and kids – they didn't really want to know him. I wonder how they're feeling now.'

'What life can do to us, aye?'

'Don't you wonder why we do it, why we get married in the first place?'

'You mean fall in love in the first place?'

'Be better off just leading our own lives, wouldn't we?'

She smiled. 'Eeh, I remember when me and Walt got together. You think today's youngsters are promiscuous. He only went and booked us a hotel room without asking. Scruffy place an' all. Mr and Mrs Wensleydale, he called us. How we got away with it, I'll never know. Told my parents I was staying with Florence Oxley for the weekend. Oh my God, Enid – I can picture it now. Him in his great big pants, coming at me like a dog on heat.'

It's not like Peggy to talk about her married life, or her sex life, come to that. Must have been the wine talking.

'Me and Peter were both virgins. Got married in white, I did.'

'But it's much more fun when it's not allowed.'

'Did you ever meet anyone else – you know, after you and Walt got divorced?'

'Not really. The love of my life, he was.'

'Didn't you ever want kids?'

She paused for a second, her eyes going off to some faraway place. Then she straightened up and looked me square in the face.

'No,' she said. 'They're not for me, kids. I'm far too self-centred for all of that.'

'It's a shame. You'd have made a good mother.'

'Thanks, Enid, that's kind of you. Right - let's get on with this 'ere chart.'

Benjamin Bradstock came round to see Tori yesterday. I confess, it was all a bit fraught before he arrived. Expectation on my part and fear on Tori's. But when Mattie turned up with Benjamin, it turned into a kind of tea party, what with my Victoria Sponge and my freshly baked cinnamon shortbread.

Mattie took to Tori like a duck to water. 'Come on, let's eat some of Enid's cake before we start, settle our tummies a bit.'

'I am feeling a bit sicky,' Tori admitted.

I made tea for us all. Benjamin's a really lovely man, you know. His soft voice is a mixture of Cornish, where he grew up, and Scottish, where he now lives. Quite a mixture, that. He has big blue eyes that peer at you above his rosy cheeks, and he puts you right at ease. I can see how he became a hypnotherapist.

'So, Tori,' he said, 'I understand you've been in hospital.'

She looked completely embarrassed. Poor girl.

'I know. It was stupid. I won't do it again.'

'I should hope not. There are reasons why we do these things, you know. And they're not always the obvious ones.'

'What do you mean?' she asked.

'Do you believe in reincarnation, Tori?'

'Not you as well!' she exclaimed. 'Enid's already asked me that one.'

'I take it the answer's no, then.'

'I don't believe in it, no. It's not something I've ever thought about. I mean, it's totally something I'd want to have time to think about, if I ever decided to.'

'That's fine. It's not a problem.' He placed his empty cup upon the table. 'So would you mind if I hypnotised you, tried to take you back to a previous life? If indeed it exists?'

She hesitated, looked at Mattie, then across to me.

I smiled and nodded my agreement. 'I'll be there with you, Tori.'

She smiled. 'Okay. Let's do this thing.'

There are moments in life when you feel as if you're the tiniest being on the planet, as if everything else is greater than you, that you're the most insignificant thing here and nobody cares. Then there are days when you feel like the most special person in the entire world. Yesterday was one of those days. Unbelievable. It was a privilege to witness such a wonderful transformation.

It began with Benjamin hypnotising Tori, which took only minutes. That in itself was amazing enough. But then he invited her to go back to a previous life, and to describe what she could see. What happened next was unbelievable.

'Annie's in the kitchen making tea. We've got pork sausages from the farm, a real treat, what with this rationing.'

I gasped, couldn't help it. Tori's voice was deeper, older, with a strong Yorkshire accent.

'Then there's jam and bread. You'd think we'd lost the war, the way they treat us. Can't buy this, not enough of that. Even potatoes now.' She turned her head to look at the wall behind me. 'And Tom and Michael are late home from school. Again.'

'What's your name?' asked Benjamin.

'Elizabeth Salter.'

'And what's the date?'

'The sixteenth of January.'

'The year?'

'1948, of course.'

'Elizabeth, what were your children wearing when they left for school this morning?'

'Their uniforms. Grey suits and caps, brown shoes. Leather satchels. Michael scuffed his knee yesterday, so he's got a good, clean bandage on it.'

'What can you see now?' asked Benjamin.

'We've got the fire lit, it's been really cold. And I can see the newspaper on the side, ready for when he comes home.'

'When who comes home – your husband?'

'Yes.'

She didn't look like Tori. She'd become very serious, very grownup.

'What does he do, your husband?'

'He's a banker, does very well for himself. He's paying for the boys to go to boarding school in September ...'

She began to cry suddenly, her hands covering her face in embarrassment.

'Tori – Tori – stop. Come away from this life. Go back, further back, to another lifetime,' Benjamin urged.

She stopped immediately, sat up straight in her chair, and smiled.

'Where are you now? What can you see?'

'The tower. The Eiffel Tower. It is very beautiful, so tall and *élégant*.'

Astounding. Her voice had completely changed. Tori was speaking English with a French accent, full of charm and vivacity. A young girl again.

'What is your name?'

'Clotilde Dourdos.'

'Thank you. And what is the date?'

'December twelfth, 1914,' she replied, but her expression said, *don't you know*?

'Look around you, Clotilde. Look at where you are sitting. Whereabouts are you?'

'I'm in the office. The taxis are outside waiting. I can hear them.'

'What are they waiting for?'

'The passengers, of course.'

'How many taxis are there?'

'Only two. Papa has taken the other one – he's got a pickup at Gard du Nord. It's not too far, he should be home soon.'

'What would you do if he asked you to drive one of his taxis?'

There was silence. She closed her eyes slowly, and when she opened them again they were full of tears.

'I have driven one.'

'When?'

'I have driven one and it did me no good. I will not be driving another.'

'Why not, Clotilde?'

She began to cry, holding her stomach with both hands.

'I'm having a baby. A baby ...'

'How lovely.'

'No, it is not! It is not lovely! I will not have it! I cannot have it!"

'So what will you do about it, Clotilde? What will you do with this baby?'

'No-one must know. *Personne!*' she screamed.

'How will that happen, Clotilde? What will you do?' Benjamin reiterated.

'I must go away.'

'How will you go away?'

'Papa's morphine.'

'No.'

'What do you know? It is the only way.'

'But there is another way, Clotilde. You don't have to kill yourself.'

'Not me. The baby. I have to kill the baby. It is a bastard, *n'est ce pas*?' Crying, distraught, her face red with anger, she leaned towards him. 'Do you hear me?'

'Clotilde, you must go forward in time. Go to your death.'

Immediately she rolled up the sleeve of her hoodie and made as if to inject something into her left arm.

I gasped so loudly that Benjamin put a finger to his mouth to quieten me. But I had every reason to gasp. Tori had a birthmark on her left arm, just above the crook of her elbow. It was a perfect star-shape. She was injecting into a star-shaped birthmark, a perfect replica of the one I saw when I was seven years old.

I stood up, my mind whirling in shock.

Coincidence, it was saying. Pure coincidence. My mind playing tricks.

Yet there was something there. I knew it.

Tori made as if to inject herself, before pulling away.

'There. It is done,' she sighed, soft tears streaming down her face.

But Benjamin was getting hot under the collar, both hands gripping the chair arms.

'No, Clotilde. It is not done. You will move away to another lifetime. To this lifetime. But you will remember. You will remember that there was an alternative, there is always an alternative. You could have, you should have, told your parents what had happened. About the soldiers, about the baby.'

'No. No baby. Not now.'

'Your parents love you, you know they love you, they would have taken care of you. Suicide is never an option. You only have to keep coming back to relearn your lesson. It is a way out, yes, but not the only way out. There are always other paths to follow, other ways to choose. Don't stop believing, Tori – in magic, in starlight, in love. There is always love. You only have to look for it.'

Tori's head fell forward and she began to cry uncontrollably.

'Tori, I'm now going to count from five down to one. When I reach one, you will be wide awake. You will be back in Enid's house, in this very room, as Victoria Seaborne. It is five to three, it is Friday the first of January, and there is some delicious sponge cake on the table.'

I sat down, watching as he counted. This prim and proper Parisian girl, so unhappy at her unwanted pregnancy, became sixteen-year-old Tori again, the twenty-first century girl with ripped jeans and a blue hoodie, right in front of my very eyes.

But I was still staring at her arm.

Does that star-shape mark the place of the injection that killed Clotilde? Is it a constant reminder of the pain she suffered during that lifetime? Did she have that same birthmark all through her other lifetimes, including the one where she threw herself off the bridge rather than divorce her husband?

Is she the same girl I saw in that house in Dorset all those years ago?

Could she have reincarnated more times than we know?

26

Tori

Sunday January 3rd

THE church bells are going off on one again . I wish someone would switch them off. I wish they could be switched off. Yeah, I know. It's my own fault. I'm still recovering from last night's party at Emily's. She's an old friend of Olly's, though, and really nice. So I wore my new dress again, with my new boots. Looked *totally* amazing. I felt just awesome, as if I could touch the sky, swim the channel, do anything I wanted.

The landlord at the Royal Oak was right, though. Gigi says Raff is seeing someone else. The two-timing sleaseball. I wonder when it all started, then. Was it the night I went to Nicole's party, because I swear he was fine before that? But I wonder what she looks like. Is she different to me, cleverer than me, prettier than me? Total bastard.

My God, we're all back at school tomorrow. It's mocks and I'm literally shitting myself, but I am working really hard. Because I've finally decided what I want to be. I want to be a politician like Olly. I think I could do it, too. Well, why the hell not? I'm joining the Debating Society at school when we go back. Sounds posh, doesn't it, but I need to practise. And if I can sort out all this bullying that's been going on, then I'll have totally proven I can do it. Poor Ross. Just because he's black. People can be really nasty to him, especially the boys. The girls quite like him because he's kind of cute. The boys are just horrible, though, ignoring him at lunchtime and refusing to sit at the same table. I actually think it's jealousy because he is cute. I mean, they're okay with the other black kids. But it needs to stop. It's so obvious, that's the problem, and it totally upsets him. Me and Danielle sit with him if we can. Otherwise he goes and sits on the stools near the canteen entrance, eats his food really quickly, and disappears.

That hypnotherapy stuff at Enid's was totally amazing. I felt so relaxed afterwards, like I could fly. I mean, how does he *do* that stuff? It's really scary if you think too long about it. But it does kind of explain why I'm scared of taxis. It brought it all back – the soldiers and the baby and everything. And the drowning. My God. I don't want to think about it, to be honest. I mean, I nearly did that again, didn't I? But it's amazing stuff, this hypnotherapy, has defo made me feel better about everything.

Enid's got no guests coming over this weekend, so I've got loads of revision time. It's English Language on Wednesday, and I should be fine with that. It's the Comprehension I usually get stuck on, but I've practised enough now. Confidence, I've realised. That's the key.

Enid's told me about Bill Mitchell dying. I can't quite believe it. That poor bloke, dying all on his own, nobody there to hold his hand or anything. I'll bet his ex-wife and kids feel dead guilty. I know I would.

I've been told about three deaths in two weeks now. I'm starting to wonder if this village is built on ley lines or something. I mean, it's happened before, but not like this. It's usually old people who die, and then only now and again, not all at the same time.

But I have a confession to make. I've done something totally weird. Enid's told me I was a white witch (they're actually called wiccans) in my past lives, and that wiccans always reincarnate as wiccans.

She says I'm a wiccan! Can you believe that? Ha! Me a white witch, dancing around a fire and chanting! I mean, what's that all about?

So my confession is this. I've chanted a spell. It's a wish for Enid to meet someone nice. Well, I feel sorry for her. She's all on her own, and she's so, so nice. The thing is, if the spell works it'll prove I'm a wiccan. And not only that, I can use it on my mum too. And Nan. Who knows – I may just end up with a huge extended family, everyone happy, everyone settled and content. Wouldn't that be totally *awesome*?

I do love my Nan. I mean, she can talk about absolutely anything. Says I should live for myself, not go chasing boys all the time, because you can't rely on them. I think I can rely on Olly, though. He's genuinely nice, and kind and thoughtful. And his eyes. I could literally sink into them. Green and hazy with long dark lashes. He's not good-looking in a Greek God kind of way, not like Raff, but in a boy next door kind of a way. Kind of cute. He says he only dumped me before because he didn't want me waiting for him while he was away at uni. And I believe him. Anyway, I'll take Nan's advice and wait until I'm at least twenty-five before settling down. But she says Mother Nature's unkind in that respect, because it's difficult for girls to get their careers going properly before they need to start having babies. She says that's why there's so much money spent on IVF these days, because some women leave it too late. But I won't. I want it all. I want a career *and* babies. And a gorgeous husband. Not Raff, though. I could never, ever trust him again. No, I mean someone gorgeous in the right way. Inside, where it matters. Just you wait and see. I'm going to be Mrs Victoria Seaborne (I'm keeping my name, I love it), MP for Grantham and Stamford. But Labour or Conservative? Or Lib Dem? Or even UKIP? Oh, my God. How am I supposed to know that? I'm only sixteen. Time enough yet, Nan would say.

Olly's on his way back to Edinburgh. He says he'll stay in touch and will come to see me at Easter, but if I want to see someone else, it's okay. He says I need to sow a few wild oats. Personally, I think I've sown enough already. I hope that doesn't mean he's going to sow a few wild oats too.

Danielle's been brilliant over the hols. Every time I get stuck on something, usually Maths or Physics to be fair, she talks me through it and shows me how to do it for myself. She's helped me with my French, too. Obvs. Although I'm pretty good at that myself now. Not surprising, considering the stuff I was coming out with on Friday. My God. That Benjamin Bradstock. How does he *do* it? Do you think it's all made up? But it can't be. It was coming from my own mouth, in my own words. *Totally* amazing! I mean, to have lived before, to have lived another life. To have been

French. I can't really remember now why I wanted to kill myself, just that it was the wrong thing to do, that I would have had other choices, that I'd only have to go through the pain again so I can learn whatever it is I'm supposed to learn.

Now I've been thinking about this. A lot. I think I'm here to learn patience. I mean, I'm always in such a rush to do everything, aren't I? Nan says I need to slow down, not live life in the fast lane. I suppose I've *always* wanted everything now, could never wait for tomorrow. But I'm waiting now, aren't I? I'm waiting for Olly to come home at Easter. But while he's away I'm going to study like mad, I'm going to do really well in my exams, and I'm going to make him so proud of me. That's patience enough for anyone, isn't it?

Yesterday was *totally* awesome. Danielle and I caught the early bus to Grantham, and who should be there, standing at the bus stop, waiting for us? Only Gigi, the girl Danielle had told me about, the girl who knows Raff. Danielle invited her along without telling me. I confess I was a bit hurt at first, because I'd thought it would just be me and Danielle going shopping. But we all had such a good time together I didn't mind in the end. I've never met Gigi before, she goes to Raff's school, but she's nice, with bright red hair and freckles. Her mum's a teacher and her dad's a doctor, the kind that replaces broken knees and stuff.

'River Island first, then Costa for coffee,' announced Danielle.

'Oh, why River Island?' moaned Gigi. 'I went there last week, there'll be nothing new.'

'Because Tori's *only* got a hundred and fifty quid to spend, that's why.'

'Wow,' replied Gigi, smiling.

I bought everything. They were practically giving stuff away. Jeans - okay, they've still got rips in them, they literally don't sell anything else, but they're proper rips with white lacy stuff around the edges. And actually, Nan's okay with it, despite what she said. And I got some tops and a hoodie, and undies and socks and bras and PJs. Everything. It was totally *unreal*.

It turns out Danielle had invited Gigi for a reason. After over two hours of shopping and trying on, and contemplating and queuing, we got to Costa, the one on the High Street. To be honest, I was having such an awesome time I could have taken all day and not eaten a thing. But the other two were hungry, so, loaded up with shiny new carrier bags, we found a window seat and sat down. Danielle bought the toasties and cappuccinos as her mum had given her some money to treat us all, which was really nice. I had cheese and mushroom. Totally dee-lish.

‘So what’s happening tonight?’ asked Gigi, tucking into hers.

I pulled a face. ‘Sorry, can’t come out. I’m studying. I promised Mum.’

‘What A levels are you planning on doing, then?’ she asked.

‘French, English and Maths. Assuming I get my GCSE’s.’ I shrugged nonchalantly, but secretly I’m really worried about the whole thing.

‘You know you’ll do well,’ said Danielle. ‘You’re working really hard these days. Anyway, Gigi’s here for a reason. Aren’t you, Gigi?’ and she poked her arm.

‘I’m here to tell you about Raff,’ said Gigi.

The toastie turned to plastic in my mouth. I’d not heard anything about him in days, had assumed he was just hanging out with that new girl.

‘What? What about him? Is he alright?’

‘It wasn’t his decision to dump you.’

‘What?’

‘His mum talked him into it.’

I thumped the table with my fist. ‘I knew it!’

‘What?’ asked Danielle.

Sorry tears filled my eyes. ‘I knew she’d had a hand in it! How could he be so fucking stupid?’

Trying to calm me, Gigi placed her hand on mine. ‘It wasn’t just her idea, though. I know. She told my mum she’d been talked into it by a friend of hers.’

‘What?’

'She has a friend who suggested you weren't good enough for Raff, that he should look for someone else. Someone in his own class, so to speak.'

I was literally shaking with anger. 'What business is it of theirs, anyway? Why would anyone else get involved like that? It's nothing to do with them.'

'I'm confused,' said Danielle, shaking her head.

'Do you know who this friend is?' I asked.

'Mrs Bruneski or something. An unusual name.'

'Nicole's mum! That's Nicole's mum!' Fear clutched at my stomach as I realised how easily Nicole had pushed herself into my life. 'What a nerve. I don't believe it.'

'Are you sure?' asked Danielle. 'Isn't she the one whose party you invited me to?'

I nodded, anger filling my every thought as I realised how they'd used me, how they'd befriended me in such a short space of time. But why the hell would they want to split us up? What advantage would that give them? Did Nicole fancy Raff or something?

'I don't understand,' I murmured, feeling sick now. 'Is he seeing Nicole, then? Is that it?'

Gigi shook her head. 'It's not Nicole, Tori. It's Charlotte Smith-Jenkins. But he's way out of her league. She's going places. It won't last long, so don't worry.'

'I am worried, though. Why would they do this to us? We were really happy. We had something.'

But this was it. The last straw. I began to sob uncontrollably, right there, right in the middle of Costa. I just couldn't stop myself.

Danielle hugged me. 'Tori, don't. Come on, he's not worth it, is he?'

'You deserve better than him,' said Gigi. 'Someone who can be told what to do by his mother defo isn't worth it.'

'Sorry, I need to go ...'

Wiping my eyes, I gulped down my coffee, grabbed my bags and left. Danielle and Gigi, now really upset, could only sit and watch.

Danielle rang later, just as I was getting into my Stats homework.

'Did you get my texts?' she asked.

'Yes, of course,' I snapped.

'Why didn't you reply, then? I mean, I was really worried …'

'What - worried I'd do something stupid?' I interrupted.

'No … I …'

'Danielle, just why did you want me to know about Raff? Why did you invite Gigi along?'

'Oh God, Tori, I'm so sorry. I so didn't mean to upset you. I just didn't want you thinking it was you, that it was your fault. It's nothing to do with you, you see – it was his mum. Because you're such a lovely person, and Raff was totally an idiot to dump you.

But it wasn't your fault. I only wanted you to know that. That's why I invited Gigi. I thought you'd believe her more than me, because I'm your friend and I might just have said it to make you feel better.'

I suddenly felt really bad. 'Okay. Thanks. I'm sorry, Danielle.'

'But don't you think it's weird? I mean, why would this woman want him to dump you? Have you done something to upset her or anything?'

I shook my head at the phone. 'Not that I'm aware of. I mean, I only know her through Nicole. And I've only known *her* a couple of weeks.'

'So why would they *do* something like that?'

'I don't know. But I'm going to find out.'

'Are we still friends, then?' she asked.

'Danielle, you're the best friend I've ever had. We'll always be friends.'

With the sound of the bells echoing through my head, I crawl out of bed, get dressed and go to get breakfast. It's Weetabix today. They must have had no *specials* on. Nan's ironing and Mum's in the shower, getting ready for a hot date.

'What you up to today, then?' asks Nan, one eye on the telly.

'Studying. Enid's got no guests this weekend, so I've got all day.'

'Good for you. You show 'em what you can do, my love.'

History first, then Chemistry, reading around the Earth's crust and the atmosphere. I think I'm doing okay. I just need to do a couple of English papers ready for tomorrow.

At eleven o'clock, Enid knocks on the front door. She's wanting to chat to Nan. But I pop into the kitchen to say hello and end up telling her all about what Gigi said yesterday, about Raff being *forced* to dump me. She and Nan are both shocked, but nothing like as much as I am. I mean, what's it all about? Why would a complete stranger tell another woman what to do with her son?

Enid waits until Nan pops to the shop for more milk and biscuits before opening up and telling me the truth.

'The idea was to get you to harm yourself, Tori. I've already told you there's such a thing as witchcraft, that the people who practise it can have a great influence. And because you've been a wiccan and have tried suicide before, they're out to destroy you. Getting Raff to finish with you was the last straw in a list of attempts to belittle you.'

'But why me?'

'Well, Peggy says the first time you killed yourself was the time you were raped. Apparently, you were all set to help the French defeat the Germans. You were bilingual, young and very brave. Living in the centre of Paris you may have gained information that could have helped decide battle strategy. If you'd lived, you might have shortened the war by years.'

'Wait. How does she know all this? It was a century ago.'

'She has contacts.'

'Contacts?'

'I don't want to frighten you, Tori.'

Is she kidding me?

'You don't want to frighten me? What – you've told me I've lived before, that I'm a wiccan and now witches are out to get me to kill myself? And you don't want to frighten me?'

She looks slightly embarrassed. 'Shush, Tori. Calm down now.'

'I need to know. Everything.'

'Okay. But if your Nan walks back in, we were just talking about boys, okay?'

'Okay,' I agree.

'The thing is, Peggy can contact the spirit world. Well, in fact they contact her.'

I laugh out loud at that. 'What? You're joking me.'

'No, Tori. You have a great uncle who's watching over you, looking out for you. He's the one who contacted Peggy when you …' but she stops, unable to say the words.

I fill them in for her. 'When I tried to kill myself.'

'He woke Peggy in a dream. She rang me. That's how we got you to hospital in time. Otherwise I don't know what …'

Soft tears fill her eyes. I never realised she cared so much. I begin to cry, too.

'I'm sorry, Enid.'

'Don't be. Just promise me you'll never do it again.'

'I promise.'

'Thank you.'

'So who is this great uncle? I didn't know I had any ...' then an awful thought strikes me. 'Oh, my God - no!'

'What?'

'He's the one who's watching me all the time, isn't he?'

'He is.'

'I can sense him, standing at the door, or outside the bathroom. Oh, my God, it's so weird.'

'He's just keeping an eye, that's all.'

Just then Nan walks in with a bag full of food. I spot chocolate digestives straightaway. Placing it onto the table, she looks at me carefully.

'I heard you talking.'

'The bloke – the one I can sense – apparently he's my great uncle.'

'Enid's already told me.'

'But Nan! Why the hell didn't you tell *me*?'

'I didn't want to scare you, my darling.'

'So *he's* not been scaring me for years, then?' I complain.

'He's been looking after you. Enid's right.'

I stand up. 'So, right, let's get this straight. He's been freaking me out because?'

Enid smiles. 'Because you're set for great things, you're going to sort this country out, you're going to bring the people of this country together. There are certain people who don't like it, they want chaos, disorder, fighting, murder and mayhem. They want evil.'

That stuns me. I sit back down.

'So just how the hell am I supposed to do that, then?'

Nan grins. 'Tori – just what is it you've decided to do with your life? You were only telling me the other day.'

'A politician. I want to be a politician like Olly.'

'There you go, then,' says Enid, folding her arms and smiling. 'There you go, then.'

27

Melissa

Monday January 4th

IS there anything worse than a son who mopes around the house all day? Okay, so bloody Charlotte's finished with him, we know that. But there are other fish in the sea. Plenty of them in fact, where my Raff's concerned. Good-looking boy, he is. Takes after me.

The Brunewski family, the whole lot of them, have left the village, would you believe. Lock, stock and barrel. Ed rang me earlier. They're all talking about it at work. Rumours fly from one thing to another, he says. Some say the police are after her, something to do with drug trafficking. As if. Others say she's come into money (yes, *more* money) and has gone abroad to be with her family. The drugs rumour's a load of rubbish, I'm sure. The other is possible, I suppose, but why would she just up sticks like that? Why not take a few weeks to pack, say goodbye to us all, throw a leaving party (she's got the money, after all) and arrange things properly? All very strange, if you ask me. Mind you, those friends she brought round on New Year's Eve left a lot to be desired. I must say. I wasn't sure about them at all. Now they *could* have been on drugs for all I know. Not that I know much about drugs, you understand. I know what I'll do. I'll ring Maxine later, get all the goss.

Raff's first driving lesson went very well. He's a clever boy, his instructor was very impressed. He's not happy though, I can tell. He went back to school today, but instead of walking in at five o'clock starving hungry as usual, he went straight to his room. He's there now, headphones on, watching some film or other and texting his friends. That's what gets me about teenagers, all this multi-tasking. Is that a good or a bad thing, I wonder? He really should be doing his homework, but I don't like to nag. He needs cheering up, that's for sure. So I'm making his favourite. Shepherd's pie, then chocolate cheesecake for dessert. Poor Raff, though. Dumped on the fifth date. But we all have to go through it. Life's not perfect, is it? Never was. No, I'll have a chat with him later, when he's calmed down a bit. He's angry with me for some reason. Men, aye?

It's snowing outside, a blizzard, whipping at the windows and filling up the garden chairs so you can hardly see them. Ed will be on his way home. I do hope he's careful. There have been so many deaths in this village just lately I'm becoming superstitious.

So.

Just the mashed potato to do.

Isn't that a dance?

28

Enid

Tuesday January 5th

MY little chat with Tori proved quite an eye-opener. So Eva talked Melissa into getting Raff to finish with Tori, did she? What else had she been involved in, I wondered? Could she have been responsible for the other awful things that have happened round here?

So we called on Eva and Nicole on Sunday afternoon. Just for a chat, you understand. I must admit, though, I was very impressed with their house. Magnificent, it was. Old-fashioned streetlamps in the garden, a huge front door with leaded lights, *the* most amazing conservatory stuck onto the side.

Peggy rang the doorbell. 'Nothing like practising evil for making money,' she whispered.

'We don't know that yet, Peggy.'

'Don't we? Julia rang me last night. Turns out Josie's car was forced off the road by a shiny new black Megane. The police have narrowed down the paint on her car. Now, who do we know who has a black …?'

The door was opening. Eva stood there in a crimson kaftan, long nails and all the makeup.

She smiled. 'Hallo,' she murmured throatily. 'It's Enid, isn't it?'

I couldn't speak. My mouth had gone suddenly dry and my heart was thumping wildly. I just wanted to run. What the hell are we doing here, anyway, I thought? What on earth am I supposed to say?

But Peggy took over.

'Hello, Eva,' she replied in her confident, theatrical voice. 'We were in the area and thought we'd pop in for a chat. If that's okay?'

'Well, I am waiting for some friends, as you can see,' and she indicated her dress. 'But it's alright, come on in. It's lovely to see you.'

She led us into the kitchen where Nicole was rolling pastry at the long pine table. Whatever she was making, the smell was divine, and I immediately regretted having a measly egg salad for lunch.

'Nicole's just making herby sausage rolls. We're having a buffet. When they arrive.' She glanced at the clock on the wall. 'Now then, tea or coffee?'

She offered us a seat at the table and we sat down at one end, careful not to disturb Nicole's baking.

'Tea, please,' I replied, quietly.

'The same, not too much milk,' said Peggy.

Minutes later, we were drinking tea and chatting as if we'd known each other for years. But Eva's smile was greasy, too white, her red lipstick thickly painted. I'd thought before that she looked elegant, but was now changing my mind. Up close, her teeth are perfect, but huge like a horse's. And she has this awful habit of rolling her tongue around them absentmindedly, the veins beneath it a silvery blue colour. It really freaked me out, to be honest, and I confess I did not like the woman.

The feeling was mutual, I was to discover.

'So how are the grandchildren, Enid? I understand you had them over for Christmas?'

I had the sudden sensation of being on a boat, of rocking with the waves, up and down, back and forth. I placed my hands upon the table to steady myself. Get a grip, Enid, I thought.

But how the hell did she know that? How on earth did she even know I had grandchildren? It had been such a last-minute decision I was sure I'd never mentioned it to anybody.

Then I saw the callous look in her eyes. Oh, she knew alright. She was playing with me like a kitten plays with a ball.

Nervous as hell, I coughed to clear my throat. 'They're fine, thank you. We had a lovely few days.'

'That is good, then.'

'Do you have grandchildren, or is Nicole your only child?' I found myself pressing my left thumb into the palm of my right hand. It gave me some confidence.

'She is my only child, yes. But precious, nevertheless. Aren't you, my dear?'

Nicole, her slender hands covered in flour, smiled and nodded. 'Yes, Mum. If you say so.'

Eva smiled, a sickly smile, and turned to me once more. 'So, what can we do for you, Enid?'

I was not happy. She was completely ignoring Peggy. So I turned to my friend, anxious not to say the wrong thing, mentally asking her to fill in for me.

Which she did.

'It's very kind of you to invite us into your home, Eva. Thank you.'

Eva smiled questioningly. 'My pleasure.'

'But Enid and I were wondering,' Peggy continued, 'exactly what your connection *is* with Victoria Seaborne.'

Eva was suddenly agitated, anxious, her eyes narrowing, scanning the room behind Peggy, looking for a way out. And beneath all the makeup I'm sure she'd turned white. Nicole stopped rolling pastry, her eyes searching mine and Peggy's.

'Victoria Seaborne?' Eva repeated, picking up her coffee with a nonchalance that wasn't at all convincing.

'She means Tori, Mum,' interrupted Nicole. 'You know - the girl I invited to the party, the one I met at the Christmas Fayre?'

Eva smiled greedily. 'Oh, yes, I remember. A little darling, isn't she? Bit skinny though, looks like she could do with a bit of feeding up.'

Peggy nodded. 'She is rather vulnerable, I'm afraid. A child of the times. But you've met her before, haven't you? You've met her before Nicole got to know her?'

Fear filled her eyes, but she blinked it away. 'Are you stupid? How could I? How could I have met her before?'

'We understand you persuaded her boyfriend's mother to get him to finish with her. Now why would you do that?'

'What? What boyfriend? She doesn't look old enough to have a boyfriend.'

'Rafferty Slater. His mother's Melissa Slater. She and her husband own Slater Motors.'

'Oh yes, I know her. Lives on Peterborough Road. Not that she's a proper friend, you understand.'

'Friend enough to be talked into doing something. You suggested Tori wasn't good enough for her son, didn't you? You got him to finish with her?'

'Okay. Now I'm offended. That is not only an untruth, but a very strange accusation to make.'

'It's not an untruth, though, isn't it?'

Nicole had by this time sat down, the pastry all forgotten.

'Now for goodness' sake! Why on earth would I *do* that?' cried Eva. 'I hardly know the girl. How can you even say such a thing? And in my house, too?'

I found my voice at last, raising it just a little to emphasise my point.

'We know you had a hand in getting Raff Slater to finish with Tori. We also know you managed to infiltrate my guesthouse with a so-called Mr and Mrs Taylor, who left an offensive letter behind on purpose, making Tori out to be bad at her job and *a dowdy schoolgirl, ugly as sin*. A letter that Tori found and read, as you knew she would.'

'What?' she screamed.

'I also know from Tori that you made her feel completely worthless when she came to your house on Christmas Eve, that you and your friends didn't make her welcome, looked down your noses at her and made her feel so bad that when Raff finished with her - at your command - she took an overdose.'

She stood up indignantly. 'What? What a load of rubbish. Did she tell you that? Well, the girl's deranged!'

'She's not the accuser. I am,' said Peggy.

'I'm sorry?'

'I'm accusing you of getting Tori to harm herself. I'm also accusing you of forcing Josie Timmins and Mr and Mrs Hardy off the road, and I'm accusing you of trying to harm Enid's grandson.'

'No!' she screamed. 'It's not Tori who's mad! It's you! Get out of my house! Now!'

She pulled at Peggy's coat sleeve, forcing her to stand upright. But Peggy resisted and sat back down.

Nicole was by now very agitated, her face pale, her expression shocked. She moved towards her mother.

'Eva!' she cried.

Disbelief echoed through the room.

I stared at her. 'What? She's not your mother, then?'

Tears filled her eyes. 'Just go, will you - just go!' and she ran out.

Satisfied, Peggy sat back and folded her arms. 'So. The truth will out.'

'I'm ringing the police,' said Eva, fishing in her handbag. 'If you won't go of your own accord, then I'm ringing the police.'

'No. I'm the one who will ring the police. Just as soon as I'm out of this place.'

'Out then! Get out!'

'We'll go. But before I do, just one little thing. You're the reincarnation of Flora Middlewood, aren't you? You can use magic, witchcraft, evil spells. You can do anything you want. So why do you have to kill people? Couldn't you just have threatened them? Why did you have to bloody well murder them?'

'What the hell? *Now* what are you accusing me of?'

She was really angry now, her tongue rolling around her teeth in fury. But there were no veins beneath her tongue this time. Just the slippery, slimy scales of a black snake.

Shocked, my legs like jelly, I stood up and opened my mouth to scream.

But Peggy caught my hand. 'It's okay. She's just trying to frighten us.'

Eva laughed. A huge, roaring, menacing laugh. 'You don't know the meaning of the word. Yet!'

Peggy continued. 'So, Josie, Mr and Mrs Harvey, Bill Mitchell. All those deaths on your conscience. Why?'

She was clutching at straws, and she knew it.

The tongue retreated. 'What? I had nothing to do with Bill Mitchell. Who is he, anyway?'

'You do know about Josie and Mr and Mrs Harvey, then?'

The kitchen went dark, heavy and dark. Thick grey smoke began to rise from the Aga and the roar of thunder echoed around us.

I screamed with fear, my throat and lungs hurting with the effort.

A deep crack began to run slowly along the table, splitting it in two. The two pieces remained upright, the yawning space between them filled with a darkness that seemed never-ending, that looked as if you might never return from it, that looked like hell itself. Pushing back my chair I stared at it, mesmerised. But two crows flew at the kitchen window, gaining my attention. More crows, big and black and ferocious, began to circle the garden outside, pecking at one another, huge lumps of feather falling to the ground. Then my chair began to rock viciously, back and forth, back and forth, back and forth. Desperately, I managed to stand up, clinging onto the cooker behind me. I pushed away the chair with my foot and it clattered to the floor. Shaking, confused, my heart pounding, I ran towards the hallway.

'Come on, Peggy,' I called.

But suddenly she was far, far away and the kitchen was a cold black room, huge and dark and echoing, like a cave. A thick fog descended, and I collapsed in a heap.

I came to with the most thumping headache. Peggy was sitting on the armchair opposite while I lay on her sofa, feeling rather sick and very, very tired. The welcoming aroma of patchouli pulled at my nostrils.

'Oh...' I tried to sit up.

'Don't,' said Peggy, quietly. 'You've had a nasty bump to the head. I've put some arnica on and had the doctor take a look at you. You'll be fine, just a bit of concussion. But you do need to rest.'

My hand went straight to my forehead. There was a sizeable bruise, but no damage to my skin. Gratefully, I lay back beneath the covers, tartan throws that had seen better days.

'What time is it?' I asked.

She checked her watch. 'It's just after nine. You can stay here the night. There's some lavender oil on the side there if you need it. But I promised the doc I'd keep an eye on you.'

'What the hell happened, Peggy? What did she do to me?'

'Magic. Dark, nasty magic. She tried to use Dim Mak, the death touch. She tried to send us away. But it failed, thank God. She just wanted me out of the house, but she was more angry with you for having saved little Tori there. Thank God you're still with us.'

'So how did you get us out?'

She nodded mysteriously. 'Ways and means, Enid. Ways and means.'

'Where is she? Did you get the police?'

'Well, I had to get you home first, get you checked out. But then I left you to sleep while I drove over to the station. I did try ringing them, but honestly they were useless. They went straight round there, Enid, but she's gone. Packed her bags and gone.'

Angry tears came, and I managed to sit upright this time, fiddling in my bag for my frankincense and sweet orange. I was completely distraught.

'But she'll just go and do it all again. Can't they trace her?' I asked.

'They've contacted Interpol in London. She's wanted in five bloody countries. Drug-dealing, prostitution, embezzlement of a university that was stupid enough to employ her, and art theft. And now murder.' She counted them off on her fingers. 'If they can prove it. And she's not called Eva Brunewski. She has three different names, one of which is Laura Middleton. No doubt she'll adopt another. Tori must have done something awful to her in a past life.'

'She is the reincarnation of Flora Middlewood, then?'

'She didn't deny it, did she? Going on her past history, I think there's every chance that's who she is. I mean, why else would she be trying to get rid of Tori?'

'So what about Nicole?'

'Nicole isn't her daughter, as you so rightly pointed out. She's a hanger-on, an assistant if you like. Same with her so-called husband, Philip. Some kind of minion, I would imagine. God knows what they'll all be up to now.'

'But they can't just be let loose,' I cried. 'They can't, they can't get away with it. All those murders. And poor Josie.'

'I know, I know,' she soothed. 'If it's any consolation Eva's known to have family in Switzerland, so she may have headed there. They'll track her down.'

I felt sick all over again. 'Megan's parents were in Switzerland …'

'I told the police that. In fact, I've told them everything. Apparently, Megan's mum had some kind of high-up position in Oxfam. And I know Nicole was looking for work in the charity business, so whether it's coincidence or not, I don't know. But if she was applying for work and Megan's mum turned her down, then …'

'She was. I know she was. She told me she'd had an interview with Oxfam. Down near London somewhere. Oh, my God. That poor girl.' My head began to thump again, so I lay down, curling onto my side, feeling very sorry for myself.

'What's done is done, Enid. And it can't be undone, I'm afraid.'

'I know.'

But there was a place in my heart that said I wish it could. That Josie could be brought back, and Megan's parents could be brought back. That evil doings can be undone. But they can't. They never can.

And that's the point of karma, I suppose. At some point Flora Middlewood will get her comeuppance. We must all pay for our misdeeds eventually, in some way or other, in this lifetime or the next.

'Right,' sighed Peggy. 'I'm going to make some tea. Fancy a cup?'

Yesterday I walked round to see Tori. It was still quite early and the pavements were white with a thin layer of snow, but I'd had a chap on the phone asking to book a room, so thought I'd let her know in person.

Just as I was turning the corner, however, I noticed a light in Bill Mitchell's house. Concerned, thinking there might be squatters, or even burglars, I banged on the door loudly.

It opened quickly and a man stood there, tall, tanned and slim with neat grey hair.

He smiled. 'Yes?'

'Sorry,' I mumbled. 'I just saw a light on ...'

'And you thought I was a burglar?'

His soft blue eyes creased at the edges and I suddenly saw the resemblance.

'You're related to Bill.'

'You must be a friend of his. Come on, come on in. I'm just putting on the kettle.' He held out his hand. 'The name's Harry.'

The kitchen was clean and fresh, cleared of all the mess and all the accoutrements Bill liked to have around. My nose wrinkled at the scent of bleach.

'Sorry,' Harry said. 'It needed a really good spruce, and I couldn't just leave it. Not if I'm going to be comfortable.'

I was surprised. 'Are you moving in, then?'

He began to make tea. 'Once I've got it sorted. Well, I've been paying off the interest to make sure Bill had somewhere to live, so he's left it to me in his will.'

'He never was very good with money.'

'Couldn't hold down a job, no matter how hard he tried. Not a very happy life, I'm afraid. Marie and the kids are devastated. I spoke to her yesterday.'

'Yes, a very sad life,' I agreed. 'Such a nice man, though. He'd do anything for anyone.'

'I'm glad you've said that. I wouldn't want to think he'd been all alone.'

'So why are you moving in? Why not just do it up and sell?'

'I've been looking to move out of London anyway, now I'm retired. So it's just the thing.'

'What did you do?' I asked, now warm and comfortable, sipping on Earl Grey. Not my favourite tea, mind.

'Quantity surveying. Fairly interesting work, and it earns a decent living. I still take on the odd job occasionally, contracting, but I can work from home so it doesn't matter where I live. But it is lovely round here, and there's always the train to London if I need it.'

'So what relation are you to Bill?'

'I'm his brother. Four years his junior. Did he never mention me?'

'No.' I shook my head.

'He didn't have much to do with me, really, apart from asking for money. Not after my wife moved out.'

'Oh?' The Earl Grey was becoming much more interesting.

'They had an affair, you know. Years ago now, it was. His wife and kids had left, he was homeless, so he moved in with us for a while.' He sighed deeply. 'They had the motive, the opportunity, and the time.'

'I'm sorry,' I whispered.

'Don't be. It's in the past, gone, obliterated from memory. Well – almost.'

He smiled, and his smile was so warm and caring I could have stayed there all day, could have forgotten all about Tori and the B&B and drunk Earl Grey 'til the cows came home. But no, I thought, I'm far too old for that kind of thing. Aren't I?

'He always seemed angry, somehow,' I replied. 'Deep down. Other than that, he was lovely.'

'Our parents,' he explained. 'They died when we were quite young. Bill took it badly, took it out on the people he loved. Wanted to control the things he could control because he couldn't do anything about the things he couldn't.'

'He always said his wife left him because he lost his job?'

'No. It was the other way round. He lost his job *after* she left him. And she left him because he was a control freak. She was such a free spirit when he met her, but he had to control everything. What she bought, where she went, who she saw. And when the children came along, he was even worse. No, he drove her away, turned to drink, then lost his job. Such a shame.'

Upset at Harry's revelation, I made my excuses. I needed to get to Tori's. We had matters to discuss, and not only about the bed and breakfast. Peggy and I had decided, as painful as it might be, that the ninth wiccan of the Sleaford Coven should be appointed to replace Josie. And it was to be Tori. If she'd accept. Obviously the appointment would only come into force on her eighteenth birthday.

So I finished my tea, said thank you, and left.

'Come and visit again,' he said, as I closed the garden gate.

Today Peggy and I are booking tickets to Dorset. She popped round to see me last night. All dolled up in her new sheepskin coat, she was. Well, it is the weather for it. And we got to talking. Or as my old dad would have said, rabbiting. Rabbit and pork – talk. Anyway, we were sitting there, a bottle of Pinot Grigio between us and Genevieve stretched out in front of the roaring fire. Peggy only had the one glass, of course, she was driving. But what I learned, what we both learned, was absolutely fascinating.

It began with Tori. We were talking about Tori, about her enthusiasm at being asked to become a wiccan, and I just happened to mention the birthmark on her arm. Peggy had seen it too, up at the hospital.

'You know, Peggy, this may sound really strange, but I think I've seen that birthmark before. On a small child a long, long time ago.'

'Well, I suppose Tori doesn't have exclusive access to star-shaped birthmarks.'

'It was very strange, though. She wasn't just an ordinary small child, you see.'

'Oh?'

'She was a ghost.'

She wasn't a bit surprised, having seen plenty of ghosts herself.

'Not that strange, then.'

'It was in Dorset. I was seven years old. The house … even the house was a ghost. Right beside the sea, it was.'

Peggy had been busy playing with the edge of her thick brown cardigan, but she looked up at that, her face completely white. Even her carmine-red lipstick had gone pale. Genevieve and I both stared at her.

'What?' she whispered.

'Are you okay, Peggy? Can I get you anything?'

'Whereabouts in Dorset?'

'Pinhock. A beautiful little place. We only lived there six months, not long.'

'What did the house look like?'

'Oh, it was lovely. I remember it like it was yesterday. Huge, it was, with a black front door and wide windows either side, with two enormous steps leading up. There was an apple tree in the front garden and loads of land round the side and the back. I loved that house. I wanted to move in when I grew up. Until I realised it wasn't real.'

'You mean because it was a ghost house?'

'Yes.'

'So where was this child?'

'Inside the house. I went inside. She was there.'

'What?'

'She was crying, said she was looking for her mummy. Then she just disappeared.'

Peggy began to cry. I've never seen Peggy cry.

'So you let her go, just like that?' she said. 'Didn't you go looking for her?'

I pushed my glass onto the side table. Genevieve looked up knowingly.

'Peggy – what is it? What's wrong?'

So she told me. About the house she'd lived in from the age of ten, about the little girl she gave birth to at the age of fifteen, about how her parents supported her, let her keep the child, despite the shrewd looks and the cheap remarks of so-called friends and neighbours. And about how the child died.

'It was suicide, Enid. She was only four …' and she broke down, and sobbed and sobbed and sobbed, ended up crying herself to sleep on my sofa.

I sat beside her, afraid to leave her, afraid of what she might do, afraid of her waking up alone.

She awoke at ten past three in the morning.

'Sorry, Enid, I'm so sorry. I didn't mean to stay, I just … I'll get on home …'

'You're not going anywhere, Peggy Fleming. Not until you've told me exactly what happened. And if there is anything we can do.'

'There's nothing to do, is there? Once a person's dead, they're dead. Reincarnation doesn't really bring them back, does it?'

'Maybe we can do something, though. Maybe we can lay your ghosts to rest. Maybe I can help. What do you think?'

She sat up, her hair a mess, her makeup washed away with tears. For the first time since I'd known her, she looked old.

'Wait here,' I said. 'I'll fetch in some logs and make us tea and biscuits.'

So I built up the fire and we sat on the floor with tea and home-made cinnamon biscuits. Genevieve looked a little put-out, but she did make some room for us, for Peggy to tell her tale.

'Her father was a black Spaniard, in England to study medicine. He came to Dorset on holiday and we fell in love. I was fourteen when I met him. He seduced me.'

'Oh, Peggy …'

'It was a gloriously warm summer's evening, the kind you usually find on the Continent. He'd brought red wine, two glasses, and a box of chocolates. We sat on the beach and ate and drank. And one thing led to another. I know …' and she nodded miserably.

'You're not the only one, Peggy. Hundreds of girls end up in the same boat.'

'But it didn't stop there. I let it happen again and again. It was wonderful, I was madly in love, besotted. Stupid.'

'No precautions?'

'I didn't really know about such things. I hadn't even begun my periods. To be honest, I don't know what the hell I *was* thinking.'

I was speechless, didn't know what to say. Trying to comfort her, I took her hand and held it.

'When my periods didn't start, Mum became worried. I was fifteen by this time, so should by rights have been menstruating, so she took me off to the doctors. Who of course found I was expecting, four months gone.'

'So where was the father?'

'No sign of him, not anywhere. He'd said he was studying at Cambridge, but when Dad went up there, they'd never heard of him.'

'Oh, Peggy ...'

'So I had the baby. Abortion was illegal then, anyway.'

'So what happened? I mean, after she was born?'

'She was so beautiful, Enid. I loved every tiny inch of her. Mum and Dad had looked into adoption, but I cried so much, wanted to keep her so much ...'

'What about school?'

'I went to school every day, as usual. Mum looked after Millie until I got home. They weren't going to let it affect my schoolwork. After all, I had a baby to bring up when I left.'

I smiled. 'That was really good of them, you know.'

She nodded. 'I know. They were wonderful.'

'So what went wrong?'

'She ran down to the beach one day and walked into the sea. An old man was watching, but he thought she could swim, he said, thought she'd be okay, he didn't think. Until she didn't come out.'

'Oh, no ...'

She began to cry again. 'She'd had people, other kids, chanting at her, saying unkind things. That she was a nigger, she didn't belong, she was a bastard. A nigger bastard, that's what they called her. She went in on purpose, Enid. She wanted to die.'

'She had a star-shape on her arm?'

Tears roared down her cheeks and she nodded, her eyes red and swollen. 'Just where Tori's birthmark is now.'

29

Tori

Wednesday January 6th

ENGLISH this morning was easy-peasy. I mean, the comprehension was to do with oranges and orange farms, which I know nothing about, but I knew what they were getting at straightaway. The trouble with comprehensions, though, is you can't tell how well you've done until you get your mark. To be fair, I actually felt I did okay.

I've been wearing my new stuff to school all week. I feel totally awesome and am just loving my jeans. And my fave top at the moment is the tee-shirt with the drawing of Minnie Mouse on. It's kind of grey with little blue beads on the front. Love it, love it, love it!

So I've joined the Debating Society, as I said I would. Cool, huh? We had our first meeting tonight, straight after school. Before it started, we had to stand up and introduce ourselves, which felt really awkward, to be fair. But Miss Farrell says I'm a natural, especially when I said I was there because I wanted to put the world to rights and get rid of racism in school. She says it's inspired next week's class. Which is totally awesome and I can't believe it. Me, inspiring next week's class! She wants a debate on how racism began, and why we hold onto it in today's liberated society. Oh, my God.

Defo need to work on that one.

There's a hot bloke in the Debating Society, too. He's called Nathan, he's tall and dark and shy, and he only joined our school in September, so I've not had much to do with him until now. But we got chatting over tea and garibaldi. Miss Farrell says she always brings garibaldi to Debating – it's her fave biscuit. They're alright, actually, especially if you dunk them. Anyway, Nathan lives in this cute little village on the way into Grantham and gets really bored as he used to live in Manchester, a great big city full of stuff to do. So I've asked him if he wants to go out somewhere after the mocks have finished. To celebrate, kind of thing. And he's agreed. Yes!

I do feel a bit guilty, though. I mean, about Olly. But he did say I could sow my wild oats, didn't he? And Nathan looks like he needs a friend or two. That's why he's joined the Debating Society. He's also joined the Badminton Club, so looks like I'll be going along to that, too. Well, can't do any harm, can it?

I've actually started *talking* to Great Uncle John. So has Nan. It creeps Mum out, but we're making a big joke of it. He doesn't seem to mind, and it makes him a lot less scary. It feels quite nice, knowing someone's watching over me. And I've stopped having such weird dreams since Benjamin hypnotised me. To be fair, Great Uncle John isn't here so much now anyway. I think he just pops in now and again, keeps an eye out.

Nan's been doing a bit of research on him. She's actually paid for *Ancestry*. And it turns out he's on my dad's side of the family. He's my dad's great uncle. If she's right about this, he was born in Camden in 1912, became a sailor in the Second World War and died at sea in 1943. So he was only young when he died. I wonder why he's taken on the task of looking after me. Nan thinks it's because he remembers what it feels like to be a child.

'But I'm not a child!' I exclaim.

'You were when he began visiting. Maybe he feels for you because you don't have a father - at least, not one who cares a hoot. Maybe he's taking his place, keeping an eye out.'

'Don't you think it's weird, though, that our surname's Seaborne and he was a sailor?' I ask.

She smiles. 'Trust you to think of that one, Tori. But yes, your dad's family might all have been sailors, for all we know. Why on earth not? If they go back generations, that could be where the name comes from. The salty Seaborne sailors. Or maybe it's just pure coincidence. We'll have to do a bit more digging on that there Ancestry, won't we?'

'So those marks on the floor, Nan. Is it salt or something? Could it be sea salt? And the smell – rum or brandy or something? They used to drink stuff like that at sea, didn't they?'

'It could be any kind of alcohol, I suppose, something to warm their cockles. But I'm glad you're questioning things. You've got a brain in that there head of yours, Tori. You're going to go far, my love.'

Raff's started messaging me again. He's on his own now, just spends time at the Royal Oak with his pals. He'll get someone else soon enough, but it won't be me. I really thought he was the one, though. Just shows how wrong you can be. Too much up his own arse for my liking. And he had no respect for me, though I couldn't see it at the time. Thought I was a little working class tart, someone to practise on til he meets the real thing. Well, I'll show him.

No, I can live my life without him, thank you very much. I'm okay.

Enid came round yesterday. She's got someone staying for bed and breakfast this weekend, so she wants me to help out. I just hope they're nicer than the last lot. She says she's going to start showing me how to use herbs. It's oregano this weekend, which is supposed to be good against the flu. Awesome!

Enid's been eyeing up that bloke at Bill Mitchell's house, you know, says she got talking to him on the way here. He's Bill's brother and he's moving in, once he's done the place up.

Unbelievable. Is that me? Have I made that happen? Have I been able to influence Enid's life? Awesome! Again!

I'm going to try it out on Mum. That bloke she's been seeing, that Mike somebody, is defo a bit of a loser. Talks like he owns half of Sleaford. But he doesn't, he just works in the council offices. I don't like him, and he's not right for her, he doesn't make her happy.

So I'll do a bit of wishing. It's in the hands, I've found. It's a bit like praying, but you have to really, really believe in it.

30

Melissa

Thursday January 7th

THE more I think about it, the more I realise it *was* Eva Brunewski who forced me to get Raff to finish with that Tori. And now he's so unhappy and it's breaking my heart. I wonder what that was all about. Why would she have done that? It's all very strange.

So now I have a son who, instead of studying really hard and making the most of the private education we're paying thousands for, is hanging around the pub all night. I really need to have words.

Ade and Imogen came over for dinner on Sunday. He's on this special diet and can't drink, but he's looking a whole lot better. So we've booked our weekend in Bruges, finally. We're leaving it until Easter, so Ade can be sure he won't need hospital visits or anything. The insurance are making a bob or two out of it, though. Topped up his premium by a third. I don't know, the cheek of it. On the other hand, the local gym gives him a discount if he's had heart problems. So it's swings and roundabouts, I suppose. I've been on at Ed to join the gym, too. We're not getting any younger, after all. Imogen and I have decided to join, so it'd be nice if we all went along together.

Ade's using the NHS this time, you know, because it was an emergency. They're not that bad, actually, when push comes to shove, when it's something really important. In fact, Imogen and I are thinking of doing some fundraising - you know, for the cardio team. I was thinking of coffee mornings, but she wants to do a sponsored cycle. More in keeping, she says, than eating a load of cake that's bad for you. Looks like I need to get into training, then. One more reason to join the gym. Need to find a sexy leotard or something.

Imogen and I are meeting for lunch in town again today. The January sales are amazing, I can't wait to get back there. I might buy Raff something nice to cheer him up this time. Maybe a couple of nice shirts.

I know he's upset at me, but really, that girl was never going to be right for him. Best to cut his losses now, I think.

So.

A squirt of *Clive Christian.*

Then I'm off.

31

Enid

Tuesday February 2nd

THE train was nearly empty, just a few people on their way down to London for the day. We quickly found a table-seat near the toilets and sat down, our Starbucks coffee and cheese and chutney baguettes at the ready.

It took us nearly five hours to reach Weymouth, and then we needed a taxi. And as for taking the tube through London to get to Waterloo Station – well now, don't get me started. Good job Peggy's been there before and knows the ropes.

We'd booked ourselves into a bed and breakfast in Pinhock, not far from the beach. It had a four star rating and was friendly and warm, with comfortable beds, huge white baths and soft pink towels. Doreen Atkinson, the landlady, was a smiling, jovial type, so invited us in for coffee after showing us our rooms. But we declined. We wanted to explore the area before it got dark.

The air was alive with the sound of seagulls and the all-pervading scent of fish and chips. We walked along the main road to find Cove Lane, exactly where Peggy had lived, exactly where I'd seen Millie's ghost. There's now a coffee shop opposite and a shop selling expensive artwork behind. The plot of land itself has been used to build a dormer bungalow, long and expensive-looking, in stone with black ash windows and wide patio doors. But the car on the drive said it all. A brand new silver Audi TT.

'Must have made a bob or two to retire to this,' murmured Peggy.

'What makes you think they've retired?'

'Well, there's not much work around here, is there? It's either coffee shops or trinket bars.'

'Or art dealers. But you never know - there might be a few solicitors, or an investment guru or two.'

'They could commute to London, I suppose.'

'True,' I agreed. 'What did your dad do for a living, then?'

'He was an investment banker. Now he *did* commute. Left the house at six in the morning, got home eight o'clock at night. But he sometimes had to stay over for meetings and things, so it wasn't ideal. But come on, let's ask round. I need to know about my house, what happened to it.'

'We could have asked the landlady.'

'No. Doesn't look old enough.'

'If you're expecting to meet someone who was alive in 1959, is still living here, and has a good enough memory to remember what happened after you left, then good luck with that one.'

She smiled. 'And I always thought you were the optimistic type.'

'I am.'

'I mean, look at you, Enid. You're on the cusp of the greatest romance of your life, and you can't see it. He's crazy about you. I saw the look in his eyes when we called round with Genevieve.'

Harry had offered to look after Genevieve whilst we were away. Not that she needs much looking after. But I thought it was really kind of him, so I accepted. But Peggy's right. We are getting along really well, and I find myself popping in there nearly every day on my way back from the greengrocer's. The house is starting to look very nice, with fresh paint and original pine flooring instead of the dirty old carpets Bill had down. It's still very sad, though, Bill's heart attack, and I know

Harry would much rather he was here, alive and kicking.

We went to his funeral, Peggy and I. It was beautiful, full of anecdotes about Bill and the honey-coloured lab he had when he first moved to Pepingham. His wife and the two girls were in church, along with a chap who might have been her husband, but I couldn't see a ring on her finger. She looked upset, as were the girls. Well, I should hope so.

But Harry was kind, didn't mention anything about Bill's affair with his wife, just read a piece saying what a lovely man he had been, how he'd always looked out for people, how he could grow fruit and veg with just a few seeds, and how he always shared whatever he had. Which was true.

But I laughed out loud at Peggy's comment. 'I'm hardly headed for a great romance, Peggy. Not at my age, I'm not.'

She grinned. 'Well, we shall see, Enid Phelps, we shall see.'

I chose merely to ignore her. 'So, come on then. Exactly where do you suppose we'll find someone who knows what happened to your old house?'

'We can ask in the pub tonight – how about it? I fancy a pub meal and a pint of something strong and dark.'

'Like your men,' I interrupted, before she could say it.

She giggled. 'You know me far too well, Enid, my love.'

The pub was bustling, despite it being the beginning of February. There was a log fire burning and we headed towards it to find a table for two, a chunky white candle at its centre. The air was thick with the scent of wood-smoke and steak pie gravy. A couple of blokes, a few years younger than us, propped up the bar nearby. One of them, a skinny country yokel type, winked as we sat down.

'I could eat him for dinner,' murmured Peggy.

'Ooh, it's nice to have someone take notice now and again. Shows we're not too old.'

'Well, you're certainly not. Not the way Harry's taking notice, you're not.

I blushed hotly. 'Peggy, stop that, will you? We're just good friends.'

She grinned. 'Sorry, love. I'm just excited for you, that's all.'

'Yes, well, we're here to find out about your old house, not chat up a couple of locals.'

'Come on then,' and she stood up.

'What?'

'Let's go and ask them.'

'Peggy – no! I'm ordering food, I'm absolutely starving.'

'Must be the sea air. Come on then.'

We ordered fish and chips, a Guinness for Peggy and white wine for me. The fish was delicious, freshly caught, and I sat back afterwards, satiated, relaxed, the warm fire and the candlelight making me sleepy.

'Come on then – let's go and ask them,' insisted Peggy.

'Ask them what?'

'About my house.'

I was amazed the two men were still there, but they were, and after a little persuasion from Peggy we crossed to the bar, ordered more drinks, and began chatting.

One of them, the one who'd winked at us, was a local from the next village along. The other was his brother, visiting from some place in Kent. As it turned out, neither of them knew the history of the village, never mind the house. But we had a lovely evening and as they walked us back to the Bed and Breakfast we agreed to meet up the following day for a walk along the beach, then lunch.

It was as we were making our way up to bed that Doreen Atkinson appeared. Tall and slim with perfect teeth, her golden hair tied back, a glass of whisky in her hand, she invited us into her lounge for a nightcap.

She smiled at our reticence. 'Just the one, you know. I like to get to know my guests if I can. They may just decide to come back one day.'

'Oh, we probably won't be back,' Peggy replied, pausing at the bottom of the stairs. 'We're just here to gain a little knowledge, that's all.'

'Oh?'

'I lived here as a child, you see, but the house I lived in is no longer there. I'd just like to know what happened to it.'

'Is that the only reason you're here? My, my.'

'There's more to it,' I offered.

'Which house was it?'

'At the top of Cove Lane,' said Peggy.

'The bungalow?'

'Yes. Only it wasn't a bungalow then. It was an old house, two storey.'

She indicated the lounge with a tilt of the head. 'Come on in.'

We sat down on the long grey leather sofa, expensive, designer. Doreen poured us two whiskies and we accepted.

The room was large but cosy, with pink lamps on low tables and red velvet curtains drawn across the window. Doreen sat opposite us on an armchair and looked directly at Peggy.

'I knew you reminded me of someone when you first came in, you know. I just couldn't place my finger on it.'

Peggy wriggled a little. 'Oh?'

'Your mother. You're a little older, but you're the spitting image.'

Peggy nearly dropped her glass. 'What? How did you know my mother?'

'I actually checked your name after you'd gone out, but it's different. I guess you must have married.'

'My maiden name was Broadstairs.'

She looked suddenly thoughtful. 'Hannah Broadstairs. I remember you sitting backstage while she rehearsed. A pretty young thing, you were. All the men fancied you, but you'd have nothing to do with them. Not that you were shy.'

Peggy wriggled some more. 'You don't look old enough to know my mother.'

'Oh, don't be fooled by my looks, dear. Never be fooled by people's looks. No, I confess I've had a little help over the years.'

'You mean cosmetic surgery?'

'That's exactly what I mean. In my profession it helps keep the money rolling in if you're not seen as being past it.'

'You were a dancer like Mum, then?'

'I was her choreographer. For a while. After she moved back to London with you.'

'You mean after we left here?'

'She was an amazing dancer, came back to work at the Theatre Royal once she felt you no longer needed her, once she knew you could be left alone. We were so overjoyed to see her out there again. Marvellous, she was. Still lithe, supple, perfectly balanced, even though she'd not danced in years. We became really good friends, you know.'

'Did she ever tell you what happened here, in Pinhock?'

'All I know is you all left in a hurry, that something bad had happened and you needed to get away, to start again.'

'Oh.' Peggy downed her whiskey in one.

'Here – let me top you up,' and she poured more whiskey for us both. 'She did tell me what happened to the house, though,' she continued. 'Your parents had managed to sell it through an agency, but Hannah saw it in the papers afterwards. A massive fire, there was. Luckily the new owners hadn't moved in, were still at the doing-up stage. No-one had any idea what started it, except there'd been an electric storm that night. But it didn't hit the other houses in the area – no trees, nothing. The place was just a heap of ash in the end.' Doreen looked at the floor suddenly. 'There were rumours, though.'

'What rumours?'

'That the house was haunted. That ghosts set the house alight. A load of rubbish, of course. Just people's wild imagination. Ridiculous.'

'What happened after the fire?' I asked. 'Do you know?'

'Only what I've heard. They say the place was haunted, that even after the fire a small ghost was seen wandering through the gardens. That bungalow took its time being built, I can tell you. The new owners wouldn't live there after the fire and no-one would buy up the land.'

'When was it built, then?'

'Late last century, it was. I'm not sure when, exactly. Maybe you could pop along in the morning – there's a date etched into the stonework.'

We decided not to meet up with Phil and Brian, as planned. Peggy texted to let them know, and we walked along the seafront towards the small harbour. A large building on the left called itself The Yacht Club. We pulled up our scarves against the cold breeze.

'What is that chinking sound that boats make?' I asked. 'It always sounds lovely.'

'Metal ropes. They're called shrouds.'

I smiled. 'Do you know everything, Peggy?'

'Nearly everything. When you get to my time of life …'

'They didn't have such things as yacht clubs when I lived here.'

'When was that, then?'

'1959. We were only here six months.'

'Millie died in 1958. Autumn was just beginning, and ...'

'Peggy – don't,' I pleaded.

'It was a Monday, the eighth of September. A beautiful sunny day, and my first day back at college.

I was at Secretarial College by this time, in Dorchester. I left that morning, all happy, full of the joys. I'd got one more year to do, then I'd have been working full-time, earning my own money. Mum was at home, looking after Millie for me. They only went out for an hour or so. Mum let Millie run down to the park while she chatted to a friend. She wasn't that far away, really.'

'Oh, Peggy …'

'She never saw her run off, never heard a thing, not the taunting of the children, not the screaming of the woman in the park when she realised what had happened. Nothing.'

I walked beside Peggy, tears rolling down my face. I had to keep wiping at them with my scarf.

'It killed Mum,' she continued. 'She went back to London and danced until she could no longer dance. So she could forget. As long as she was dancing, she could forget. She was never really the same person again.'

'I'm so sorry, Peggy.'

'And Dad – I never heard him utter Millie's name again. Not ever. Pushed it to the back of his mind. So did I.'

We had to stop walking at that point. It was all too much, too painful, too heartbreaking.

'There's a coffee shop ahead,' I said. 'Come on, let's get something to eat.'

We ordered crisp, toasted sandwiches and steaming hot coffee. Not another word was said about Millie and I could understand why Peggy had never uttered a word about her until now, until the day we discussed Tori's birthmark. It was much, much too painful.

Mr Jackson's field, the one I lived in as a child, no longer exists. It would have been just beyond the coffee shop, so we checked. It's a car showroom with a couple of warehouses alongside. But the scent of honeysuckle still lingers, and the roar of the waves continues to fill the air. Never-ending. Eternal. And if I breathed in and cleared my mind, I could still smell the sweet scent of Topper's harness oil, still feel the touch of his soft warm nose beneath my fingers.

'Come on, let's get back,' I said. 'We've a train to catch.'

'The weather's turning, anyway,' Peggy replied. 'A good time to be leaving.'

'We need to check the date on that bungalow first.' The house was quiet as we walked by. The apple tree was still there, and the path with the white pebbles was pretty much in the same positon. We checked the apex of the house, but there was no date written.

'Here,' said Peggy, stepping back. 'It's by the name. On the wall.'

It read *The Chalet*, and beneath that, *1999*.

'It's the year of Tori's birth,' I murmured. 'She was sixteen at the end of November.'

'So maybe Millie's spirit left here when they began building. What do you think?'

'I think she's finally at peace, Peggy, that's what I think.'

With soft tears in her eyes, she smiled. 'Come on, let's go and get packed.'

'A quick paddle before we go!' I called, running down the road towards the beach. 'There's still time.'

'What?' she shouted after me. 'Enid, you're mad! It's freezing!'

Throwing myself onto the sand, I removed my shoes and socks, rolled up my trousers and, holding my handbag high so it didn't get wet, walked into the sea, to just above my ankles. It was icy cold, but I loved it.

I turned, elated at doing such a stupid thing on such a sad day. I wanted to show that life goes on, that nothing can bring us down.

But Peggy was just standing there, sobbing her heart out, so lost and helpless and miserable that my heart ripped into tiny pieces. I stopped paddling, walked out of the sea and took her hand. We sat together on the beach and I hugged her close.

'What is it, Peggy?'

'This will be where she stood. This is where she would have taken that final decision.'

'Peggy, please don't. Let's give her leave to go. Let's rejoice in the fact that she's here with us again, that she's living her life to the full, that she'll never want to kill herself again.'

'It was her, you know. I'm sure she was the old man who watched her go in.'

'What?' I asked, puzzled.

'I think it was Flora Middlewood, come back as a man. He just stood there, and he watched her. He watched her walk into the sea and never come out.'

'Is this why you became a wiccan, Peggy? To find her, to find Flora Middlewood?'

She nodded tearfully. 'I was contacted after Millie died, you know. Frightened to death, I was. She just appeared, right there in front of me, as I was coming home from work one night. Said she was a white witch and had something to tell me. She told me all about Flora Middlewood, but she never said anything about Millie having killed herself before.'

'So what *did* she say?'

'She said that Millie had lived before, that she was a wiccan, destined to do great things, but Flora Middlewood, an awful, evil spirit, had stopped her, would carry on stopping her. I don't know what great things they would have been, mind. I often think about it, but nothing ever springs to mind.'

'A lot's happened since 1958, Peggy. It could have been anything. But you've found the woman now, and the authorities will find her, too. And Tori will never be persuaded into committing suicide again.

She's stronger, much stronger, than she was. So don't torment yourself. Please.'

Wiping her face with her hands, she smiled. 'You're right. I'm sorry. I know she's gone and there's nothing I can do about it. But she's here again. She's not mine, but I know she's safe. She's safe from harm. At last. Thank God.'

'You're a strong woman, Peggy Fleming. You can do this, you know.'

Standing up, she brushed the sand from her coat. 'Come on then, let's go.'

'Good, because I'm ready for a cuppa.'

'Enid, do we have to go home today?'

Puzzled, I looked up. 'No. Why?'

'There's somewhere I'd like to go.'

The churchyard was bleak, desolate. It was getting on for five o'clock by this time, and a storm was brewing. The leaves in the trees swirled to the ground as we walked along, and we crunched them beneath our feet.

'Here,' said Peggy. 'We buried Susie, her doll, with her. She just loved that doll.'

We'd reached the statue of a stone angel, its curved wings spreading out to welcome us. The words below it read: *Millicent Agatha Broadstairs, Born 1954, Died 1958. Resting in the arms of Jesus.*

Peggy had brought white roses from the florists along the road. She placed them upon the gravestone and prayed.

I stood beside her with tears in my eyes. I prayed too, for Millie's soul, now Tori's. I prayed for her to be safe from the powers of evil, from the ones who would prevent her from doing good things. I prayed for all those people who need help, all those in peril, all those whose lives are so affected by evil.

The journey home was uneventful. We did feel a huge sense of release, however. As though a weight had been lifted. For Peggy, it was a form of closure. For me, I felt as if every event in my life had somehow led to this moment.

I discussed it with Peggy as we sat there, eating the pasties we'd bought at the station.

'Don't you think it's strange, though? Don't you think it's strange I saw Millie's ghost when I was only seven, and now here I am, sitting opposite her mother?'

'I've been thinking just the same thing, Enid. And I've come to the conclusion that it was all meant to be.'

'I know, but …'

'After my divorce from Walt, I was distraught. I just wanted to lose myself, move to a place where no-one would know me. So I packed in my job in Kensington and moved to Folksbury. But I always felt as if I was waiting for someone. Or something. It was as if I had to stay there, working at the veg shop, fulfilling my role as the village wiccan, becoming the old spinster everyone knows me as. Until you came along.'

'Oh, Peggy ...'

'No, it's true. When you advertised for help at the B&B - well, I just had to apply, didn't I? I felt it in my bones, that if I didn't get to know you better, I would always regret it.' She sighed deeply. 'And now I know why.'

'Why me, though?'

'Because you had already made that connection. Because you can see ghosts, people after they've died. Because Millie's soul trusts you.'

I smiled. 'That's lovely, Peggy. Thank you.'

'Great Uncle John's told me why Flora Middlewood's so busy trying to get rid of Tori, you know.'

'Oh?'

'The thing is, Tori's been through so much in her previous lives that now she understands, she can connect. All the lessons she's learned are coming together. And we need someone to bring the people together too, to heal the rift in this country, to stop the hatred. That's what we need, what the world needs, actually. And Tori's the one to do it.'

'What, a girl from Grantham? A politician? You mean like Maggie Thatcher?'

'I suppose. But better, more a politician for today. Someone who truly understands.'

Today we've been to Flauson's, the travel agents in Grantham. Peggy doesn't do online. Wendy rang me last night to say we'd been left some money in Josie's will. Her solicitors in Sleaford read it out yesterday, while we were on our way home.

So I've booked flights to see Jonathan in Dubai, and Peggy's booked her holiday to St Tropez. That silver bikini will cost an arm and a leg at this time of year. A pity the top will never be used.

And if the idea of a seventy-four year old sunbathing topless like the film stars distresses you, concentrate your mind on the carmine-red lips and nails. They can cover a multitude of sins.

Especially if you're a witch.

THE END

Made in the USA
Columbia, SC
20 November 2017